I0646005

Secret Service

A PATRIOT'S PROMISE

ZOE NORMANDIE

ENTWINED PUBLISHING

A Patriot's Promise
ISBN # 978-1-80250-290-9
©Copyright Zoe Normandie 2025
Cover Art by Kelly Martin ©Copyright October 2025
Interior text design by Entwined Publishing
Published by Entice, an Entwined Publishing imprint

This is a work of fiction. All characters, places and events are from the author's imagination and should not be confused with fact. Any resemblance to persons, living or dead, events or places is purely coincidental.

All rights reserved. No part of this book may be used, reproduced, or distributed in any form or by any means, including but not limited to electronic, mechanical, photocopying, recording, or by any information storage and retrieval system, without prior written permission from the publisher. This book and its contents are expressly reserved from use in training artificial intelligence technologies or systems. Furthermore, this work is expressly reserved from the text and data mining exception, in accordance with Directive (EU) 2019/790 of the European Parliament and of the Council.

Applications should be addressed in the first instance, in writing, to Entwined Publishing. Unauthorised or restricted acts in relation to this publication may result in civil proceedings and/or criminal prosecution.

The author and illustrator have asserted their respective rights under the Copyright Designs and Patents Acts 1988 (as amended) to be identified as the author of this book and illustrator of the artwork.

Published in 2025 by Entwined Publishing, United Kingdom.

Entwined Publishing is a division of Totally Entwined Group Limited.

Entwined Publishing books by Zoe Normandie

Unbreakable Heroes
Under Control
Under Pressure
Under Fire

Secret Service
His American Oath
The President's Bodyguard
A Patriot's Promise

A PATRIOT'S PROMISE

Chapter One

Palm Beach, Florida

Pixie's three-inch patent heels clicked through the halls of President Armstrong's Palm Beach estate. Four years of serving the First Lady in this fortress of security.

A low murmur of voices and the hum of authority filled the air. With the president entering campaign mode, the Secret Service was running on high alert, updating risk assessments.

She rounded the corner — and there he was. Wyatt Steele. At the center of a group of agents, giving orders with effortless command.

Broad-shouldered, impossibly self-assured, his gray suit tailored to perfection, he radiated quiet intensity, making everyone snap to attention.

Pixie pressed herself against the wall, unnoticed for now. She'd known he was here — but seeing him again still sent a jolt through her.

Wyatt Steele was dangerous. Not in the obvious way, but in a way that could unravel everything. A rogue who didn't play by the rules. Every time she tried to rein him in, he ignored her, argued her down, or made her feel like she was the one out of line.

And it drove her mad that it worked.

The agents around him nodded, muttering acknowledgments before scattering, leaving Wyatt standing alone, his back to her. His stance was relaxed, his hands in his pockets, but there was an undeniable alertness to him, like he was ready to spring into action at any moment.

Pixie straightened her posture, schooling her expression into its usual mask of scorn, and stepped forward.

"Steele," she called out, her tone clipped and professional.

Wyatt turned slowly, and for a moment, his gaze locked with hers. His blue eyes, as piercing as ever, scanned her face, lingering just long enough to send a ripple of heat down her spine. Then his mouth curved into a faint, maddening smirk.

"Sinclair," he drawled, his voice low and deliberate. "To what do I owe the pleasure?"

Pixie's jaw tightened. "I assume you've been briefed on the First Lady's expectations for her detail this week."

Wyatt tilted his head, a mock-thoughtful expression crossing his face. "Oh, you mean the list of rules you sent over? Yeah, I saw them."

"And?"

"And I'll take them under advisement," he said with a casual shrug, the corner of his mouth twitching like he was trying not to laugh.

Pixie's hands tightened around the folder she was holding. "This isn't a suggestion, Steele. Those expectations are nonnegotiable."

His smirk widened, and he took two steps, closing the space just enough to make her pulse quicken. "Nonnegotiable?" he repeated. "That's cute, Sinclair. But you know I don't work for you, right?"

Pixie's nostrils flared, her calm slipping. "No, you work for the First Lady. And as her Chief of Staff, I represent her interests, which means—"

"You get to boss me around?" he interrupted, his tone laced with sarcasm. "Is that it?"

Her lips pressed into a thin line. "I expect you to respect the chain of command."

Wyatt leaned in slightly. "And I expect you to stop wasting your breath trying to control things you can't."

For a moment, the air between them crackled with tension, sharp and heavy. Pixie's heartbeat thundered in her ears, but she refused to back down, lifting her chin in defiance.

"You're a liability, Steele," she said, low and cutting.

Wyatt's smirk softened into something harder, his gaze unwavering. "And you're still trying to figure out why that bothers you so much."

Before she could respond, he turned and walked away, leaving Pixie standing there, her carefully maintained composure shattered.

She hated him.

And most of all, she hated that, for all her disdain, he still got into her head in a way no one else ever had.

* * * *

Wyatt Steele stood at the edge of the great room, his sharp eyes cutting through the crowd. His team was in perfect formation, guarding every angle of the First Lady's appearance. Caroline Armstrong was the picture of grace, her smile magnetic, her poise effortless, charming donors and supporters.

But Wyatt's focus wasn't on her tonight.

It was on Pixie Sinclair.

Wyatt's gaze lingered on Pixie longer than he intended, his trained eyes taking in every detail with the precision of a man who noticed everything—whether he wanted to or not. Her bleach-blonde hair was pulled into its usual perfect coiffe, not a strand out of place, a sharp contrast to the dark, enigmatic eyes that could cut through him with a single glance. That skin of hers, always tanned to a golden olive tone, made her seem like she lived in perpetual sunlight, though her personality was anything but warm.

Wyatt had dealt with every personality imaginable during his career in the Secret Service—politicians who thought themselves untouchable, celebrities who couldn't stop testing the boundaries of their protection, even the occasional agent with a chip on their shoulder. But Pixie Sinclair? She was a different beast altogether.

The First Lady's Chief of Staff was supposed to be diplomatic, someone who could effortlessly navigate the tightrope of politics and public scrutiny. Pixie, however, wielded her words like weapons, cutting sharp and clean. There was no tact in her commands, no deference in the way she addressed people.

Wyatt's jaw tightened as he watched Pixie approach Caroline, her black heels clicking like gunfire against the marble floor. She leaned in close to the First Lady, whispering something into her ear. Caroline laughed, her eyes lighting up, but Wyatt didn't miss the faint exasperation that grew across Pixie's expression.

Concern? Empathy? No. That wasn't a word he'd use with Pixie Sinclair.

The First Lady needed a Chief of Staff who understood her, someone who reflected her grace and priorities back into the world. Pixie was more like a bulldozer, smashing through subtlety with a confidence Wyatt might have admired if it weren't so grating.

And then there was the matter of respect.

Pixie had none for him.

Wyatt clenched his fists at his sides, careful to keep his expression neutral. He could recall half a dozen instances in the last two weeks where Pixie had overstepped. She barked orders at him like she ran the Secret Service. She didn't just question his decisions — she outright undermined them.

Like last week.

Wyatt's jaw ticked at the memory. They'd been preparing for Caroline's visit to a new children's hospital. He'd outlined security in painstaking detail, accounting for every possible risk. But Pixie had breezed into the room, glared at his plans, and called them 'overkill'. She'd insisted the First Lady didn't need to be treated like a 'fragile doll', and when he'd tried to calmly explain why each precaution was necessary, she'd cut him off with a sharp, "You work for me, Steele. Not the other way around."

I don't work for you, he'd wanted to snap. But he hadn't. Because Wyatt Steele didn't lose his cool, not even when someone like Pixie Sinclair made it damn near impossible not to.

He sighed, his gaze flicking back to Caroline. She deserved better. She deserved someone who could be assertive without being a tyrant, someone who could advocate for her without stepping on everyone else in the process. Someone who didn't make him grit his teeth every time they walked into a room.

As if summoned by his thoughts, Pixie appeared at his side.

"You're standing too close to the First Lady," she said, barely sparing him a glance.

"I'm exactly where I need to be," Wyatt replied, his tone calm but firm.

She crossed her arms, her icy blue eyes narrowing at him. "Well, your 'need' is obstructing her photo ops. Shift back."

Wyatt held her gaze, refusing to move. "Her safety comes first. The cameras can work around it."

Pixie huffed, her irritation radiating off her in waves. "You're impossible," she muttered, spinning on her heel and stalking away.

Wyatt watched her retreat, biting back the urge to say something he'd regret. She was svelte and fit, the kind of woman who moved with the fluid grace of someone who cared about every inch of herself. And tall—taller than most women, especially in those ridiculous heels she wore like weapons.

He took a slow, deep breath, forcing himself to refocus. He should have been thinking about Caroline Armstrong, the First Lady he was sworn to protect. About the entrances, the exits, and the agents stationed at each. About the shifting crowd dynamics and the potential threats lurking in plain sight.

But instead, his attention was stuck in one place.

Pixie moved like she owned every room she entered, chin high, shoulders squared, her sleek pencil skirt highlighting how her hips swayed with an infuriating kind of rhythm. Even in retreat, she was impossible to ignore.

And that was the damn problem.

Wyatt gritted his teeth, his jaw clenching as he forced his eyes to track the room again, scanning for potential threats. *Focus, Steele. Do your job.* But his gaze betrayed him, flickering back to her.

It wasn't just her disdain for him — though there was plenty of that. It was the way she carried herself, with all the subtlety of a lightning strike. The way she seemed to thrive in conflict, like sparring with him was less about the job and more about sheer enjoyment. She wasn't deferential, not even a little, and maybe that's what gnawed at him. He was used to people treating him with respect, acknowledging the weight of his position. Pixie Sinclair didn't just ignore that weight — she stomped all over it with her designer heels.

And yet, despite everything, she *fascinated* him.

Wyatt hated that word. Fascinated. It made him sound like some starry-eyed rookie instead of the hardened professional he prided himself on being. But how else could he describe the way his attention snagged on her whenever she entered the room? It wasn't her looks — though she was beautiful, objectively speaking. Blonde hair always swept into a no-nonsense bun, sharp cheekbones that looked like they could cut glass, and those cold eyes that could freeze him in place with a single glance. No, it wasn't that.

It was the fire underneath it all. The passion in the way she argued with him, the way her lips pressed into a line when he pushed back, like she wanted the fight but hated to admit it. She was so tightly wound, so fierce, that Wyatt couldn't help but wonder what it would take to crack that icy exterior. To see what was beneath all that armor she wore so well.

He dragged a hand through his short, dark hair, exhaling slowly. This wasn't the time or place to dissect his feelings — or whatever the hell this was. He had a job to do, and getting tangled up in his fascination with Pixie Sinclair wasn't part of it.

But damn it, she was under his skin.

As if she could feel his gaze, Pixie turned, her cold gaze cutting across the room to meet his. For a moment, neither of them moved, the distance between them crackling with unspoken tension. Then she lifted one perfectly sculpted eyebrow, a challenge clear in her expression, before spinning on her heel and disappearing into the crowd.

Wyatt sighed, shaking his head.

"Get a grip, Steele," he muttered under his breath.

But deep down, he wasn't sure he wanted to.

Chapter Two

Wyatt keyed his radio, issuing a quiet update to his team. The First Lady's exit was set, the motorcade in position. All that remained was keeping the final stretch smooth—no surprises, no unnecessary delays. As he reattached the radio, Jamie Gray, the White House Social Secretary, materialized at his side, clipboard in hand.

"Fifteen minutes," Jamie said without preamble. "She's heading straight back to the residence, correct?"

"That's the plan," Wyatt replied. "We'll take her through the east corridor to the loading zone. Five-minute buffer before the crowd moves."

Jamie frowned, tapping his pen. "Small change. She wants to stop in the side lounge to thank the event organizers."

Wyatt's brow furrowed. "That wasn't in the itinerary."

"It never is," Jamie said. "You know how she operates."

Wyatt exhaled. "Fine. But she's in and out in three minutes. Anything longer, and the corridors won't stay clear."

Jamie smirked. "You tell her that."

"I will," Wyatt said. "She respects the risks. But make sure Sinclair doesn't throw in any more last-second adjustments."

Jamie's smirk widened. "Not a Pixie fan, I take it?"

Wyatt glanced past him, his gaze landing on Pixie Sinclair as she conferred with the First Lady across the room. "It's not about liking her. She complicates things."

Jamie chuckled. "She complicates everyone. But she gets results. Caroline wouldn't keep her around otherwise."

Wyatt's jaw tightened. "Her delivery isn't just difficult, it's reckless. And you're not the least bit curious about her? No one knows where she came from. No backstory, no connections, nothing. How's everyone so comfortable with that?"

Jamie shrugged. "Caroline vetted her. That's enough for me."

"Is it?" Wyatt asked, his tone edged with skepticism. "You ever wonder how much vetting was done? Mysteries come with complications, and the First Lady doesn't need either."

Jamie tilted his head, studying Wyatt with faint amusement. "Sounds like you've got a theory—or maybe just a fixation."

Wyatt scowled. "Focus on your job, Gray."

Jamie laughed quietly. "I am. You, on the other hand…" He trailed off, arching a brow before disappearing back into the crowd.

Wyatt shook his head, turning back toward Pixie. She stood near Caroline, gesturing as she spoke, her movements deliberate and controlled. She was a mystery—one Wyatt couldn't ignore. And for a man trained to trust his instincts, that was more troubling than he wanted to admit.

* * * *

The First Lady's residence had stilled, the evening settling into quiet. Wyatt stood by the entryway, twirling his phone in his hand, scanning the dark grounds one last time before passing the shift. The overnight team was in place. He was ready to clock out.

Then, a faint murmur of voices reached him. Wyatt froze, ears straining. The sound came from the gardens, where shadows stretched long under the dim security lights.

He moved silently toward it, instincts on high alert.

He rounded the corner, shoving his phone back into his pocket, and there they were—Jamie Gray and Pixie Sinclair, standing close, their heads bent in deep conversation. It was an odd mix—Jamie's curly brown mop against Pixie's bleach-blonde locks. Wyatt's jaw tightened as he stopped just out of sight, watching them.

Conniving.

It wasn't just the proximity that bothered him—it was the intensity. Pixie's usually sharp gestures were subdued. Jamie stood with his arms crossed, nodding, his expression serious but relaxed. Whatever they were discussing looked intimate, deliberate. Too deliberate.

Wyatt felt the familiar rush of adrenaline, the same gut instinct that had saved his life more than once. With Pixie involved, he couldn't dismiss the worst.

He stepped forward, his boots crunching against the gravel.

"You two look cozy."

Both heads whipped toward him, the low murmur cutting off. Jamie sighed, rubbing a hand over his face like he was already exhausted by the conversation. Pixie, on the other hand, straightened her posture, her sharp eyes narrowing as they locked on Wyatt.

"Steele," Jamie said. "Always a pleasure."

Wyatt ignored the attempt at humor, his gaze fixed on Pixie. "What's this about?"

Jamie rolled his eyes and stepped back. "Nothing that concerns you, Wyatt. It's been a long night, and I'm heading out. You should do the same."

Wyatt's lips thinned as Jamie brushed past him, leaving the two of them alone. Pixie didn't move, her arms crossing as she met Wyatt's accusing stare head-on.

"Well?" she said, arching a brow. "What's your problem now?"

"My problem," Wyatt said, his voice low and controlled, "is you. Whispering in the dark. Plotting with Gray. You've been scheming since the day you walked into this job, and I'm not letting it go unchecked."

Pixie's laugh was sharp, humorless. "Scheming? You really think I'm plotting some grand conspiracy? What exactly do you think I'm doing, Steele? Enlighten me."

"You tell me," Wyatt said, stepping closer. "You keep secrets. You operate on your own terms, without regard for anyone else. You undermine the team, and you expect everyone to trust you without question."

Her chin lifted, defiant. "And why does that bother you so much? You don't trust me? Fine. But last I checked, I don't answer to you."

"It bothers me," Wyatt said, his voice rising slightly, "because you're too close to the First Lady, and I can't afford to have someone in her orbit who I can't figure out. You're unpredictable. Dangerous."

Pixie scoffed, throwing her hands in the air. "Dangerous? You really think that low of me?"

"I don't know what to think of you, Sinclair," Wyatt said, his frustration slipping into his tone. "You're a mystery. A walking question mark. And that's a liability."

"Two words— Fuck you." Pixie gave him a scornful look and spun to march away, classically her, when her heel caught in the uneven stone of the path. She stumbled, her balance shifting, and she squeaked.

Wyatt reacted. He shot his hands out, catching her at the waist as she fell forward, grabbing at him to steady herself. For a moment, neither of them moved.

"Easy, tiger," Wyatt said, his voice rough, his grip tightening a touch as he steadied her.

His gaze betrayed him, drifting lower, to her lips. He'd never really noticed them before—full, softly curved, with a slight sheen catching the light. Kissable.

Pixie's breath hitched, her face inches from his. Wyatt could feel the warmth of her body through the thin fabric of her blouse, the rapid beat of her pulse against his hand.

Wyatt didn't give her a chance to catch up.

His hands tightened on her hips, pulling her roughly against him, his body pressing her into the unyielding wall. He surrounded her, and her heart raced as her breath came in shallow, uneven gasps. The look in her eyes was blistering, as his lips hovered just a whisper away from hers.

"You don't get it, do you?" he growled, his voice a low, feral rasp that clearly sent a shiver straight through her. "You think you can fight me, push me, and I'll just back off? Not happening, Pixie."

Her lips parted to argue, but the words seemed to catch in her throat as his hand slid up her thigh, rough and demanding. He gripped her leg, pulling it around his hip, and her body arched instinctively toward him. His other hand twisted her hair, tugging just hard enough to make her gasp. He liked that sound. The immediate intimacy sent a shockwave through them both, and he watched her as she bit her lip, as if refusing to give him the satisfaction that she wanted this too.

"Oh, no, sweetheart," he said, his voice dripping with dark amusement. "You don't get to play coy now. You've been asking for this."

Her defiance flared. "You're full of yourself," she said, her voice trembling but edged with fire. "You think you can just—"

His mouth crashed down on hers, cutting off her words in an instant. The kiss was fierce, consuming, and so raw it left her trembling. His teeth scraped against her lower lip, demanding entry, and finally she couldn't hold back the moan that escaped her as his tongue swept inside, claiming her. It was a battle, every movement charged with frustration and need, but he was relentless, kissing her like he owned her.

When he pulled back, his breathing was ragged, his lips curling into a wicked smirk. "What was that?" he asked, his tone taunting as his hands moved to her waist, gripping her with a possessiveness that made her head spin. "Something about me being full of myself?"

Her glare was weak at best, her chest heaving as she tried to catch her breath. "You're insufferable," she said, though her trembling hands clinging to his shoulders betrayed her.

"And you love it," he said, his voice low and dangerous. His hands slid down, grabbing her other thigh and hoisting her up completely. Her legs wrapped around his waist, and he pinned her harder against the wall, his hips pressing into hers in a way that made her gasp.

"Wyatt—" she started, her voice breaking as his lips trailed down her neck, hot and insistent. He nipped at her skin, soothing the bite with his tongue, and her nails dug into his shoulders as the sensation sent fire racing through her.

"Say my name again," he growled, his voice rough with barely restrained desire. "But say it like you mean it."

He didn't wait for her, kissing her again. He'd never forget the feeling of her moaning his name off her lips as he tasted them with his tongue. And in that moment, all he could think of was kissing down her neck and tasting every inch of her body.

The world around them fell away. The cool night air, the faint hum of the evening lights, the weight of their roles—none of it mattered. It was just her, tasting like defiance and something sweet he couldn't name, melting into him in a way that made his head spin.

When he finally pulled back, he was breathless, his hands still cradling her face. Pixie's wide, dark eyes searched his, her cheeks flushed, her lips slightly swollen.

Everything about her shifted. He felt it—fast. She wasn't the sharp-tongued, unyielding Chief of Staff who seemed to live to make his life difficult. Right now, she was something else entirely—softer, almost fragile in a way that contradicted everything he thought he knew about her.

Her lashes fluttered as she blinked up at him, the dark pools of her doe-like eyes catching the faint glow of the evening lights. Those eyes — they were deeper than he'd ever noticed before, wide and unguarded. For the first time, it struck him — she was younger than he'd assumed. Mid-twenties, maybe.

"Well," she breathed, her voice barely a whisper. "That's one way to settle an argument."

Wyatt let out a low growl, shaking his head as he took a step back. "Learn your lesson, sweetheart."

Pixie smirked, her usual edge returning as she tilted her head, watching him like he was a puzzle she'd just figured out. "This never happened," she said, her voice tinged with something he couldn't quite place. "Never speak of this to me again."

And with that, she turned and walked away, leaving Wyatt standing alone in the dark, every instinct telling him he'd just made the worst mistake of his career — and the best decision of his life.

Chapter Three

Six months later

Pixie Sinclair straightened the stack of notes in her hand, every move tense, though her mind raced. The warm morning light poured through the Armstrong estate's windows, the soft ocean breeze outside offering a calm she couldn't quite feel. This place was a far cry from Washington's cold efficiency, but then again, everything about Caroline Armstrong defied convention.

Caroline sat at the marble vanity, golden silk robe draped over her shoulders, sipping coffee as Pixie ran through the day's agenda. The First Lady's reflection remained serene, almost detached.

"Your call with the education initiative is at eleven. Fifteen minutes—quick and to the point," Pixie said, flipping to the next page. "Then lunch with the Palm Beach Arts Council, low-key, limited press. After that, your fitting for the gala."

Caroline's lips curled into a faint smile as she set her cup down. "And what would I do without you, Pixie?"

"You'd survive," Pixie replied, then added with a touch of softness, "but it wouldn't be nearly as seamless."

Caroline turned in her chair, her discerning gaze landing on Pixie. "You're tense today."

Pixie hesitated, gripping her folder a little tighter. "There's a lot to coordinate. The gala's coming up fast, and—"

"It's not the gala," Caroline interrupted, her smile widening. "I know you better than that. What's wrong?"

Before Pixie could respond, a knock echoed through the room. One of the estate staff opened the door a fraction, leaning in just enough to speak.

"Ma'am, Agent Steele has arrived. He's waiting downstairs."

Pixie froze. She hoped it was subtle, but Caroline caught it. Her dark eyes flickered with curiosity as she looked back at her Chief of Staff.

"Agent Steele?" Caroline asked, though there was a knowing edge in her voice. "Why does that name sound familiar?"

Pixie forced her expression into neutral territory, though her pulse was hammering in her ears. Six months. Six months since the kiss, since Wyatt Steele had all but disappeared from her orbit and into the President's campaign detail. Six months since she'd convinced herself that whatever had passed between them was done and buried.

"He was your detail lead last summer," Pixie said, her voice even. "Looks like he's been reassigned."

Caroline studied her, one eyebrow arched. "And is that a problem?"

"No," Pixie replied too quickly, standing a little straighter. "Of course not."

Caroline didn't look convinced, but she waved a hand dismissively. "Well, if it is, I'm sure you'll manage. You always do." She stood, setting her cup aside. "I'll leave you to deal with whatever it is that's tying you in knots, Pixie."

Pixie nodded, swallowing hard as Caroline breezed past her, leaving her alone in the quiet of the room. She exhaled, her fingers brushing over the stack of papers as if grounding herself.

Wyatt Steele.

The name alone sent a ripple through her carefully constructed composure. She'd spent months telling herself the kiss had been a lapse in judgment, a fleeting moment that meant nothing. But the thought of seeing him again—of facing those steady blue eyes, the ones that had looked at her like she was both infuriating and irresistible—made her stomach twist in a way she hated.

She didn't want him back here. Not in this house. Not in her well-ordered world.

Pixie squared her shoulders, forcing the panic down. She was better than this—stronger, sharper. Whatever unresolved mess lingered between them, she'd deal with it like she dealt with everything else—efficiently and without emotion.

But as she stepped into the hallway and made her way toward the grand staircase, her hands felt unsteady, her breathing a little too quick. His voice carried from the lobby. She paused, turned back up the stairs and decided it was time for a break.

Perhaps time to read a novel.

A tome.

The Bible.

Anything that could keep her occupied and out of his sight.

* * * *

The Armstrong estate was as grand and pristine as Wyatt remembered, a blend of luxury and Florida charm. But he barely noticed. His focus was elsewhere. He moved through the house with practiced efficiency, nodding at staff, scanning every corner for a glimpse of her.

Six months. Six long months since he'd last seen Pixie Sinclair. Since that kiss that had burned into his memory. Now that he was back, the need to find her gnawed at him.

His sharp blue eyes darted around as he passed through the living areas, steps quickening despite himself. He told himself it was just a routine check-in, part of his job.

But deep down, he knew better.

Where the hell is she?

Wyatt ascended the stairs, his polished shoes silent on the plush carpet. His pulse quickened as he rounded the corner and pushed open the door to the second-floor library. The room was still, bathed in sunlight streaming through the tall windows, the scent of old books hanging in the air.

Then he saw her—someone, with short, dark hair.

He froze in the doorway, his breath catching.

She sat by the window, legs crossed, one sleek leg exposed as her skirt rode up. Her fingers trailed absentmindedly along her shin as she pushed a pair of glasses higher up her nose, absorbed in the book in her lap.

Is it her?

She's different.

It wasn't the coiffe of blonde hair he remembered but a sharp, dark bob framing her face. The color was a deep, rich blend of black and brown, cropped just above her shoulders.

He took a step forward, the floorboard creaking under his weight.

Her head snapped up. Their eyes locked.

"Pixie," he whispered, the name barely escaping his lips as his chest tightened.

She stared at him for a moment, her dark eyes narrowing, then her lips pressed into a thin line. "It's you," she said, her voice clipped, her tone laced with annoyance.

Wyatt blinked, still thrown by the sight of her. "Your hair...your hair...it's changed."

She closed the book in her lap with a snap, setting it aside as she uncrossed her legs and leaned back in the chair. "Nothing gets past you, Steele."

"What happened?" he asked, taking another step into the room.

"To?" she replied, tilting her head, her expression as sharp as her tone.

"Your hair," he said, softer, almost hesitant.

She exhaled, clearly irritated. "I had an allergic reaction to the bleach. This is my natural color. Satisfied?"

Wyatt's gaze swept over her, taking in the unfamiliar hair and how it changed her. It changed her more than it should, made her look younger, more vulnerable, yet just as striking. His chest tightened again, and he couldn't tell if it was relief, longing, or frustration that he felt.

"It suits you," he said, his voice low and genuine.

Her eyes flicked up to his, and for a split second, something flashed in her expression—something he couldn't quite name. But then it was gone, replaced by her usual guarded irritation.

"Is there a reason you're here, Steele, or are you just making the rounds to critique people's hairstyles?"

Wyatt smirked, though his chest still ached. "Just checking in on the staff."

"Well," she said, standing and smoothing her skirt. "Consider me checked in."

She stepped past him, her scent brushing against him as she moved toward the door.

"Pixie," he said softly, stopping her in her tracks.

She turned her head slightly, but not enough to meet his eyes. "What?"

His throat tightened, but he forced himself to speak. "It's good to see you."

Her shoulders stiffened, and for a moment he thought she might say something. But then she walked out without another word, leaving him standing alone in the quiet library, her absence hitting him harder than he'd expected.

It's not just the hair that's changed, he realized, his jaw tightening as he stared after her. *Something else is different. And I'm going to figure out what it is.*

Chapter Four

Pixie kicked off her heels the moment she hit the sandy path toward the beach. The sun was dipping, painting the Atlantic in gold and pink, the waves lapping gently. Out here, it was quiet — far enough from the estates to escape the chaos of the day.

The cool sand soothed her frayed nerves as she walked, her thoughts knotted around the same thing. Wyatt Steele was back. Six months of peace shattered in an instant. And it wasn't just anger she felt — it was something else, something she couldn't name.

She shook her head, trying to clear the thought. That's when she saw it — a flash of dark fur, strong legs, and unbridled enthusiasm.

Pixie froze as a German Shepherd skidded to a halt in front of her, a stick in its mouth. Its tail wagged furiously as it dropped the stick at her feet, eyes wide and eager.

"Uh…" Pixie took a cautious step back. "Where did you come from?"

The dog barked once, a sharp, happy sound, then nudged the stick closer with its nose.

Pixie's heart thudded in her chest as memories flickered at the edges of her mind—memories she didn't want to relive. She'd avoided dogs ever since that incident as a teenager, the one that left her with scars both physical and emotional. They were unpredictable, wild, and far too capable of harm.

But this dog didn't seem wild. It seemed…insistent.

"I'm not playing with you," she muttered, folding her arms across her chest.

The dog tilted its head, tail wagging harder, as if it hadn't heard her—or didn't care. When she didn't move, it picked up the stick again and dropped it at her feet with even more enthusiasm.

Pixie sighed, glancing up and down the empty beach. No owner in sight. Just her and this persistent dog.

"Fine," she said finally, bending down to grab the stick. The dog's ears perked up, and for a moment, she couldn't help but be charmed by its sheer excitement. "Just once."

She threw the stick as far as she could, and the dog bolted after it, kicking up sand in its wake. Pixie watched, almost in spite of herself, as the dog raced back to her, stick in tow, tail wagging like mad.

"You're relentless," she said, laughing despite herself as she threw the stick again.

The dog came back just as quickly, dropping the stick at her feet once more. And again. And again.

Pixie found herself laughing harder than she had in months, each throw loosening the weight she carried a little more. For a moment, she wasn't the razor-sharp Chief of Staff, always composed and in control. She was just a woman on a beach, playing fetch with an unexpectedly sweet dog.

But as the minutes passed, the dog's energy didn't wane.

"Okay, that's enough," Pixie said, holding her hands up as the dog dropped the stick again. "You've had your fun. Go back to wherever you came from."

The dog barked, wagging its tail, entirely unbothered by her dismissal.

"I'm serious," she insisted, trying to sound stern. "Shoo. Go home."

The German Shepherd sat, cocked its head, and stared at her like she was the one being ridiculous.

Pixie sighed, crouching down to look the dog in the eye. "Look, you're adorable, and clearly very persistent, but I'm not your person, okay? Find someone else to bother."

The dog barked again, as if laughing at her, before leaning forward and licking her cheek.

"Ugh, gross!" Pixie snarled, pushing the dog's face away as it wagged its tail even harder. "Fine. You win. But just for the record, you're so annoying."

She sat back on her heels, shaking her head as the dog leaned against her side, tail still thumping against the sand. For the first time in what felt like forever, the tension in her chest eased, replaced by something lighter. Something she didn't quite know how to name.

"Who do you belong to, huh?" she asked softly, scratching the dog's ears. "And why do I feel like I'm the one who's been claimed?"

The dog barked again, as if it had the answer, and Pixie couldn't help but smile.

"Nova!"

The sharp call carried over the sound of the waves, making Pixie turn toward the voice. The dog—Nova, apparently—perked up, ears swiveling before bounding off toward the figure walking down the beach.

Her stomach dropped when she saw him.

Wyatt Steele, striding toward her with that same confident, easy gait that made him look like he owned every space he stepped into. He was dressed casually, in a plain white T-shirt and dark jeans, but his presence was anything but casual. His blue eyes locked on her as he approached, and the air between them seemed to tighten.

"Of course," Pixie muttered under her breath. "Because who else would it be?"

Nova ran up to Wyatt, circling him in excited loops before sitting obediently at his side, looking back at Pixie like she was part of some unspoken agreement.

"She yours?" Pixie asked, folding her arms as Wyatt stopped a few feet away.

He nodded, crouching down to scratch behind Nova's ears. "Yeah. Sorry if she bothered you. She's supposed to stay by my side, but…she gets ideas."

Pixie raised an eyebrow, her heart still racing from the sight of him. "She's a little persistent. And by 'a little,' I mean a lot."

Wyatt smirked, glancing up at her. "She gets that from me."

Pixie rolled her eyes, but her gaze softened as she watched Nova lean into Wyatt's hand. "I didn't know you had a dog."

Wyatt straightened, his expression shifting into something quieter, more thoughtful. "She wasn't planned. One of my buddies found her while on deployment in Syria. She was just a pup—alone, malnourished, no one to claim her. They got her stateside, but she didn't adjust well. Too wild. Too much for anyone to handle."

Pixie glanced at Nova, who was now sitting at Wyatt's feet, wagging her tail happily. "And you took her in?"

"She was on the list to be put down," Wyatt said simply, shrugging like it wasn't a big deal. "I figured if she had any fight left in her, maybe she just needed someone who knew what to do with it. Spent a year training her, getting her steady. She's certified now—part of the team. But mostly, she's just mine."

Pixie stared at him, caught off guard by the unexpected tenderness in his tone. She looked back at Nova, her earlier wariness fading into something warmer. "You saved her."

"She saved herself," Wyatt said, giving Nova a pat. "I just gave her a shot."

For a moment, they stood there in silence, the waves rolling in softly behind them. Pixie could feel the tension in the air, the unspoken weight of their last encounter hanging between them like a storm cloud.

Pixie folded her arms tighter across her chest as Wyatt's gaze locked onto hers. His blue eyes were unreadable, the faintest flicker of something dangerous lingering in their depths. But it wasn't his eyes that snagged her focus—it was his mouth.

That mouth. Those maddeningly kissable lips that had haunted her for six months. She could still remember the exact feel of them, the way they'd pressed against hers with a mixture of hunger and control, leaving her breathless and dizzy in a way she hadn't been able to shake. She hated that she remembered it so vividly, hated that just looking at him now made the memory bloom all over again.

She cleared her throat, forcing her gaze back up to his. "Why did you come back?"

Wyatt didn't hesitate, didn't flinch. His answer was simple, steady. "You know why."

Her heart stumbled, the weight of his words hitting her harder than she wanted to admit. She forced herself to scoff, tilting her chin higher in defiance. "I don't."

"Yes, you do," he said, his voice softer now, low and resolute.

Pixie clenched her fists, willing herself not to break under the intensity of his stare. He looked at her like he knew every thought racing through her mind, like he could see the tug-of-war between wanting to push him away and wanting to pull him closer. He was dangerous—chaotic—and she couldn't afford to let him back into her life, not after the last time.

She told herself to focus on the facts. Wyatt Steele was a man who didn't play by the rules. He thrived in chaos, flouted authority, and lived to make her job harder. He was a rogue in every sense of the word, and giving him even an inch of trust was asking for trouble.

But none of that logic could quiet the part of her that remembered how his hands had felt on her waist, how his lips had tasted of salt and certainty, how he'd kissed her like she was the only thing that mattered in the world.

"No," she said finally, shaking her head as if to shake the thought away. "I don't know why. And I don't care."

Wyatt's mouth curved into the faintest smirk, and the look in his eyes shifted—still steady, but with a spark of something more dangerous. "You don't care?"

he asked, his tone almost teasing. "You sure about that?"

"I'm sure," she snapped, her voice sharper than she'd intended.

Wyatt stepped closer, his gaze narrowing just slightly, his voice dropping even lower. "Want me to remind you?"

Her breath caught, her heart pounding in her chest. She opened her mouth to fire back, to tell him no, but the words tangled on her tongue. For a second, she thought he might actually do it—close the distance between them, kiss her again, ruin what little control she had left.

Nova barked, breaking the moment, and Pixie exhaled, the tension snapping like a taut wire. Wyatt smirked, as if the dog had spoken for him, his gaze flicking to Nova before settling back on her.

"See you around, Sinclair," he said, his tone light but his eyes anything but.

Pixie stood frozen, her fists clenching at her sides as she watched him turn and whistle for Nova to follow. The dog bounded after him, tail wagging happily, while Wyatt strode up the beach, every step radiating the same infuriating confidence he always carried.

The weight of his words pressed heavily against her chest, and she clenched her jaw, forcing herself to breathe.

He was dangerous. Reckless. Unpredictable.

And yet, as he disappeared from sight, she couldn't stop herself from wondering how it would feel to be reminded.

Chapter Five

Wyatt stood at the edge of the estate, the faint glow of the Atlantic visible over the dunes. The shadows of the estate stretched long in the moonlight as he leaned against a stone pillar, arms crossed. Salem Briscoe approached, boots crunching on gravel.

"Boss," Salem said, tipping his hat back. "I've got something for ya. You're gonna want to hear this."

Wyatt straightened, eyes narrowing. "You dig into Sinclair's file?"

Salem nodded, pulling out a folded piece of paper. "Yessir. Just like you asked. Girl's got holes in her history bigger than the craters on the moon."

Wyatt unfolded the paper, scanning it. It was a thin, neat summary of Pixie's clearance record. "What kind of holes?"

Salem scratched his chin, clearly enjoying the intrigue. "Here's the kicker. Pixie Sinclair only starts existing about ten years ago. Nothing before that—no school records, no address history, not even a birth certificate we can verify. It's like she just popped up outta nowhere, full-grown, and slid into her shiny career path."

Wyatt's jaw tightened, his mind already spinning. "That's impossible. Someone would've flagged it during her vetting process."

"You'd think," Salem agreed, shrugging. "But whoever filed her paperwork was real careful. There's just enough there to pass the sniff test—degrees from big schools, glowing references. But when I looked closer, it's all surface-level. Nothing concrete. Like it was designed to hold up under a glance but not much more."

Wyatt tapped the paper against his palm, a gnawing suspicion growing in his gut. "And her age?"

"Form says mid-thirties," Salem said, his tone skeptical.

Wyatt's mind snapped back to the kiss—the softness of her skin, the faint flush of her cheeks, the youthful spark in her dark eyes. She wasn't in her thirties. Hell, she barely looked like she'd crossed into her late twenties.

Wyatt folded the paper and shoved it into his pocket. "Keep this between us," he ordered.

Salem tipped his hat. "You got it. Anything else you want me to pull?"

"Not yet," Wyatt said, though his voice was tight with unspoken resolve.

Salem nodded and turned to leave, his boots echoing softly against the stone.

Wyatt stayed where he was, staring out at the dark waves as they rolled in. The dots in his mind were starting to connect, but the picture wasn't clear yet. He knew one thing for sure, though—Pixie Sinclair was hiding something big. And whatever it was, it wasn't just about her past. It was about why she was here, in the First Lady's inner circle, with no one questioning her.

His fists clenched at his sides. That kiss had told him more than she realized—not just about her age, but about the fire she worked so hard to bury. She wasn't just a mystery—she was a contradiction, a living puzzle he was damn determined to solve.

* * * *

The motorcade rolled through Palm Beach, black SUVs gliding silently against the sunny backdrop. Wyatt drove the First Lady's vehicle, scanning the streets with practiced precision. It was a simple route to the Palm Beach Children's Hospital, where Caroline Armstrong was scheduled to speak and visit patients.

Caroline sat in the back, poised in a navy dress and pearls, hands neatly folded in her lap. The morning light filtered through the tinted windows, softening her sharp but kind features.

"Agent Steele," she said, her tone light but curious.

Wyatt glanced at her in the rearview mirror. "Yes, ma'am?"

"You're, what—mid-thirties?" she asked, voice casual, but the question clearly leading somewhere.

"Yes, ma'am," Wyatt replied, already bracing for what was coming.

She smiled, her eyes studying him in the mirror. "And not married."

Wyatt blinked, momentarily thrown off by the sudden shift. "No, ma'am."

Caroline leaned back in her seat. "So who are you bringing to the gala?"

Wyatt's brow furrowed. "Excuse me?"

"The Valentine's Day gala," she clarified, her tone light but insistent. "It's in two weeks, and I assume you're attending. I was just wondering who your plus-one is."

Wyatt resisted the urge to sigh. "I wasn't planning on bringing anyone."

Caroline gave him a look of mock disapproval, her lips curving into a small smirk. "A handsome man like you, showing up alone to a Valentine's gala? I'll have to warn the ladies of Palm Beach to brace themselves."

"I'll be working, ma'am," Wyatt said, keeping his tone professional, though her teasing set him slightly on edge. "Not exactly the time for a date."

"Nonsense," Caroline replied with a wave of her hand. "You'll be there in a protective capacity, yes, but even Secret Service agents deserve a personal life. Doesn't anyone ever catch your eye? Someday there will be a Mrs. Steele?"

Wyatt clenched his jaw, his grip tightening slightly on the armrest. "With respect, ma'am, I don't think it's for me."

She leaned back in her seat, crossing her arms as she regarded him. "You're going to need to settle down someday, Wyatt. Especially if you want to climb in your career. A man in your position—dedicated, successful—he's expected to have certain things. A stable home life, for one."

The words sat uncomfortably in Wyatt's chest. It wasn't that he hadn't thought about it—marriage, kids, a white-picket-fence kind of life. But every time the thought crossed his mind, he pushed it away. That wasn't his path. His life was built on control, precision, and staying untethered.

"I've done fine on my own," Wyatt said, his tone a touch sharper than he intended.

Caroline smiled knowingly, clearly not deterred by his frustration. "For now, maybe. But life has a way of changing those plans."

Wyatt said nothing, his jaw tight as he stared out at the passing scenery. Her words rattled around in his head, uncomfortably close to things he didn't want to think about. He'd always been fine with the occasional fling, something short-lived that didn't leave any strings attached. It was clean, simple. Exactly the way he wanted his life to stay.

The idea of anything else—something permanent, something that required him to be vulnerable, to let someone into the messy corners of his life—felt impossible. And more than that, it felt dangerous.

Caroline's voice broke into his thoughts, softer this time. "You might surprise yourself, you know."

Wyatt didn't answer, keeping his gaze forward as the motorcade pulled into the hospital's private entrance. His earpiece crackled with updates, and he used it as an excuse to refocus, giving quick instructions to his team as they prepared for Caroline's arrival.

But as he stepped out of the SUV and opened the door for the First Lady, her words lingered, gnawing at the edges of his carefully constructed world.

And somewhere in the back of his mind, unbidden and unwanted, he thought of dark eyes, soft lips, and the undeniable spark that had haunted him for six months.

Chapter Six

Wyatt adjusted his earpiece, eyes scanning the chaotic construction site. Scaffolding rose haphazardly around the half-built veterans' center, machinery scattered at the edges, debris everywhere. Not the ideal setting for a high-profile event, but the schedule was set, and his job was clear — make it go smoothly.

Pixie stood nearby, dressed in a tailored navy suit that looked effortlessly chic, even in the dust. She was talking to a local official, her voice steady, heels wobbling slightly on the uneven ground.

Wyatt smirked. Typical Sinclair — always commanding attention, even at the risk of a twisted ankle.

He kept his distance, focus never wavering. He didn't like this. Too many moving parts. Too much unpredictability.

His earpiece crackled with a status update from one of his agents stationed near the perimeter. He acknowledged it with a clipped response, his gut already prickling with that familiar sense of unease. It was the kind of feeling he'd learned to trust—the one that had saved him more times than he could count.

Then he heard it.

A groan of metal straining under pressure.

Wyatt's head snapped toward the source, his eyes locking onto a stack of heavy steel beams perched precariously on the edge of a high scaffold. A worker nearby, distracted and oblivious, had bumped into the machinery holding it in place, causing the beams to shift.

"Shit," Wyatt muttered under his breath, already moving.

It happened fast. Too fast. The beams tilted, the balance giving way, and they started to fall.

"Pixie!" he barked, his voice cutting through the chaos.

She turned toward him, her dark eyes wide with confusion, and for a split second, everything slowed. She didn't see it. Didn't realize what was happening above her.

Without thinking, Wyatt lunged forward, closing the distance between them in seconds. He grabbed her waist and shoved her hard, sending her stumbling out of the danger zone.

The beams came crashing down before he could fully clear the space.

Pain exploded in his shoulder as the edge of one beam clipped him, its weight tearing through fabric and skin before slamming into the ground. Another beam grazed his back, leaving a deep, burning gash that sent fire coursing through his body.

He hit the ground hard, his vision blurring as dust and debris filled the air.

"Wyatt!" Pixie's voice cut through the haze, sharp and panicked in a way he'd never heard before.

He groaned, trying to push himself up, but his left shoulder screamed in protest, and he collapsed back onto the ground. He felt the warmth of blood seeping through his shirt, the sting of the gash spreading across his back like wildfire.

"Damn it," he muttered through gritted teeth.

Pixie dropped to her knees beside him, her face pale and her hands hovering as if she didn't know where to touch him without making it worse.

"Don't move," she ordered, her voice shaking slightly. "You're hurt."

"No kidding," Wyatt rasped, his tone rough but laced with the faintest hint of humor.

"You—" Pixie's voice cracked, and she shook her head, her usual sharpness replaced by something softer, something raw. "Why the hell did you do that?"

Wyatt met her eyes, his own swimming with pain but steady. "Because I saw it coming. And because it's my job."

She swallowed hard, her hands still trembling as she reached for her phone, barking orders at someone on the other end to get a medic immediately.

Wyatt let his head fall back against the dusty ground, his breath coming in shallow bursts. The pain was excruciating, but what unsettled him more was the look in Pixie's eyes—a mix of fear, anger, and something else he couldn't quite name.

"Pixie," he said, his voice low.

She stopped, her gaze snapping back to him.

"You're okay," he murmured, his lips quirking into a faint, pained smile. "That's what matters."

She didn't respond, her expression unreadable as she shifted closer, her hand brushing against his uninjured arm.

"Stay awake," she said firmly, her tone brooking no argument.

Wyatt chuckled weakly, the sound more of a rasp. "Don't worry. I'm not going anywhere."

But as the sound of approaching medics filled the air, he couldn't help but wonder if he'd regret throwing himself in harm's way — not because of the injury, but because of the way Pixie Sinclair was looking at him now, as if he'd just turned her perfectly controlled world upside down.

* * * *

The flashing lights of the ambulance painted the construction site in sharp reds and whites. Wyatt sat on the edge of the stretcher, gritting his teeth as Salem tried to maneuver him into the back of the ambulance.

"I'm fine," Wyatt growled, waving off Salem's attempt to steady him.

Salem, his cowboy hat shoved back on his head and his expression a mix of frustration and concern, didn't budge. "Fine? You're covered in blood, boss," he said, gesturing to the deep crimson stain spreading across Wyatt's shirt and down his side.

"It's not as bad as it looks," Wyatt said, though the sharp pain in his shoulder and the burning gash across his back told a different story. He winced as he shifted, his body betraying him with every movement.

"Not as bad?" Salem scoffed, his hands on his hips. "You've got a shoulder that looks like it's been through a meat grinder, and you're leakin' blood like a stuck pig. Now, get in the damn ambulance before I throw you in myself."

Wyatt glared at him, but the dizziness creeping into his vision dulled the effect. "I'm not leaving until—"

"You're not leaving?" Pixie's voice cut through the commotion, sharp and unmistakable. She stormed into view, her suit dusted with debris, her hair disheveled but her eyes blazing. "You're not in a position to decide anything right now."

"I don't need—" Wyatt started, but the words faltered as a wave of nausea hit him, his vision tunneling slightly. He blinked hard, trying to push it back, but the pain was becoming impossible to ignore.

Pixie turned to Salem, her tone clipped and furious. "Why isn't he already in the ambulance? He's losing blood!"

Salem held up his hands. "Believe me, I've been tryin'. But the man's as stubborn as a mule."

"Stubborn doesn't matter when he's about to pass out!" Pixie snapped, her voice shaking.

"Stop yelling," Wyatt muttered, though the sound came out weaker than he intended. His head drooped, his strength ebbing as his body finally betrayed him.

"Wyatt." Pixie's voice was softer now, closer. He felt her hand on his uninjured arm, firm and steady. "You need help. Let them take you."

He opened his mouth to argue, but another jolt of pain shot through him, forcing a groan from his lips. His head tipped forward, the edges of his vision going dark. The last thing he saw was Pixie and Salem's faces—Pixie pale and furious, Salem grim and determined.

And then there were voices.

Familiar.

Concerned as hell.

"Call Caroline," Pixie was saying, her voice urgent. "Get her on the phone. She'll—"

"I'm already here," came Caroline's commanding tone, cutting through the chaos like a knife.

Wyatt vaguely registered her presence as she stepped forward, the First Lady's elegant figure somehow impervious to the surrounding mess.

"Agent Steele," she said, her voice laced with both concern and authority. "You're going to be fine. I'm making sure of it."

"Ma'am—" Pixie started.

"The President's medical team will see him," Caroline said firmly. "No arguments. He's getting the best care available. Take him there immediately."

The last thing Wyatt felt was the soft pressure of Pixie's hand on his arm as the medics lifted him into the ambulance. Her voice, sharp and insistent, followed him as he drifted into unconsciousness, but he couldn't make out the words anymore.

All he knew was that Pixie was fighting for him, and for some reason, that made the darkness feel a little less heavy.

Chapter Seven

The Armstrong estate's guest quarters were eerily silent, broken only by the hum of the air conditioner and the soft murmur of the visiting nurse. Pixie stood at the edge of the room, arms crossed, eyes fixed on Wyatt. He lay motionless in the oversized bed, his usually sharp features slack with exhaustion and pain. His left shoulder was heavily bandaged, chest rising and falling steadily under the light blanket.

Twelve hours had passed since the accident, but Pixie couldn't shake the image of Wyatt pushing her out of the way, the steel beam slamming into him, his blood soaking through his shirt.

"Ms. Sinclair?"

The nurse's voice snapped her back to the present. Pixie blinked, focusing on the petite woman standing nearby, clipboard in hand. Her expression was patient, but expectant.

"Yes?" Pixie's voice was sharper than she intended.

The nurse didn't flinch. "Mr. Steele's injuries are serious but manageable, as long as he rests and avoids strain."

Pixie raised an eyebrow. "You know who we're talking about, right?"

The nurse allowed a small smile. "I've dealt with more than my share of stubborn patients. Trust me, I'm prepared. But it's up to you to enforce the rest. The next three to four days are critical. He needs to stay in bed, keep his shoulder immobilized, and take the pain medication and antibiotics on schedule. No arguments."

Pixie glanced back at Wyatt, who shifted slightly in his sleep, wincing even in unconsciousness. Guilt twisted in her stomach, sharp and insistent.

"I can manage," she said finally, though her voice lacked its usual edge.

The nurse nodded, handing her a printed list of instructions. "Call me if you notice anything concerning—fever, excessive swelling, or signs of infection. Otherwise, he just needs time and care." She paused, glancing at Pixie. "And patience."

Pixie let out a humorless laugh. "Patience isn't exactly my specialty."

The nurse smiled, then packed up her bag and left, the door clicking shut behind her.

For a moment, Pixie just stood there, the silence pressing in on her as she looked at Wyatt again. He seemed so different like this—vulnerable, human. Gone was the cocky smirk, the infuriating swagger, the maddening glint in his blue eyes that always made her want to slap him and kiss him at the same time.

Now, he was just a man who had thrown himself into harm's way to protect her.

Pixie sank into the chair beside the bed, gripping the arms tightly. She hated this feeling — this gnawing guilt that wouldn't let her go. She wasn't used to feeling like she owed anyone anything, least of all someone like Wyatt Steele.

Her eyes drifted over him, as much as she hated herself for letting them. His roguish brown hair was longer than it had been last summer, a little unruly now from the sweat and strain of the accident. It framed his face in a way that softened his usual sharpness, making him look almost boyish. Almost. But then there was the faint stubble along his strong jaw, dark and rugged, as though he couldn't be bothered to tame it.

Her gaze lingered on his lashes — longer than they had any right to be, fanning over his high cheekbones — and the unreadable blue of his eyes, even though they were hidden now. She could still see them in her mind, though, sharp and unwavering, the kind of gaze that pinned her in place and made her feel seen in ways she didn't want to be.

And then there was his frame. Wyatt was tall, too tall, and broad-shouldered in a way that made the oversized guest bed look small. The blanket rested across his chest, doing little to hide the sheer size of him. His shoulders, one of them now bandaged and immobile, seemed like they were built to bear the weight of the world. He wasn't the kind of man who could blend into a crowd — he was a presence, commanding and solid.

Even now, injured and asleep, he radiated that same infuriating pull. She hated it — hated that her chest stirred with something she couldn't control every time she looked at him.

Pixie's jaw tightened as her gaze returned to his face. Despite the bandages and the paleness from blood loss, Wyatt Steele still looked maddeningly handsome. Rugged in a way that felt almost deliberate, as though the world conspired to make him the kind of man who got under her skin.

She leaned forward slightly. "You're an idiot," she muttered, the words tinged with more frustration than she meant. "You could have been killed."

Wyatt shifted, his brows pulling together like he'd heard her, even in his unconscious state. A quiet groan escaped him, his head turning slightly to the side. But he didn't wake.

Pixie exhaled slowly, leaning back in the chair and folding her arms tightly across her chest. She needed to get a grip. This was Wyatt Steele — chaotic, impossible, and reckless. He was infuriating in every way, and yet here she was, sitting by his side, unable to leave.

She told herself it was guilt. He'd risked himself to save her, throwing his body into harm's way without a second thought. She owed him, if nothing else, for that. And Caroline had asked her to ensure he recovered, a task she couldn't exactly refuse.

But as her eyes flicked back to him, she knew it wasn't just a favor keeping her there.

He stirred something in her, something she didn't want to acknowledge. Watching him like this — so vulnerable, so human — tangled her emotions into a knot she couldn't untie. She remembered how his blue eyes, as if lit from within, had burned into hers, how his rough hands had steadied her in the chaos, how his very presence had felt like a shield.

Pixie clenched her jaw, shaking her head as though she could shake off the thought. No. She wasn't going to do this. Wyatt Steele was chaos, and she couldn't afford to let him into her life, not in any way that mattered.

She leaned back in the chair, letting out a slow breath. For now, all she had to do was make sure he got through the next few days in one piece. After that, she could walk away again.

At least, that's what she told herself.

Chapter Eight

Sunlight poured through the tall windows, casting a warm glow over the room. Pixie stood by the bedside table, holding a small orange pill bottle, glaring down at Wyatt with her best no-nonsense look.

Propped up against pillows, Wyatt's face was pale, jaw tight with pain. Despite the bandages, he still looked frustratingly handsome—his tousled brown hair, piercing blue eyes locked on hers with defiance…and something darker.

"I said no," he growled, voice rough but firm.

Pixie's patience was running thin. She crossed her arms, the pill bottle rattling in her grip. "You're in pain, Steele. These will help. So stop being stubborn and take them."

His gaze hardened, fingers tightening on the blanket. "I'm not taking them. End of discussion."

She huffed, hands on her hips. "Why? Because you'd rather suffer and prove some macho point? You can barely sit up without wincing."

Wyatt's jaw clenched, eyes flicking away before meeting hers again. Something in his expression shifted — unease, vulnerability.

"It's not about that," he muttered.

"Then what is it?" she asked, tone softening just a fraction.

For a moment, he didn't answer, his gaze fixed on the far wall as though he were trying to avoid her entirely. Then he sighed, running a hand through his unruly hair.

"When I was in the military," he began, his voice low and rough, "I got injured during a mission. Pretty bad. Ended up on opioids for months while I recovered."

Pixie stilled, the tension in the room shifting.

"It got...out of hand," Wyatt admitted, his lips pressing into a thin line. "At first, it was just to manage the pain. But it didn't stop there. Took me a long time to get off them, and even longer to get back to myself." He looked at her then, his blue eyes sharp but tinged with vulnerability. "I can't go back to that, Pixie. Not for anything."

She stared at him, the pill bottle suddenly feeling heavy in her hand. She hadn't expected this — hadn't expected him to lower his walls like this, to admit something so raw.

"I didn't know," she said softly, her voice lacking its usual edge.

"Not exactly something I advertise," Wyatt replied, a faint, bitter smirk tugging at his lips. "But there it is. That's why I won't take them."

Pixie bit her lip, her fingers tightening around the pill bottle as she searched his face. He looked exhausted, the pain etched into every line of his features. She hated seeing him like this, hated that he was suffering because he refused to accept help.

"What if…" she started, hesitating before pushing forward. "What if I stayed? Just for a few days. I'll keep an eye on you. Make sure you only take what you need, when you need it. You won't be alone, Wyatt. I won't let you fall back into that."

His eyes locked onto hers, something unreadable flashing in their depths. "You'd do that?"

"Yes," she said firmly, surprised by how much she meant it.

Wyatt let out a slow breath, his shoulders sagging slightly as if the weight of the decision was pressing down on him. "It's a big promise, Sinclair," he said, his voice softer now.

"I know," Pixie replied, her chest tightening. She wasn't sure if he was talking about the promise itself or something deeper — something neither of them was ready to name. "But I'll keep it."

He studied her for a long moment, his piercing blue eyes searching hers as though testing her resolve. His eyes made her feel like drowning — beautiful, bottomless, and entirely unforgiving. Finally, he nodded, though the tension in his expression didn't fully ease.

"Fine," he said reluctantly. "But only because you promised."

Pixie exhaled, relief washing over her as she handed him a single pill and a glass of water. As he took it from her, his fingers brushed against hers, sending a spark of warmth up her arm that she ignored as best as she could.

"Thank you," he murmured, his voice barely audible.

She nodded, stepping back as he leaned his head against the pillows, his eyes already closing as the medication began to take effect.

But as she sat back down in the chair by his bed, watching his breathing slow, she couldn't shake the weight of the promise she'd made—or the feeling that it wasn't just for the next few days. It felt bigger, heavier. And it scared her more than she wanted to admit.

* * * *

The guest quarters were unusually still, the soft rhythm of rain tapping gently against the large windows. Wyatt lay on the oversized bed, his injured shoulder supported by pillows, the warm weight of Nova curled against his thigh. The faint sting of pain still lingered, but the painkillers had long since dulled it, leaving him warm and comfortably loose, sinking deeper into the plush sheets.

Across from him, Pixie sat in the armchair by the window, a spot she'd unofficially claimed. Her legs were tucked beneath her, and a sketchpad rested on her knee, the tip of her pencil moving quickly in swift, fluid marks. The quiet scratch of graphite on paper was the only sound, broken now and then by her low hums of satisfaction or disapproval as she adjusted her work.

The scent of the ocean wafted through the open window, mingling with the soft, earthy scent of rain. The air felt thick and warm, the sound of the storm outside a constant reminder of the storm that had passed between them.

"You know," Wyatt said lazily, his words slightly slurred, "you're real bossy, but you've got a good eye."

Pixie glanced up at him, her lips twitching into a smirk. "I'll take that as a compliment. You're not exactly the easiest subject."

"Why?" he asked, grinning despite himself. "Too handsome?"

She rolled her eyes but didn't argue, her focus returning to the page. "More like too fidgety. Hold still, Steele, or you'll end up looking like a Picasso."

He chuckled, sinking further into the pillows. The loose, light feeling was something he wasn't used to, and it unnerved him. He didn't like letting his guard down, especially around Pixie, who always seemed to know exactly how to dig under his skin. But the combination of the painkillers and her unexpected presence was doing strange things to his usually impenetrable walls.

"So," Pixie said after a moment, not looking up from her sketch. "Why'd you join the military?"

Wyatt blinked, his smile fading slightly. His instinct was to deflect, to change the subject, but the words came tumbling out before he could stop them. "Didn't have much of a choice. Small-town kid, nothing but trouble in my future if I stayed. The Army felt like a way out."

Pixie tilted her head, her pencil pausing mid-stroke. "A way out of what?"

Wyatt hesitated, staring at the ceiling. His voice softened. "Everything. My old man was a drunk, my mom couldn't handle him. I didn't want to end up like him, you know? Thought the Army would fix me. Give me some kind of purpose."

She didn't respond immediately, and when he glanced at her, her expression wasn't pitying—just thoughtful. She nodded, returning to her sketch. "Did it work?"

He let out a breathless laugh. "Define 'work.' It gave me direction, sure. But it also made me into someone else. Someone harder. Good for the job, not so good for real life."

Pixie looked up again, her dark eyes searching his. "You seem pretty good at real life to me."

"Yeah, well," Wyatt muttered, shifting uncomfortably against the pillows. "You don't know me as well as you think."

"Then tell me," she said softly, her voice devoid of its usual sharpness.

Wyatt froze, his heart skipping a beat. He wanted to, for reasons he couldn't quite explain. But the thought of laying himself bare in front of Pixie—of giving her a glimpse of the man he kept hidden—felt too dangerous.

Instead, he deflected. "What about you, Sinclair? What made you decide to rule the world as the First Lady's Chief of Staff?"

She smiled, but there was a flicker of something guarded in her eyes. "That's a long story."

"So's mine," he said, raising an eyebrow.

She hesitated, and for a moment, he thought she might actually open up. But then she shook her head, a teasing smile tugging at her lips. "I'm the one asking the questions, remember?"

Wyatt smirked, though it didn't reach his eyes. "Of course you are."

As Pixie returned to her sketch, he watched her, his gaze lingering on the curve of her lips, the way her hair fell across her cheek, the determined focus in her expression. She stirred something in him—something that went beyond attraction, beyond the usual pull he felt for women who caught his eye. She made him feel, and that terrified him more than anything.

"You're quiet all of a sudden," Pixie said, glancing at him. "Unusual for you."

He shrugged, wincing as the movement tugged at his injured shoulder. "Just thinking."

"About?"

"You."

The word slipped out before he could stop it, and the room seemed to still. Pixie's pencil froze mid-stroke, her gaze snapping to his.

"Wyatt…" she started, her voice uncertain.

"Don't," he interrupted, his voice low but steady. "Don't make me explain. Not now."

She stared at him for a moment longer, her expression unreadable, before she nodded and looked back down at her sketch.

Wyatt let his head fall back against the pillows, his chest tight despite the haze of the painkillers.

The room felt like it was spinning, warm and soft at the edges, and Wyatt knew he was way too high. The painkillers coursing through his system dulled the throbbing in his shoulder, but they also loosened his tongue in a way that was getting dangerous.

Pixie was sitting in the chair by his bed, her legs tucked beneath her, sketching something on her pad. The quiet focus on her face made her look younger, softer. She was full of contradictions, and right now, those contradictions were driving him insane.

"I didn't know you could draw," he said, his voice slow and slurred. "You're full of secrets."

Pixie glanced up, arching a brow, but didn't stop sketching. "Hm, you seem pretty intent on finding all of them."

"Damn right," he said, leaning his head back against the pillows. "I won't stop until I know them all."

This time, she stilled, her pencil pausing mid-stroke. For the first time, she looked...unnerved. Her dark eyes searched his, her lips pressing into a thin line. "What exactly do you mean by that?"

He blinked at her, the haze in his head making it hard to focus. His lips moved before his brain could stop them. "Just tell me how old you are."

Pixie frowned, sitting up straighter. "What?"

"How old are you?" he repeated, his tone as serious as he could manage.

"Thirty-three," she said, her voice clipped.

"Bullshit," Wyatt said, letting out a rough laugh that sent a sharp pang through his shoulder.

Nova grunted and rolled on her back, demanding a belly scratch from Wyatt.

Her frown deepened. "Wyatt, seriously."

"You aren't older than twenty-six, twenty-seven tops," he said, waving a hand as if it were an indisputable fact.

Pixie's lips parted, her brow furrowing. "How are you so sure?"

He smirked, though the effect was softened by the drugs. "I have eyes. And I pulled your file to prove it."

Her sketchpad slipped from her lap, landing on the floor with a muted thud. She stood up abruptly, her movements sharp. "What the hell, Wyatt?"

"I just need to know," he said, as he tried to sit up, only to wince and sink back down. "Tell me what's going on."

Her arms crossed tightly over her chest, her gaze narrowing. "Why do you care so much?"

He opened his mouth, then closed it, the words slipping away before he could grab them. The room tilted as he tried to think straight. "Because..." He paused, licking his dry lips. "Because you."

Pixie's brows knitted together, her frustration giving way to confusion. "That doesn't make sense."

Wyatt exhaled, the weight of the confession too heavy to stop now. "Because you've burned a hole in my brain, Sinclair. And I just can't stop thinking about my tongue in your mouth—" He stopped, running a hand over his face, but the filter was long gone. "I just want to grab you and bend you over this bed and unravel you, piece by piece—"

Pixie's gasp was audible, her cheeks flushing a deep red as she took a step back. "Wyatt!"

"I'm not sorry," he muttered, his head falling back against the pillows, his chest heaving. "One day, I'm going to show you."

Her jaw worked as if she wanted to say something but couldn't find the words. The tension between them was electric, suffocating, and for a moment, neither of them moved.

Then she spun on her heel, her voice tight. "You're high, and this conversation is over."

She stormed out, leaving the sketchpad abandoned on the floor and Wyatt staring at the ceiling, the heat of his words still burning in the air around him.

Chapter Nine

The estate was still, the quiet of the early hours pressing in. Pixie paced her guest room, bare feet gliding over the cool hardwood floor. Anger simmered beneath her skin—anger at Wyatt for being an arrogant idiot, at herself for still caring enough to check on him. But mostly, she was unsettled. The things he'd said—*burned a hole in my brain*—kept circling in her mind, forcing her to face feelings she didn't want to acknowledge.

She ran a hand through her hair, frustrated, before grabbing her robe and heading down the hall toward Wyatt's room. She'd promised to check on him. She always kept her promises, even when she wanted to strangle the man she'd made them to.

The door to his room was cracked open. She peeked inside. Wyatt lay on his back, chest rising and falling in a slow rhythm, with Nova curled on the rug by the window.

The moonlight filtering through the curtains cast shadows over Wyatt's face, highlighting the sharp planes of his jaw and the unruly mess of his brown hair. He looked younger, his usual hard edges softened by sleep. Vulnerable. Human.

For a moment, she hesitated. Seeing him like this stirred something uncomfortable in her — something raw. She wasn't used to vulnerability, in others or herself. It reminded her of things she'd tried to bury long ago.

She stepped inside quietly, her eyes scanning the room for the pill bottle on the bedside table. The nurse had said the drugs could make him restless or disoriented, and the last thing she needed was for him to hurt himself further.

As she approached the bed, Wyatt shifted, his face tightening in a grimace. A groan escaped his lips, and her heart clenched involuntarily.

She leaned closer. "Wyatt?"

His eyes fluttered open, glassy and unfocused, but he managed to find her face. "Pixie?"

"It's me," she said, crossing her arms defensively as she stood over him. "I'm just checking on you. You okay?"

He blinked a few times, the haze of the painkillers evident in his slow response. "Yeah. Just hurts like hell."

"Good," she said, though her voice wavered. "You deserve it for being reckless."

A faint smirk tugged at his lips, even through the pain. "You're mad."

"Of course I'm mad," she snapped, hugging herself. "You scared the hell out of me. You could've died, Wyatt."

The smirk faded, replaced by something more serious. "Didn't, though."

She exhaled, her gaze dropping to the floor. "No thanks to yourself."

He shifted again, wincing, and she instinctively reached out to steady him, her hand brushing against his uninjured arm. The warmth of his skin startled her, and she pulled back quickly.

"Pixie," he murmured, his voice low and rough. "Why do you care so much?"

Her chest tightened, her carefully constructed walls threatening to crack. She opened her mouth to respond but couldn't find the words.

He studied her, his blue eyes clearer now, though still heavy-lidded from the drugs. "You act like you don't, but you do. Why?"

Pixie stiffened, forcing her mask back into place. "Don't flatter yourself, Steele. I'm here because I made a promise. That's it."

"Nice try," he said, his gaze unwavering.

She turned away, her hands trembling as memories bubbled to the surface—memories of another man, another time, when vulnerability had cost her everything. The scars weren't visible, but they were there, woven into the fabric of who she was now. Serafina Romano didn't survive. Pixie Sinclair did.

She swallowed hard, forcing the memories back down. "You don't know anything about me," she said as she leaned in, inches from his face, to check the dressing on his shoulder.

"You're wrong," Wyatt said. "I know more than you think. And I'm not stopping until I figure out the rest."

"Why are you doing this?" she asked, her voice barely above a whisper. "Why are you looking at me like that?"

"Because I can't stop," he said simply.

Her hands froze mid-motion, her breath hitching in her chest. She forced herself to focus on the dressing, but before she could pull away, his hand shot up, gently wrapping around her wrist.

"Wyatt," she started, her voice uneven.

He didn't let her finish. With a careful but insistent pull, he brought her closer, guiding her down to his uninjured side. Her knees buckled, and she caught herself with her free hand against the mattress, her body suddenly pressed against his.

"Stop," she whispered, though her voice lacked conviction.

"Tell me you don't feel this," he said, his voice husky.

She opened her mouth to argue, to deny it, but the words caught in her throat as his other hand slid around her waist, anchoring her to him. His lips were on hers before she could think, capturing her in a kiss that was all fire and desperation.

Her first instinct was to push him away, but the moment his lips moved against hers, she melted. The kiss was nothing like she expected—demanding yet gentle, filled with a need that mirrored her own buried emotions.

She let herself sink into it, gripping the sheets beside his head for balance.

Wyatt's grip on her wrist tightened just enough to hold her steady, and in one fluid motion, she found herself half on top of him, her hand pressed against his chest for balance.

"Pixie," he murmured, his voice low and gravelly, the sound of her name sending a shiver through her.

Before she could respond, his free hand slid to her waist, fingers curling around her frame with a firmness that made her heart race. Then his lips were on hers, and all her protests, all her carefully constructed walls, shattered in an instant.

The kiss was intense, consuming. His lips moved against hers with a desperation that matched the fire building in her chest, his stubble rough against her skin. His tongue swept across her lower lip, seeking permission, and before she could think, she opened for him, her resolve crumbling completely.

His tongue slid into her mouth, warm and insistent, exploring her with a slow, deliberate rhythm that made her knees weak. She couldn't stop the soft, involuntary gasp that escaped her as he deepened the kiss, his hand sliding up her side, tracing the curve of her waist and ribs through the thin fabric of her blouse.

His touch was maddening, firm yet gentle, his fingertips brushing just below her shoulder before trailing back down her frame, his palm spreading against her lower back to pull her closer. Her body responded without hesitation, leaning into him, her free hand finding its way to his chest.

Wyatt groaned softly against her lips, the sound reverberating through her as his grip tightened, his thumb tracing the edge of her blouse where skin met fabric. The heat of his hand burned her, sending a jolt of electricity down her spine.

The kiss grew hungrier, his tongue tangling with hers in a way that left her breathless, her pulse thundering in her ears. His injured shoulder barely seemed to hold him back as he shifted slightly, pulling her further onto the bed and into his uninjured side, anchoring her to him.

Her body molded against his, her curves aligned with his hard frame. His hand slid lower, tracing the dip of her waist and holding the curve of her hip, his touch igniting a fire in her she hadn't felt in years.

When she finally pulled back, gasping for air, her lips were swollen, her chest heaving as her forehead rested against his. His hand remained on her waist, holding her close, his thumb idly stroking small circles on her side.

"Pixie," he whispered again, his voice rough and filled with something raw, something dangerous.

Her eyes fluttered open, meeting his gaze. Her heart pounded as his lips tilted into a faint smirk, and his fingers ran along her side again, sending another wave of heat through her.

"You feel that too," he said softly, his voice a low rumble. It wasn't a question—it was a statement, one she couldn't deny.

She didn't respond, couldn't respond, because her body had already betrayed her. The way she clung to him, the way her breathing quickened, the way her skin burned under his touch—it all spoke louder than words ever could.

And the worst part? She didn't want him to stop.

Pixie's breath mingled with Wyatt's as their foreheads rested together, the heat of the moment cocooning them in a space that felt suspended from reality. His hand on her waist didn't loosen—in a way that felt too intimate, too dangerous.

"Stay," he whispered, his voice hoarse, as if her name carried every emotion he couldn't quite say.

Her eyes fluttered open, meeting his gaze. Those piercing blue eyes, darkened now with something deeper than desire, locked onto hers, refusing to let her look away. She could still feel the ghost of his lips on hers, the way he'd kissed her like she was the only thing in the world that mattered.

And for a moment, she didn't want to move. She didn't want to leave the warmth of his body, the safety of his hold, the intensity of his gaze that seemed to see through every carefully constructed wall she'd ever built.

But then reality crept back in, cold and relentless.

She exhaled shakily, forcing her hands to press lightly against his chest, the steady thrum of his heartbeat beneath her palm making her hesitate.

"I... I can't," she murmured, her voice trembling.

Wyatt's brow furrowed, his hand tightening slightly on her waist, as if he could hold her there just a little longer. "Why not?" he asked, his voice low, rough.

Her lips parted, but the words didn't come immediately. She felt raw, exposed, like the kiss had stripped her bare in ways she hadn't expected. "Because...this isn't fair. To you. To me."

His other hand came up, brushing a strand of hair from her face with a gentleness that made her chest ache. "What if I don't care about fair?"

Her pulse quickened, her resolve wavering as she looked at him, his face inches from hers, his expression so open and unguarded it made her want to throw caution to the wind.

But she couldn't.

"You will," she said softly, her voice tinged with regret. "You don't know me, Wyatt. Not really."

His lips twitched into a faint smirk, though his eyes stayed serious. "Then let me."

Her throat tightened, and she shook her head, trying to ignore the way his words made her spin. "I have to go," she whispered, though she made no move to leave.

"Pixie—" he started, his tone pleading now.

She pressed her fingers to his lips, silencing him. The feel of his warm, slightly rough lips against her skin sent a shiver through her, but she ignored it, forcing herself to lean back.

"Please let me go," she repeated, firmer this time, as she gently untangled herself from his grip.

Wyatt's hand lingered on her waist for a moment before he let her go, his gaze never leaving hers as she rose from the bed. Her legs felt unsteady, her body still humming from his touch, but she forced herself to step back, putting distance between them even as every part of her screamed to stay.

"You can't keep running," he said quietly, his voice filled with something raw and vulnerable that made her heart ache.

She swallowed hard, her hands clenching at her sides. "I'm not running," she said, though it felt like a lie.

He didn't argue, just watched her with those impossibly blue eyes, his gaze burning into hers like he was trying to memorize every detail before she walked out of the door.

"I'll check on you in the morning," she said, her voice barely above a whisper.

And then, before he could say anything else, before she could change her mind, she turned and walked out, closing the door behind her.

But as she leaned against the wall outside his room, her heart pounding and her lips still tingling from his kiss, she knew she wouldn't be able to keep her distance for long. Wyatt Steele wasn't a man who let things go easily — and deep down, she wasn't sure she wanted him to.

Chapter Ten

Washington, DC

Two weeks since Wyatt's accident, and he was nearly fully recovered — something Pixie was silently thankful for.

They'd flown in from Palm Beach yesterday. Now, the First Lady was appearing at the Valentine's Day gala at the Red Orchid House.

The room buzzed with conversation, the warmth from the grand fireplace pushing back the February chill seeping through the tall windows. Pixie stood near the edge, a champagne flute in hand, eyes scanning the crowd. Veterans and their families mixed with reporters and high-profile guests. It was exactly the kind of event where Pixie thrived — polished, controlled, flawless.

Except tonight, she couldn't focus.

Her gaze kept drifting, against her will, to Wyatt. Or rather, her very grumpy patient — especially after she'd refused his late-night visits and started bringing Marcy along for the daytime check-ins.

The wall was back up between them.

Wyatt stood near the fireplace, surrounded by veterans. He looked sharp in a tailored black suit, his brown hair perfectly combed, yet still untamed. The firelight flickered in his unreadable blue eyes as he grinned, commanding the room effortlessly. Everyone hung on his every word, laughing, nodding. His charisma was magnetic — and dangerous.

Pixie gritted her teeth and turned away, gripping her glass tighter. She'd spent two weeks avoiding him — his presence, his voice, that infuriating ability to get under her skin. But here he was, larger than life in a room she couldn't escape.

She wished he'd stop existing. Or at least stop looking at her like that when he thought she wasn't paying attention.

Her attempt to blend into the crowd was thwarted as Caroline Armstrong, the First Lady, stepped gracefully onto the small stage at the front of the room. The soft murmur of conversation died down as everyone turned toward her.

"Good evening," Caroline began, her warm voice carrying through the room. "Thank you all for being here tonight to honor our veterans, their families, and the sacrifices they've made for this country. Tonight is not just about celebration — it's about gratitude."

Pixie stood straighter, slipping into professional mode. Caroline was in her element, every word carefully chosen, every gesture deliberate.

"And while we celebrate all of you tonight," Caroline continued, her gaze sweeping over the crowd, "there is one person I'd like to recognize specifically.

Someone who has dedicated his life to service, both in and out of uniform. A man who embodies courage, leadership, and resilience."

Pixie's stomach dropped. She knew where this was going.

"Agent Wyatt Steele," Caroline said, her smile widening as she gestured toward him.

The crowd broke into applause as Wyatt, looking surprised but composed, stepped forward. He moved with the confidence of someone who was used to commanding a room, though Pixie caught the faint flicker of something softer in his expression as he approached the stage.

Caroline continued, her voice warm and full of admiration. "Wyatt joined the Army at eighteen, determined to make a difference. He rose through the ranks, becoming one of the most trusted and skilled members of the special forces. But what I admire most about Wyatt isn't just his service—it's his unwavering commitment to protecting those around him, no matter the cost."

Pixie's throat tightened as the applause swelled again. She forced a sip of champagne down her throat, hoping it would quell the unwelcome knot forming there. Wyatt stood at the center of the room, accepting the honor with that maddening mix of humility and quiet confidence, his jaw set in a way that sent an irritating jolt through her chest.

Her gaze lingered despite herself, a gaze that pinned her, soft and merciless all at once. catching the way his shoulders squared beneath his tailored suit, the way his cold eyes softened as he nodded in thanks to Caroline. She hated how much this moment affected her—hated the way her chest ached at the pride she felt when she had no right to feel it.

Before she could stop herself, she glanced away, scanning the room for a distraction. The glittering crowd of veterans, reporters, and guests was a sea of chatter and clinking glasses, and Pixie was desperate to lose herself in it. She turned on her heel, heading toward the bar at the far end of the room, determined to escape before Wyatt could notice her watching him.

The bar was quieter, tucked into the corner of the room, with polished mahogany and flickering candles. Pixie placed her empty glass down and gestured for a refill, trying to steady her breathing.

"You look like you could use something stronger than champagne," came a smooth voice beside her.

She turned to see a man — mid-thirties, square-jawed, with a confident smile — leaning casually against the bar. He was dressed in a formal uniform, his chest adorned with medals that spoke of distinguished service.

"I'll stick to champagne," she replied, her voice cool but polite.

The man chuckled, lifting his whiskey in a toast. "Fair enough. Captain Greg Phillips, retired," he said, extending a hand.

"Pixie Sinclair," she replied, shaking his hand briefly.

"You here with the First Lady's team?" Greg asked, his gaze sweeping over her tailored dress.

"Yes," she said simply, hoping to end the conversation there. But Greg seemed intent on continuing.

"You must keep busy," he said, his smile widening. "I don't envy you trying to keep all of this running smoothly."

Pixie forced a small smile, the practiced kind that didn't reach her eyes. "It has its challenges."

Greg leaned in slightly, lowering his voice. "Well, if you ever need a break from all the madness, let me know. I'd be happy to buy you a drink sometime."

Pixie blinked, caught off guard by the sudden turn in the conversation. She opened her mouth to respond but felt the weight of an intense gaze on her.

She glanced over Greg's shoulder, and there he was. Wyatt Steele.

He stood across the room, his piercing blue eyes locked on her like a hawk tracking its prey. The flicker of firelight from the grand fireplace danced in his gaze, but it didn't soften the intensity. His expression was unreadable, but there was a tightness in his jaw, a sharpness in his stare that made her pulse quicken.

Pixie's throat dried as she took in the scene around him. A small group of women had gathered nearby, all leaning in a little too close, their laughter a touch too loud. One even touched his arm, and though Wyatt barely seemed to notice, Pixie's chest burned with something she refused to name.

Jealousy? Don't be ridiculous.

She turned her focus back to Greg, forcing a polite laugh at something he'd said, though she hadn't heard a word of it. The effort was excruciating, her body hyperaware of Wyatt's gaze.

Greg tilted his head, his smile faltering slightly. "You okay? You seem distracted."

"I'm fine," she lied, reaching for her newly filled glass of champagne.

"You sure?" Greg pressed, stepping closer.

The movement brought him just slightly into her personal space, and before she could react, she caught another flicker of motion in her periphery.

Wyatt.

He was moving now—cutting through the crowd like he'd parted it with a blade. Broad shoulders, long stride, too tall and too sure of himself to be missed. The women he'd left behind trailed their stares after him, hollow with disappointment, drawn to the echo of him like moths chasing smoke.

Pixie's heart leapt—then lodged hard in her throat.

Because he was looking at her.

Not just looking. Seeing.

That impossible blue gaze locked on like she was the only soul in the room—soft as a touch, merciless as truth.

Every step brought him closer, and the pull of him dragged her under.

That blue.

Not the color of eyes, but of memory. Of bruises. Of ocean graves.

Then—he looked away.

And just like that, winter.

She'd never felt so cold.

* * * *

The Red Orchid House was warm and bright, the soft crackle of the fireplace and low murmur of conversation filling the air. Wyatt moved through the room with a calculated ease, his sharp eyes scanning the crowd. He wasn't here for enjoyment—he was here for duty, to keep the First Lady safe and ensure the evening went off without a hitch. At least, that was what he told himself.

But his gaze kept straying.

And then he saw her.

Pixie.

She stood near the bar, laughing at something the man beside her said. A military guy, judging by his uniform and the overly confident tilt of his grin. Wyatt couldn't hear the exchange over the hum of the gala, but he could see the way the guy leaned closer, his hand brushing the back of Pixie's chair as if he were claiming the space around her.

Wyatt's jaw tightened. His fingers curled into a fist at his side, the low burn in his chest spreading as he watched her smile at the man, angling her head in that way she always did when she was pretending to be charmed.

She doesn't mean it, he told himself, though the thought did little to soothe the sharp edge of his irritation. He tore his gaze away, forcing himself to focus on his path through the room, but his steps felt heavier, his control more fragile.

By the time he found the First Lady, she was already preparing to leave, her polished demeanor unchanged despite the long evening. "Wyatt," she said warmly, gesturing toward him.

"Ma'am," he replied, his voice even as he opened the door for her.

The motorcade was waiting just outside, the cold February air biting against his skin as he escorted her to the SUV. The press followed at a distance, snapping photos and shouting questions that went unanswered as he closed the door behind Caroline and climbed into the driver's seat.

The quiet of the vehicle should have been a relief, but his mind was still stuck on the image of Pixie at the bar, laughing, leaning, smiling at someone else.

"You've been quiet tonight, Steele," Caroline said from the backseat, her tone light but observant.

"Just focused on the job, ma'am," he replied, his voice clipped.

"You've been focused on something," she said with a knowing smile, her reflection catching his eye in the rearview mirror.

Wyatt's grip on the wheel tightened. "Everything went smoothly tonight. That's what matters."

Caroline hummed softly, her gaze flicking out of the window. "You've been with me long enough, Wyatt. I know when something's on your mind."

He didn't respond, his jaw locking as he navigated the streets of D.C.

Caroline leaned forward slightly, her tone softening. "If I may... Whatever it is, let it go. Don't let your past keep you from your future."

Wyatt's chest tightened, her words hitting a nerve he didn't want to expose. He forced himself to nod, keeping his eyes on the road. "Yes, ma'am."

But as they approached the Blair Residence, the tension in his chest didn't ease. He parked the SUV smoothly, stepping out to open the door for her, his movements automatic.

Caroline paused as she stepped onto the curb, her hand briefly resting on his arm. "You're a good man, Wyatt. Don't forget that."

He nodded stiffly, watching as she disappeared into the residence with her detail. The warmth of her words stayed with him, but they didn't soothe the storm brewing inside.

Back in the driver's seat, alone with his thoughts, Wyatt exhaled slowly, his knuckles white against the wheel.

He hated how much it had bothered him — seeing Pixie with someone else. He hated the way it stirred something deep, something raw and painful he couldn't fully name. But most of all, he hated the part of him that wanted to fight for her, even when he knew he'd never be enough.

Let it go, he told himself, gripping the wheel tighter. But as he pulled the vehicle away from the curb, the thought of her smile lingered, refusing to let him.

Chapter Eleven

Blair House, Washington, DC

The house was quiet—too quiet. The kind of stillness that came after the chaos of a busy day. Wyatt made his rounds, checking in with the overnight staff, giving one last sweep of the wing where Pixie's quarters were.

He didn't need to go in. Just check the door.

But then he smelled it. Bleach. Sharp and acrid, cutting through the usual scents of fresh linens and wood polish.

His chest tightened. Irritation flared. He pushed open the door without knocking.

The room was dim, lit only by the harsh bathroom lights spilling into the space. And there she was, standing in front of the mirror, a plastic bowl in one hand, a brush in the other. Her hair, blonde once upon a time, was now clipped up as she carefully painted bleach onto a section.

Wyatt froze.

"Are you serious?" Wyatt barked, stepping into the room.

Pixie jumped, turning toward him with wide eyes, the brush still hovering mid-air. "What the hell are you doing, Steele?" she snapped, regaining her composure in record time.

"What am I doing?" he said. "What are you doing?"

She rolled her eyes, turning back to the mirror as if his presence were no more than a mild annoyance. "What does it look like? I'm fixing my hair."

"Fixing?" he repeated, his voice rising. He stepped closer, his jaw tightening as he caught a whiff of the bleach again. "Your hair doesn't need fixing."

"Thanks for your opinion," Pixie said, dipping the brush back into the bowl. "But I didn't ask for it."

Wyatt's patience snapped. In two long strides, he closed the distance between them and grabbed her wrist, pulling the brush from her hand. "That's enough."

"Excuse me?" Pixie said, her tone icy as she yanked her arm back.

"You heard me," he growled. "You don't need this crap in your hair. It's perfect the way it is."

"It's my hair," she said, glaring at him as she tried to snatch the bowl from his other hand. "You don't understand."

"Not tonight, you're not," Wyatt said, stepping around her to dump the contents into the sink.

"Wyatt!" Pixie shouted, her voice echoing in the small space as she grabbed his arm.

Ignoring her protests, he turned on the tap, the harsh chemical smell rising as the bleach swirled down the drain. Then, before she could react, he turned back to her, gripping her shoulders gently but firmly.

"Bend over," he ordered, his voice low and commanding.

Her eyes widened, her cheeks flushing. "What?"

"The sink," he clarified, though there was no mistaking the heat in his voice. "You're washing that out. Now."

"You're insane," she snapped, but the hesitation in her voice betrayed her resolve.

He didn't wait for her to argue further. With careful but insistent hands, he guided her toward the sink, tilting her head under the stream of water.

"Wyatt, stop!" she said, half-laughing, half-shouting as she struggled against him.

"Stay still," he muttered, one hand holding her head steady as the other worked to rinse out the streaks she'd already applied.

"You can't do this," Pixie said, water splashing onto her blouse as she wriggled beneath his grip. "You're a bully."

"And you're beautiful," he said, his tone softer now but still firm.

She froze at his words, the fight draining out of her as the water rushed over her hair.

"You don't need this," Wyatt said quietly, his voice rough. "You don't need bleach or dye or anything else to be perfect. You're already—"

"Don't," Pixie whispered, cutting him off as she straightened abruptly, pulling away from the sink.

Their eyes locked, the tension between them crackling like a live wire. Water dripped down her neck, soaking the collar of her blouse, but she didn't seem to notice.

Wyatt's hands fell to his sides, his chest heaving as he searched her face. "Why are you doing this to yourself?"

Pixie's jaw tightened, her dark eyes flickering with something he couldn't quite name. "It's not about you, Wyatt. It never was."

"Then why?" he pressed, stepping closer.

She looked away, her hands clenching into fists.

Wyatt narrowed the distance between them, his sharp blue eyes scanning her face for cracks in her armor. He wasn't letting this go. Not tonight. "Then why, Pixie? What are you running from?"

Her jaw tightened, and her lips pressed into a thin line. She didn't answer.

The silence was deafening, and it only fueled his frustration. "It's not just your hair," he said, his voice rough, pushing further. "This is about something else—something you're hiding from. Isn't it?"

"I'm not hiding," she snapped, but there was a tremor there, just enough to tell him he'd struck a nerve.

"You need a better poker face," Wyatt growled, stepping closer.

Pixie tried to shove past him, but he blocked her path, his hand darting out to grab her wrist. She yanked back, and in the movement, the bowl of bleach nearly toppled off the counter. Wyatt caught it with his free hand, his movements quick but awkward, and the effort sent a sharp stab of pain through his still-healing shoulder.

He sucked in a breath, the low groan escaping before he could stop it.

Pixie froze, her dark eyes darting to his face, her annoyance melting into concern. "You're hurt," she said, softer now.

"I'm fine," he bit out, his grip on her wrist tightening slightly as if he were holding on for control—not of her but of himself.

"You're not fine," she said, her tone laced with exasperation. "You're two weeks out from nearly being crushed, Wyatt. What are you even doing storming in here like this?"

"Stopping you from making a mistake," he said, low, though the pain laced his words.

She glared at him, her free hand pushing at his chest, trying to get him to back off. "You don't know when to stop."

"And you're hiding!" he snapped, his frustration boiling over.

Their movements became a tangle of arms and sharp words, both too stubborn to relent. He reached for the towel in her hand, intending to clean the remnants of bleach from her hair, but she twisted, sending them both stumbling out of the narrow bathroom and into the bedroom.

Wyatt's foot caught on the edge of the rug, and the strain on his shoulder pulled another low groan from him as they went down. Pixie gasped as they hit the fur rug, her weight half on top of him, her hair spilling over her face in damp strands.

The world stilled, the heat of the argument replaced by something far more electric. Wyatt's chest heaved beneath her as he fought to steady his breath, his injured arm cradled protectively at his side.

"I just want a normal life, is that too much to ask for?" Pixie muttered, her hands braced against his chest.

"Define 'normal'," he replied, his lips quirking into a faint smirk despite the pain.

Her dark eyes met his, and for a moment, the tension between them shifted. She didn't move, her breathing shallow as her gaze flicked to his lips and back up again.

Wyatt's free hand moved without thought, brushing a damp strand of hair from her face, his fingers lingering against her cheek. "I wish you'd tell me what happened, Pixie," he said softly, his voice stripped of its usual sharpness. "Who hurt you?"

Her lips parted, her expression torn between defiance and something more vulnerable. "I don't want to discuss it," she whispered.

"Tell me."

Chapter Twelve

The air between them felt impossibly heavy, charged with emotions Pixie had been avoiding for years. Wyatt's hand lingered on her cheek, his touch gentle despite the frustration that lined his face. His blue eyes searched hers with a mix of concern and determination, and for the first time in a long time, she felt like someone truly saw her—not just the carefully constructed façade she wore for the world, but the messy, broken pieces underneath.

"I can't do this," she whispered, her voice trembling.

"Yes, you can," Wyatt replied softly, steady and certain. "Tell me, Pixie. Whatever it is, just say it. I'll protect you. You know I will."

Her breath hitched, and she pulled back slightly, sitting up on the rug. Her hair dripped onto her shoulders, the damp strands clinging to her skin as she wrapped her arms around herself.

"You don't understand," she said, shaking her head. "If you knew—if anyone knew—I'd be done. Completely."

Wyatt pushed himself upright, wincing as his injured shoulder protested the movement. He didn't back down, didn't give her space to retreat further. "Then help me understand," he said. "Because I'm not letting this go, Pixie. Not until you tell me the truth."

Her chest tightened, the walls she'd spent years building threatening to crumble under the weight of his words. She wanted to believe him, to trust him, but the fear of what he'd think — what he'd do — if he knew the truth kept her rooted in place.

"I just want to be a part of this," she said finally. She looked down, at her fingers gripping the edge of the rug beneath her. "The Armstrong family, this job... It's the only place I've ever felt like I belong. Even if it's just a little longer, I need this."

Wyatt's brow furrowed. "Pixie, what are you talking about? You already belong. Caroline trusts you. Hell, she depends on you. No one's questioning that."

She shook her head, tears spilling down her cheeks now, hot and relentless. "You don't get it. I don't belong here. Not really. Not if they knew —" She choked on the words, unable to finish.

"Knew what?" Wyatt pressed gently, his free hand reaching for hers. "Pixie, whatever it is, it can't be worse than you think. You don't have to carry it alone. Tell me so I can help you."

She laughed bitterly, though it was laced with pain. "You can't fix this, Wyatt. No one can."

"Let me try," he said. "Please."

Her gaze met his, and the vulnerability in his eyes nearly undid her. She'd spent so long running, hiding, convincing herself that she could outrun her past if she just worked hard enough, stayed sharp enough. But here he was, offering her the one thing she'd never had—someone willing to stand by her, no matter what.

"I trusted the wrong person once," she admitted finally, trembling. "And it cost me everything. My name, my reputation, my life. I had to start over completely. That's why 'Pixie Sinclair' only started existing ten years ago."

Wyatt's expression didn't change, though she could see the flicker of realization in his eyes. "Go on," he said softly, his grip on her hand steady.

"I was young, stupid," she continued. "There was someone I thought I could trust. Someone who promised me the world, and I believed him. But it turned out he was...involved in things. Illegal things. And when it all fell apart, I was the scapegoat."

Wyatt's jaw flexed, his gaze never leaving hers.

"I didn't do anything," she said, her voice breaking. "But that didn't matter. I was ruined. So I left. Changed my name. Built a new life." She looked away, tears streaming down her face. "But if anyone found out—if Caroline knew—I'd lose everything again."

Wyatt's hand tightened around hers. "You're not losing anything, Pixie. Not while I'm here."

She shook her head, tears dripping onto her knees. "You don't understand. It's not just about the job. It's about surviving. If they find out who I really am, I'm done."

Wyatt leaned closer, his injured shoulder forgotten as he reached up to brush a tear from her cheek. "Pixie, listen to me," he said. "I don't care who you were. I care about who you are now. And no one—no one—is going to take this life from you. Not if I can help it."

Her breath caught, the weight of his words crashing over her like a wave. For the first time in years, the fear that had been her constant companion started to loosen its grip.

She collapsed against him, her forehead resting on his good shoulder as she sobbed quietly. Wyatt wrapped his arm around her, holding her tightly, his lips brushing against her damp hair.

The room felt impossibly small, the weight of her confession pressing against her chest like a physical force. Pixie clung to Wyatt's good shoulder, her tears soaking into his shirt as she tried to catch her breath. She couldn't believe she'd told him — him of all people — the truth she'd buried so deeply. The truth she swore no one would ever know.

But here she was, and instead of the disgust or disappointment she expected, Wyatt was holding her, his touch firm and steady as if he could somehow hold her together when she felt like she was falling apart.

"Pixie," he said softly, his voice a low rumble against her ear.

She hesitated, unwilling to pull back, unwilling to see the pity in his eyes. But when she finally forced herself to lift her head, what she saw wasn't pity — it was resolve. His azure blue eyes locked onto hers, unwavering, his expression intense and serious.

"I'm going to protect you," he said, his voice steady, each word spoken like an unshakable vow.

Her chest tightened, the warmth of his words almost too much to bear. "You don't understand —"

"I don't need to understand everything," he interrupted, brushing a strand of wet hair from her cheek. His touch lingered, his thumb grazing her skin. "All I need to know is that you're worth it. And you are."

Tears welled in her eyes again, but this time, they weren't from fear. She searched his face, trying to find some crack in his resolve, some sign that he didn't mean it. But there was nothing. Just Wyatt, as steady and immovable as ever, looking at her like she was the only thing in the world that mattered.

"You can't promise that," she whispered, her voice trembling.

"I just did," he replied, his tone resolute. "Whatever it takes, Pixie. I'll protect you. No one's taking this life from you. Not while I'm around."

Her breath hitched, her chest aching with emotions she couldn't name. Gratitude. Relief. Something sharper, more dangerous.

"Why?" she asked softly, the word barely audible.

His gaze flicked to her lips, then back to her eyes, and for a moment, the world seemed to stop. "Because you matter," he said, his voice low and rough. "More than you realize."

Wyatt's hand slid to the back of Pixie's neck, his fingers threading through her damp hair as he pulled her closer. His grip was firm yet careful, as though he feared she might vanish if he wasn't careful enough. Her breath hitched, her lips parting just slightly, and in that moment, the air between them seemed to crackle with unspoken emotion.

Then he kissed her.

At first, it was soft, exploratory, his lips brushing hers in a way that sent shivers coursing down her spine. But the second she melted into him, the second her fingers curled into his shirt, anchoring herself, the kiss deepened.

Wyatt groaned low in his throat, the sound reverberating through her, and his other arm slipped around her waist, pulling her flush against him.

His lips moved against hers with a maddening mix of tenderness and intensity, as if he were pouring every unsaid word, every unacknowledged feeling into the kiss. His tongue swept across her lower lip, teasing, coaxing, before sliding inside to tangle with hers. It was electric, overwhelming, and Pixie couldn't stop the soft gasp that escaped her.

Wyatt's hand drifted from her waist, sliding up her back in a slow, deliberate motion. His palm was warm through the thin fabric of her blouse, his touch firm and possessive, tracing the curve of her spine as though he were memorizing every inch of her.

His fingers splayed out, traveling upward to the base of her neck, then down again, his movements unhurried but insistent. She arched slightly against him, her body betraying her resolve as his touch sent heat pooling in her chest, her stomach, her very core.

His free hand stayed tangled in her hair, tilting her head just enough to deepen the kiss, to claim her fully. She felt consumed by him, his presence, his strength, the way he kissed her like she was the only thing keeping him grounded.

Her hands moved instinctively, sliding up his chest and over his broad shoulders, careful of his injury but unable to stop herself from exploring. He was solid beneath her touch, his warmth seeping into her fingertips, his body pressing against hers in a way that made her dizzy.

Wyatt's hand dipped lower on her back, brushing the small of her spine before moving up again in a maddening rhythm. His touch left a trail of fire in its wake, her skin burning with an intensity she hadn't felt in years.

"Let me in," he murmured against her lips, his voice rough and breathless.

She barely registered the sound, too lost in the feel of him, the way his lips and hands seemed to pull her apart and put her back together all at once.

When he finally pulled back, just enough to let her breathe, his forehead rested against hers, their breaths mingling in the stillness of the room. His hand lingered on her back, his fingers splayed against her spine as if he couldn't bring himself to let go.

"Damn," he whispered, his voice husky and raw. His blue eyes searched hers, his gaze darkened with emotion and something deeper, something she wasn't ready to name.

Pixie's chest heaved, her fingers still clutching his shirt as she tried to steady herself. She could feel the heat of his hand, the lingering sensation of his lips, and for a moment, she couldn't think of anything but him.

"Wyatt," she started, her voice shaky, but he cut her off, brushing his thumb against her cheek.

He rolled her onto her back, guiding her down onto the plush rug beneath them. His body followed hers, hovering above her as he braced himself on his good shoulder, his other arm cradling her waist. The movement was careful, deliberate, but every part of him burned with the need to be closer to her, to claim this moment entirely.

Pixie gasped softly as she landed on the soft fur rug, her eyes wide, her lips swollen from their kiss. Wyatt's blue eyes locked onto hers, his gaze determined and unrelenting as he leaned down, capturing her mouth again in a kiss that was absolutely consuming, his tongue teasing hers in languid, deliberate strokes that left her breathless.

His free hand moved from her waist, sliding down her belly in a slow, deliberate motion. His palm pressed gently against her mound, his fingers finding the hot core between her hips, teasing her over her pants. The motion was maddeningly tender, grounding, yet it sent sparks shooting through her.

Pixie's hands moved instinctively, one curling into his shirt while the other slid to his neck, her fingertips brushing his hairline. Her body arched slightly beneath him, her stomach tightening under his touch as his hand continued its slow, rhythmic pressure.

"Wyatt," she murmured against his lips, her voice trembling with a mix of need and disbelief.

He pulled back slightly, his lips hovering just above hers as he whispered, "Tell me to stop, and I will."

She searched his eyes, the vulnerability in his voice hitting her harder than the intensity of his touch. But she didn't want him to stop—couldn't bring herself to say the words.

Instead, she pulled him closer, her lips finding his again, her answer clear in the way she kissed him back with just as much desperation.

Wyatt groaned softly into her mouth, his hand pressing more firmly against her belly, his thumb brushing just beneath the curve of her ribs. His movements were unhurried, intentional, as if he was savoring every second, every inch of her beneath him.

The weight of him above her, the heat of his hand, the way his lips moved against hers—it was overwhelming in the best possible way. Pixie felt her walls crumbling, the fear and hesitation that had kept her guarded for so long slipping away with every touch, every kiss.

"Fuck, girl," Wyatt murmured, his lips moving to her jawline, trailing soft, teasing kisses down her neck. "You drive me insane."

Her breath hitched, her fingers gripping his shoulder as his words sent shivers through her. "You're not exactly easy to deal with, Steele," she said, though her voice lacked its usual edge.

He chuckled softly, the sound low and rough, vibrating against her skin. "Good," he said, moving his hand to her waistband and then underneath in a fluid motion that set her on fire. "Because I don't plan on being easy with you."

And then he was tearing down her pants and panties. He traced down her slit, finding her wet and throbbing beneath his touch.

Pixie's heart pounded, her body responding to every word, every touch, every kiss. For the first time in a long time, she felt completely unguarded, completely alive.

And with Wyatt above her, his lips and hands claiming her, she realized she didn't want it any other way.

Wyatt moved his palm in slow, deliberate circles against Pixie's clit, his fingers trailing lower before sliding back up, his touch firm but maddeningly gentle. Her lips parted as a soft sound escaped her, somewhere between a gasp and a sigh.

He couldn't help the smirk that tugged at his lips, the flush of pride mingling with the heat coursing through him. He kissed her again, deep and slow, swallowing her quiet whimpers as his hand continued its unhurried exploration of her wet pussy. Her skin was warm beneath his touch, every movement drawing a reaction from her that made his chest tighten with want.

Need.

"Wyatt," she murmured breathlessly, her hands clutching at his ribs, her nails digging in just enough to send a spark of pain that only fueled him further.

"This," he whispered against her lips, his voice low and rough, "is beyond what I ever imagined."

Pixie's eyes fluttered shut, her breathing uneven as his hand pressed lower, his thumb tracing the edge of her hip. Her body tensed briefly beneath him, only to soften as his touch became firmer, more insistent. The way she responded to him—her soft moans, the way her body moved instinctively to meet his touch—ignited something primal in him.

Her head was tilted back against the plush rug, her damp hair framing her flushed face. Wyatt leaned down, his tongue grazing the hollow of her throat as his hand shifted, finding the perfect angle that made her gasp loudly, her fingers clutching at his tensed abs.

"Wyatt," she gasped again, her voice trembling as the tension built higher, hotter. He could feel it in the way she gripped him, the way her breathing turned shallow and uneven, the way her legs shifted beneath him as if she couldn't control the movement.

"You're so damn beautiful," he murmured, his lips brushing against her ear as he focused all his attention on her, his hand moving with a precision that made her shudder.

Pixie's breath caught, her body tightening beneath him as she reached the peak. Her head fell back, her chest heaving, her body trembling as he held her through the wave, his hand slowing but never leaving her.

He kissed her again, soft and lingering, as her breathing began to steady, her body relaxing beneath his touch. Wyatt's chest swelled with satisfaction, the sight of her in that moment burning into his memory, perfect and raw and entirely his.

And then there was a knock at the door.

Chapter Thirteen

"Steele?" Salem's voice echoed through the door.

Wyatt froze, hand still resting on Pixie's hip, eyes snapping to the sound.

"You in there?" Salem knocked again, louder this time. "Been looking for you, man. Everything okay?"

Pixie's eyes shot open, panic flashing across her face. She pushed weakly against his chest. "Wyatt," she said, voice low but urgent. "Get up."

Wyatt cursed under his breath, pulling back. His shoulder twinged in protest, but he ignored it. Pixie's flushed face, tousled hair, and wrinkled blouse screamed everything he couldn't say. All he wanted was to kiss her again.

But then Salem knocked a third time.

With a frustrated sigh, Wyatt stood, smoothing his shirt. "Stay here," he muttered.

He opened it just enough to block the view of the room behind him, leaning against the frame as he stared down at Salem, who looked mildly annoyed.

"Salem," Wyatt said. "What do you want?"

Salem's eyes narrowed. "What do I want? I've been trying to find you for half an hour. We've got shift changes happening, and you disappeared without a word. Thought something happened."

Wyatt rubbed the back of his neck, his irritation bubbling. "I'm fine. Just checking in on things."

"In the private wing?" Salem asked, raising an eyebrow. "Alone?"

Wyatt's jaw clenched. "Is there a point to this, or are you just here to give me a hard time?"

Salem studied him for a moment, his sharp cowboy instincts clearly sensing something was off, but he shrugged. "Fine, fine. Just making sure you didn't keel over or something. You're supposed to be taking it easy, remember?"

"Noted," Wyatt said, already moving to close the door. "I'll be down in a few."

Wyatt glanced back at Pixie, still sprawled on the fur rug. She found her glasses in the rug and pushed them back onto the bridge of her nose, her lips slightly parted as if she wanted to say something but couldn't find the words.

"I've got to go," he said, his voice low and rough, lingering in the air between them.

Pixie's dark eyes flickered with something he couldn't quite name as she chewed on her bottom lip, her gaze darting away. Her silence unnerved him more than anything she could have said.

Wyatt turned and made his way to the door, forcing himself not to look back. He slipped into the hallway, his heartbeat still pounding in his ears as he straightened his shirt.

He wasn't halfway down the hall when he saw Salem leaning casually against the wall, arms crossed as he gave Wyatt a long, scrutinizing look.

"Boss," Salem drawled, stepping into his path.

Wyatt stopped, his jaw tightening. "Salem. Something you need?"

"Are we going to talk about it? Or pretend it didn't happen?" Salem said, his tone casual but his sharp eyes missing nothing.

"The latter."

"Fine. Just be aware—you've been holed up in Sinclair's room for a good while. Thought you were supposed to be recovering, not…whatever that was."

Wyatt's shoulders tensed, but he kept his expression neutral. "I was checking in."

"Well," Salem said, raising a skeptical brow, "people are talking. They don't know what to make of it. You and Sinclair, all these little… moments. You're acting weird around her, and people notice, Wyatt. It's got folks unnerved."

Wyatt clenched his fists, forcing himself to keep calm. "I don't need you playing hall monitor, Salem. Everything is fine."

"Is it?" Salem pressed, his voice still calm but pointed. "That little stunt in her room? Not helping."

Wyatt didn't respond, his jaw tightening as he brushed past Salem and continued down the hall. He didn't need this right now, didn't need anyone questioning his judgment.

But as he reached the main security post, the weight of Salem's words hung over him like a storm cloud. Whatever was happening between him and Pixie, it was starting to bleed into the world around them.

And for the first time, he wasn't sure if he could stop it. Or if he even wanted to.

Chapter Fourteen

The sun was just peeking over the horizon, casting a soft orange glow on the city outside the Blair House windows. The day had already begun with its usual whirlwind of meetings, schedules, and demands, all orbiting around Caroline Armstrong's needs as First Lady.

Pixie moved through the office in her signature sharp heels, a file in one hand and her phone in the other. She was already three steps ahead of everyone, ensuring the First Lady's itinerary for the day was airtight. Her head tilted slightly as she scrolled through her messages, her focus razor-sharp, until she heard a familiar, gruff voice behind her.

"You know, Sinclair, if you walk any faster, you might start levitating."

She didn't bother turning around, her lips twitching into a smirk. "I'm sorry, Steele. Some of us actually have work to do."

Wyatt stepped up beside her, his tall frame casting a shadow over her. He was holding his earpiece to his ear, issuing a quick directive to his team, before lowering it with a faint smirk of his own. "And here I thought nagging everyone else was your work."

Pixie finally glanced up at him. "And here I thought standing around looking intimidating was yours."

His grin widened just slightly. "Well, it works. Case in point—you're talking to me instead of ignoring me."

"I'm only talking to you because you're in my way," she said, brushing past him and heading toward the conference room.

"Of course you are," he called after her, his tone laced with sarcasm as he followed.

The day unfolded as usual—back-to-back briefings, check-ins with the First Lady, and managing the endless flood of emails and requests. But as the hours wore on, Pixie found herself unable to fully acknowledge the steady undercurrent of tension.

It wasn't until she found herself alone in the residence's library later in the afternoon, reviewing security plans for an upcoming gala in New York, that the things took a turn.

Her pen hovered over a detail she didn't like when she heard it—the steady, unmistakable rhythm of *his* boots on hardwood.

Pixie didn't look up. "Family presence at this thing is going to be big," Pixie said, scanning the document in front of her. "Caroline wants to emphasize connection and community."

Wyatt didn't answer right away. When he did, he was already leaning his hip against the edge of the table, arms crossed like he belonged there.

"Makes sense," he said. "Nothing says 'heart-warming' like a family photo op staged in front of bulletproof glass."

Pixie glanced up at him. That smirk. That voice. That frustrating way he always managed to sound like he was joking and still somehow cut straight to the truth. Something flickered in her — too fast to name. She didn't let it stay.

He caught the look anyway. Of course he did.

"What?" he asked, tilting his head, that careless charm creeping in around the edges.

She shook her head. Not because there was nothing to say — but because she wasn't about to let him be the one to draw it out of her.

Not yet.

Finally, she said, "Not everyone has that, you know."

Wyatt stilled slightly, his sharp eyes flicking to hers. "What do you mean?"

She hesitated, the weight of the admission settling heavily on her shoulders. But something about the way he looked at her — steady, unjudging — made her continue.

"I don't have family," she said.

"Don't stop there."

"The closest I ever had passed away when I was young. After that…it was foster homes."

Wyatt's brows furrowed, his usual cocky demeanor softening. "You were in the system?"

Pixie nodded, forcing a tight smile. "Yeah. It wasn't all bad, but let's just say it taught me how to fend for myself."

The room went quiet for a moment, the weight of her words hanging between them. Wyatt shifted slightly, his arms crossing over his chest.

"I get it," he said finally, his voice rougher than usual.

She acted surprised. "Don't tell me you are going to share something."

He shot her a violent look. "My dad bailed when I was a kid. Left my mom to raise me on her own. I haven't spoken to him in…hell, fifteen years? Probably longer."

Pixie looked up at him. "Fifteen years?"

"Yeah," he said, his tone sharp with bitterness. "He was a deadbeat. I don't care where he is or what happened to him. Hopefully he's dead."

Her gaze softened, though she said nothing. She could see the tension in his jaw, the way his hand curled into a fist at his side. It was clear he cared more than he let on.

"Have you ever thought about finding him?" she asked cautiously.

Wyatt's eyes snapped to hers, narrowing slightly. "Why would I do that? I'm not crying at his grave."

"Because," she said softly, "maybe you need closure. Or answers. Or maybe just…peace."

His jaw tightened, his gaze hardening. "I'm good. He made his choices, and I'm fine without him."

"But are you?" she pressed, her voice gentle but firm. "Or are you just telling yourself that because it's easier than admitting you're angry?"

Wyatt's hand shot up, fingers raking through his hair, that familiar tell when something got too close. "Drop it, Pixie," he muttered, voice already fraying. "I'm not interested in digging up the past. It's done."

She froze, mid-sentence, heart catching like it always did when he shut down. *No*, she wanted to say. *It's not done — not for you. Not the way you still carry it in your shoulders. In your silences.*

"You know," she said instead, gently, trying to meet him where the wreckage was buried, "I'm something of an amateur sleuth."

A small, cautious smile. One she hoped might coax him back.

"I could help. I have connections —"

"I said, drop it." His voice cracked like a whip.

Pixie flinched, barely. Just enough for her breath to catch. Her lips pressed together in a tight line as she stared at him, willing her expression to stay calm, to stay neutral, even as something in her chest folded in on itself.

The silence stretched between them, thick and awful. The kind that made her want to fill it with anything, even lies.

Wyatt's posture shifted — guilt settling in behind the storm. His jaw twitched. He looked away.

"Look," Wyatt said finally. "I can't go there, Pixie."

She nodded once, too slowly. "Okay," she said.

But it wasn't okay.

Not really.

And he didn't try to stop her when she turned and left the room, her heels silent on the carpet but whatever just happened still echoing in her wake.

* * * *

Sunlight flooded the Blair House, casting warm golds across the room. The historic residence exuded quiet elegance, polished wood floors gleaming under ornate rugs, and the scent of fresh coffee mingling with lemon polish. Staff moved swiftly, their steps soft on the plush carpets. Conversations hummed in the background, the rhythm of a productive morning.

Pixie Sinclair sat in the corner, legs crossed, a sleek planner open on her lap. Her manicured nails tapped lightly as she skimmed the itinerary, already three steps ahead.

Across from her sat her two closest allies.

Jamie Gray lounged in his chair, a cup of black coffee in hand, silver-streaked hair catching the light. His tailored suit and calm demeanor screamed 'chaos coordinator'.

Beside him, Marcy Rivera, poised and efficient, spun a pen between her fingers. The soft clicks echoed as she scribbled notes, stylish yet practical in her sweater. Every movement calculated, every word sharp.

The team was in sync, ready to take on whatever the day threw at them.

Pixie cleared her throat, keeping her voice deliberately casual as she spoke. "Hypothetically," she began, glancing up from her planner, "if someone wanted to find information on a long-lost relative, who would be the best person to contact for that sort of thing?"

Jamie lowered his coffee, raising one brow in curiosity. "Hypothetically?" he repeated, his voice tinged with amusement. "Are you solving mysteries in your free time, Sinclair?"

Marcy's interest piqued, her pen freezing mid-spin. "Oh, is this for Mrs. Armstrong?" she asked, her tone bright. "A special project? Like a reunion story? That could be great for optics."

Pixie gave a quick shake of her head, forcing a faint smile. "Not for the First Lady," she said smoothly. "Just something I came across. Figured someone might need help."

Marcy tilted her head, her brow furrowing as she considered Pixie's response. "There are firms that specialize in that sort of thing—private investigators, genealogists. Depends on how deep you need them to dig."

Jamie set his cup down with a soft clink, his gaze sharp. "And who exactly is this 'someone' you're helping, Pixie?"

Pixie shrugged lightly, keeping her tone breezy. "No one important. Just wanted to know what options are out there."

Jamie didn't seem to be convinced, his sharp eyes narrowing slightly. He was a man who thrived on reading between the lines. "Well, if you're curious," he said after a moment, "we'll be in New York tomorrow. The city has no shortage of discreet PIs. They're pros at keeping things quiet."

Pixie nodded as she filed the information away. "Good to know. Thanks."

Excusing herself with her usual poise, she stepped into the hallway, the polished heels of her shoes clicking against the wood. The calm, controlled environment of the Blair House enveloped her, but her mind was racing.

The truth? She was solving a mystery—but it wasn't her own. Wyatt's haunted expression and the clipped tone he used whenever the topic of family came up had stayed with her. He'd shut her down so firmly when she brought it up, but the bitterness in his voice told her more than he probably realized. No matter how much he tried to bury it, there was pain there, unresolved and festering. And Pixie couldn't ignore it—not when she knew what it was like to carry that kind of weight alone.

As she passed a portrait of a former president on the wall, her reflection caught in the glass. For a moment, she paused, studying herself. Her loose hair framed her face neatly, but her expression—calm, composed, professional—felt like a mask. She straightened her shoulders and continued down the hall, her resolve hardening.

This wasn't about her. It was about Wyatt. And she was determined to give him the closure he wouldn't ask for. Even if it meant confronting some ghosts of her own.

Chapter Fifteen

New York City

The air in Little Italy hit Pixie sharper than she remembered — smoke, fresh bread, and the buzz of life filling the streets. Locals gestured wildly, vendors shouted specials, and glasses clinked at outdoor tables. The cobblestone sidewalks felt smaller now, like the memories they held had grown too big for her.

Pixie — no, Serafina Romano, as she'd introduced herself — pushed through the door of Carmine's Café. The bell jingled softly, and the familiar, dim space greeted her. Dark wood, scuffed floors, and quiet conversation. She slid into the back booth, fingers brushing the worn leather.

A moment later, Ethan Kane entered. His tailored coat unbuttoned, blue eyes scanning the room before locking onto hers. His confidence was effortless, the kind that came from knowing every exit without needing to look.

"Serafina Romano," he said, his voice laced with curiosity.

"Ethan," she replied, forcing a smile she didn't feel.

He slid into the booth across from her, setting a small notebook and his coffee down in one fluid motion. His hair was slightly mussed, like he'd been running his hands through it, and the faint scent of aftershave mixed with the stronger aroma of espresso.

"Romano," he repeated, leaning back slightly. "You didn't mention that when you booked me. Thought you looked familiar."

She stiffened, her fingers curling slightly around her own cup of coffee. "Small world."

Ethan tilted his head, his sharp gaze assessing her. "Your family was from here, right? Your dad—" He stopped himself, his tone softening. "I heard about him. My condolences."

Pixie nodded tightly, the familiar ache of grief settling in her chest. "Thanks," she said, her voice quieter now.

For a moment, there was only the faint clinking of cups and the muted chatter of the café around them. Then Ethan straightened, pulling out his notebook. "All right, Serafina. You said you're looking for someone specific. Let's get into it."

She forced herself to focus, her fingers brushing the edge of her cup as she chose her words carefully. "It's...a relative. A father. He disappeared years ago, and I need to know if he's alive, where he is, and if he's safe to contact."

Ethan nodded, his demeanor professional but not detached. "Got it. The more details you can give me, the better. Name, last known address, connections—anything you've got."

Pixie slid an envelope across the table. Inside was everything she'd been able to gather about Wyatt's father, though it wasn't much. Ethan scanned it briefly before tucking it into his notebook.

"You want to tell me what happened there?" he asked casually, though his tone didn't push.

"It's not my story to tell," she said firmly, lifting her coffee to her lips. "Just find him."

Ethan studied her for a beat, then nodded. "All right. Anything else?"

Pixie hesitated, her heart pounding. The name was on the tip of her tongue, but the weight of it felt like it might choke her. She glanced around the café, her gaze flicking over the familiar faces and old photographs on the walls. This place was her childhood, a world she'd abandoned and yet couldn't fully leave behind.

Finally, she looked back at Ethan. "Yes," she said softly, her voice barely above a whisper. "There's one more name."

Ethan leaned forward, his pen poised. "Let's hear it."

"Raffaele Santoro," she said, the name falling from her lips like a curse.

Ethan's pen froze midair, his sharp eyes narrowing. "The designer?"

Pixie nodded, her stomach twisting as the familiar nausea crept in. "Yeah. Him. I need to know if he's still…looking for me."

Ethan didn't respond immediately, and his expression was unreadable as he studied her. "You're sure you want me to dig into this?"

"Yes," she said firmly, though her voice wavered. "I need to know if he's still connected. If he still… remembers me."

His sharp gaze softened, a flicker of concern breaking through his professional exterior. "Sounds dangerous."

"It is," she admitted, her fingers tightening around her coffee cup. "But I need to know."

Ethan nodded slowly, his pen moving again. "All right. I'll look into it. But this kind of thing might take time, especially if he's tied to…people."

"Just be discreet," she said quickly, her tone sharper than intended. "No one can know."

"You've got it," Ethan replied, his easy smile returning, though it didn't reach his eyes.

As he packed up his things and rose to leave, Pixie stayed in her seat, her chest tight and her thoughts spinning. She watched him walk out, the bell above the door jingling softly in his wake, then turned her gaze back to the worn wood of the table.

She'd started this to help Wyatt, to give him the answers he deserved. But as her own ghosts clawed their way to the surface, she couldn't shake the feeling that she was opening doors that should have stayed locked.

Her fingers traced the edge of her cup, her mind racing. Somewhere in this city, Raffaele Santoro might still be watching. And for the first time in years, she wasn't sure if she'd ever truly escaped.

* * * *

Pixie's hotel room at The Valemont exuded old-world charm with a modern edge. The thick, cream-colored curtains framed a view of midtown Manhattan, the city's lights twinkling against the inky night sky. The room was all polished wood and soft, luxurious textures. A deep burgundy armchair sat by the window, a vintage vanity gleamed in one corner, and the faint scent of fresh lilies—courtesy of the hotel—hung in the air.

Pixie stood in front of a full-length mirror, smoothing the fabric of her onyx-colored gown. The satin hugged her frame, the slit at her thigh daring but tasteful, while the off-shoulder neckline added just enough drama. A string of diamonds glimmered at her collarbone, catching the light as she moved. Her makeup was flawless—soft smoky eyes, a deep red lip—but her hands trembled as she adjusted her hair, now styled into loose waves.

"Honestly, Sinclair, if you fuss with that hair one more time, I'm cutting it off," Jamie Gray quipped from his spot by the minibar. He was nursing a glass of whiskey, his sharp suit a classic black-and-white ensemble that looked impossibly crisp. "You look perfect. Stop stressing."

Marcy Rivera, seated cross-legged on the edge of the bed, tilted her glass of champagne toward Pixie in agreement. "He's right, you know. You're going to steal the show."

Pixie managed a faint smile, though her stomach twisted with unease. "It's not that," she said, her voice quieter than usual.

Marcy arched her brow. "Then what is it? You've been fidgety all night." She took a sip from her glass before adding, "You know we won't let you leave this room until you spill."

Jamie leaned against the minibar, swirling his whiskey lazily. "It's true. We've got all night."

Pixie glanced at them, her two closest allies in the chaos of the First Lady's staff. Marcy in her sleek silver gown, her dark hair swept into a chic bun, and Jamie, ever the picture of sophistication, watching her with a mix of concern and curiosity. She wanted to tell them, to unburden herself, but the words caught in her throat.

"I'm fine," she lied, turning back to the mirror and reaching for her earrings. The diamond studs felt cool against her fingers as she fastened them. "Just a little pre-event jitters. You know how these things go."

Marcy snorted. "You don't get jitters, Pixie. You're practically robotic at these events."

Jamie smirked. "Except when it comes to Steele. Then you're a walking mess."

Pixie shot him a sharp look through the mirror, though her lips twitched into a reluctant smirk. "We're not talking about him."

"Fine," Jamie said with a shrug, taking another sip of his drink. "But whatever's got you on edge, just remember you've survived worse."

The words hit her harder than she expected, and for a moment, she froze. She had survived worse. But as she picked up her phone from the vanity, the knot in her stomach tightened. The screen lit up with a notification, and her breath caught.

A message from Ethan Kane.

Pixie glanced over her shoulder to make sure Jamie and Marcy were too distracted to notice before opening the text.

Confirmed. Santoro is asking questions about you. He's definitely still looking. Be careful tonight.

The blood drained from her face, her grip tightening on the phone as her chest constricted. For a moment, the sounds of the room — the clinking glasses, the soft hum of conversation — faded into the background. All she could hear was her heartbeat, loud and fast in her ears.

"Pix?" Marcy's voice broke through the haze.

Pixie quickly locked the phone and plastered on a smile, turning back to face them. "Sorry. Just checking the time."

Jamie squinted at her, clearly unconvinced, but he didn't press. "Well, let's get moving. Caroline's expecting us to be on point tonight. And if we're late, it's your fault, Sinclair."

Pixie nodded, slipping her phone into her clutch as she grabbed her champagne glass and downed the last sip. The bubbles burned slightly on the way down, but it wasn't enough to drown out the fear clawing at her chest.

She followed Marcy and Jamie out of the room, her heels clicking softly against the polished wood floor. As they made their way to the elevator, she forced herself to focus, to push the fear down where it couldn't control her.

Chapter Sixteen

The SUV cut through midtown Manhattan, the hum of the city just reaching the edges of the quiet ride. Wyatt kept his eyes on the road, scanning every corner for the chaos New York always delivered. The Valemont Ballroom was only a few blocks away, and the streets were already clogging with the usual event frenzy.

In the backseat, Caroline Armstrong, the First Lady, sighed contentedly, smoothing the skirt of her cream gown. The fabric caught the light, sparkling with a regal elegance. She leaned forward, eyes drifting to the city outside.

"Wyatt," she said, her voice warm. "Do you ever stop working?"

Wyatt glanced at her in the rearview mirror, smirking. "Not really, ma'am. Comes with the job."

Caroline clicked her tongue, settling back against the leather. "That's the problem. You're too dedicated. It's not healthy."

"I'll keep that in mind," he replied, the smirk lingering.

"No, you won't," she said with mock exasperation, folding her arms across her chest. "You never listen to me when I tell you these things."

Wyatt chuckled under his breath, shaking his head. "I listen, ma'am. I just don't always agree."

Caroline sat forward again, her expression softening as she looked at him in the mirror. "You're like one of my boys, you know. Stubborn as all get-out but with a heart of gold. And like them, you need a little push every now and then to do what's good for you."

Wyatt's smirk faded slightly, replaced by a flicker of something warmer, deeper. "I appreciate the concern, ma'am, but I'm fine. Really."

Caroline's brow lifted, her expression skeptical. "You're not fine, Wyatt. And you're certainly not happy. I'm a mother. I can tell." She lifted her hand to silence his protest.

The words hit him harder than he expected, and he forced himself to focus on the road, gripping the steering wheel a little tighter.

"Your accident," she continued, her voice gentle but persistent. "Didn't that get you thinking about your life? Your happiness? What you want?"

Wyatt groaned internally, his lips pressing into a thin line. "Can't say that I have. I like to live in the moment."

"That's not an excuse," she said firmly, though her tone was laced with affection. "You're a handsome man, Wyatt. Kind, loyal, dependable. Any woman would be lucky to have you. And yet, here you are, all alone, throwing yourself into this job like it's the only thing you've got."

"It is the only thing I've got," he replied, though his voice was quieter now.

Caroline shook her head, her expression softening further. "That's not true. You have us — this family. But you need more, Wyatt. A real family. Someone to share your life with."

Wyatt chuckled softly, though it lacked humor. "I'm not exactly the 'settle down and start a family' type, ma'am."

"Nonsense," she said, leaning forward again and fixing him with a pointed look. "You're exactly that type. I know you better than you think."

He opened his mouth to respond, but she cut him off, wagging a finger at him.

"Don't you dare argue with me," she said, her voice firm but fond. "You think I don't see how you look after everyone around you? How much you care? You're built for love, Wyatt Steele, whether you like it or not."

Wyatt cringed. He glanced hopefully at the sidewalks for something — anything — to break the conversation. Perhaps a drunken pedestrian veering into the street or a random knife attack.

Anything but this conversation.

"I have decided to help you," she declared, a mischievous glint in her eye. "I've arranged for you to meet a few lovely young women this evening. Intelligent, accomplished, kind. Exactly the sort of people you should be spending your time with."

His stomach sank, though he kept his expression neutral. "Please, I will do anything — "

Caroline interrupted, entirely unapologetic. "There's nothing for you to do but sit back and meet people. You will thank me later. Someone has to look out for you."

Wyatt exhaled slowly, shaking his head. "For the first time, I am seriously thinking of calling in sick for this—"

"No buts," she said firmly, sitting back in her seat with a satisfied smile. "You're going to meet them, have a drink, and enjoy yourself. That's an order. That's what you will do for me tonight."

He glanced at her in the mirror, his lips twitching into a reluctant smirk. "Pretty sure you can't order me to fall in love, ma'am."

Caroline laughed, a warm, motherly sound that filled the SUV. "We'll see about that."

Despite himself, Wyatt felt a pang of gratitude beneath the mild irritation. As much as he hated the idea of being paraded around like a prize stallion, he couldn't deny the care behind her meddling. She didn't have to worry about him—not really—but she did anyway.

As they pulled up to The Valemont Ballroom, the flashing lights of cameras illuminating the street, Wyatt stepped out and opened her door, extending a hand to help her out.

"Just promise me one thing, Wyatt," Caroline said, pausing to look up at him as she adjusted her gown.

"What's that, ma'am?" he asked, his voice softer now.

"Promise me you'll let yourself be happy."

His chest tightened, and for a moment, he couldn't bring himself to respond. Finally, he nodded, his voice low as he said, "I'll try, ma'am."

"Promise," she said with a smile, slipping her hand into his arm as he escorted her toward the entrance.

When he didn't respond, she jabbed him in the ribs with her encrusted baguette purse.

"I promise," he finally coughed out.

Under duress.

As they walked into the glittering ballroom, Wyatt couldn't help but shake his head slightly. He wasn't sure what the evening had in store, but one thing was certain—Caroline Armstrong wasn't giving up on him anytime soon.

Chapter Seventeen

The Valemont Ballroom oozed old-world glamour. Vaulted ceilings gleamed with gold moldings, crystal chandeliers bathed the room in soft light, and the polished parquet floor reflected the glow. The air was thick with roses and cologne, mixed with the lingering chill of the city.

Wyatt took it all in—entrances, exits, the staff moving through the crowd with champagne trays, and clusters of donors, politicians, and socialites mingling under the glittering lights.

The buzz of conversation mixed with the quiet strains of a string quartet. Laughter and clinking glasses punctuated the air, but the music, soft and elegant, reminded everyone just how exclusive the night was.

As head of protective detail, Wyatt had a clear focus—no distractions, no enjoyment. His job was to stay sharp, scanning for threats and ensuring the First

Lady's safety. He moved through the crowd, alert, always on edge.

His earpiece crackled softly, a voice murmuring updates from one of his agents stationed near the back entrance. Wyatt raised a hand to adjust it, his movements casual but deliberate as he surveyed the ballroom. He kept close to the First Lady, who was already making her rounds, her dazzling smile charming everyone she greeted.

But while his posture remained professional, his focus wasn't entirely on the job. He couldn't stop himself from glancing through the crowd, searching for one person in particular.

Pixie.

He hadn't seen her yet, but he knew she was here. He'd caught a glimpse of her earlier, her dark bob shining under the hallway lights as she moved briskly toward the ballroom, clipboard in hand.

Now, she seemed to have vanished into the sea of people, and Wyatt felt an involuntary tug of frustration. His gaze flitted over the clusters of guests, lingering on every flash of dark hair, every hint of movement that might be her. He told himself it was just about keeping tabs on everyone, maintaining security — but he knew better.

The truth was, she'd been on his mind more than he wanted to admit. And it bothered him.

Wyatt's earpiece buzzed again, this time with a note about a delay in the First Lady's scheduled speech. He relayed a quiet acknowledgment, his voice low and calm, before resuming his scan of the room. As a Secret Service agent at an event like this, he was both a shadow and a guardian — present but unobtrusive, his attention split between protecting the First Lady and maintaining a low profile.

He moved along the edges of the ballroom, his eyes constantly scanning. He took in the details—the overly enthusiastic donor who gestured too wildly with his champagne flute, the young catering assistant nervously adjusting her tray as she moved toward the VIP section, the security team discreetly stationed near the rear exit, their postures alert but relaxed.

And then he saw her.

Pixie was standing near the far end of the ballroom, close to the edge of the crowd. She had a tablet in hand, her focus fixed on something as she nodded along to whatever Marcy Rivera was saying beside her. Her dress was simple but stunning, accentuating her frame while still giving her the air of authority she seemed to carry effortlessly. She wore reading glasses as she thumbed through the device, shifting her weight on her heels.

Wyatt's breath caught briefly, though he masked it with a subtle shift in his stance. She didn't notice him, too absorbed in her conversation, but the sight of her—confident, composed, and utterly unflappable—made something tighten in his chest.

He forced himself to look away, redirecting his attention to the First Lady, who was deep in conversation with a prominent donor. But it wasn't long before his gaze slid back to Pixie, like a magnet he couldn't resist.

The ballroom, with all its opulence and noise, seemed to fade slightly as he watched her. She gestured with her hands, her expression animated as she spoke. She was so different here, in her element—a far cry from the vulnerable woman he'd held on a fur rug a week ago.

Wyatt's earpiece buzzed again, jolting him back to reality. "East hall clear. No issues," came the soft voice of one of his agents.

"Copy that," Wyatt replied, his tone steady as he resumed his circuit of the room.

He moved closer to the First Lady, positioning himself strategically so he could keep both her and Pixie in his line of sight. His job came first—always. But as much as he tried to focus, the pull toward her was impossible to ignore.

It wasn't just attraction—it was something deeper, more frustrating, and far more dangerous.

Wyatt clenched his jaw, forcing himself to concentrate. The First Lady was holding court in the center of the room, effortlessly charming her guests, and the rest of the security detail was in place. Everything appeared to be running smoothly. Still, Wyatt couldn't shake the unease in his chest.

His gaze flicked to the far end of the ballroom, where he'd last seen Pixie. She'd been standing near Marcy Rivera earlier, all business as usual. But now, she was gone, and that unsettled him more than he cared to admit.

He wove through the clusters of guests, his attention split between maintaining his professional focus and finding her. Then he spotted her—across the room, standing near a marble pillar. Something was different.

Pixie's usual sharp, confident posture was missing. Her shoulders were tense, her hands fidgeting with the strap of her clutch. She glanced over her shoulder, her dark eyes scanning the crowd with a nervous energy he'd never seen before.

Wyatt's chest tightened. *What's going on?*

He slowed his pace, watching her more intently now. Pixie was rarely nervous. If anything, she was annoyingly unflappable under pressure. But tonight, something was off.

Her fingers brushed her necklace absently, her lips pressing into a thin line as her gaze darted toward the ballroom's exit. Wyatt felt his gut twist. *She's scared.*

And suddenly, so was he.

Wyatt picked up his pace, angling through the crowd to reach her, his mind racing with possibilities. Was she in trouble? Did she know something he didn't? He was about to reach her when—

"Wyatt!"

He froze, turning toward the sound of Caroline's voice. The First Lady was standing just a few feet away, her radiant smile directed not at him, but at the striking young woman by her side.

"This is the man I was telling you about," Caroline said warmly, gesturing toward him.

Wyatt's sharp gaze darted to the woman. She was tall and elegant, her sleek navy gown hugging her frame in all the right places. Her blonde hair was styled into an intricate chignon, and her perfectly painted red lips curved into a practiced smile as she extended her hand.

"Isabella Wentworth," she introduced herself, her voice smooth and refined.

Wyatt took her hand, offering a polite but distracted smile. "Wyatt Steele."

Caroline stepped between them, her expression both amused and determined. "Now, Wyatt, I know you're going to say you're working, but consider this a direct order. Take a break. Isabella is delightful company, and I want you to have a little fun for once."

"Ma'am—"

"No arguments," Caroline cut him off with a sly smile. "That's an order."

Before he could protest, Isabella placed a firm hand on his arm and practically steered him toward the dimly lit hallway just off the main ballroom. The space was quieter, with the soft hum of a jazz band playing in the background and a few scattered guests lounging by the bar.

Wyatt's jaw clenched as he reluctantly followed Isabella to a small seating area near the band. The flicker of nerves he'd felt when watching Pixie hadn't faded, and now it gnawed at him even more. He needed to get back to the ballroom. He needed to know what was wrong with her.

But for now, he was stuck.

"You look like you'd rather be anywhere else," Isabella said lightly, taking a seat and crossing her legs.

Wyatt managed a polite chuckle. "It's not you," he said, his voice calm. "I'm just not used to sitting still."

"I can imagine," she replied, her eyes sparkling with interest. "Caroline speaks so highly of you. She says you're her rock."

Wyatt shifted uncomfortably, his mind still half in the ballroom. "Just doing my job."

Their conversation continued, but Wyatt barely heard her. He was too busy glancing toward the hallway, his mind racing with questions about Pixie. Why was she so tense? What was she looking for—or running from?

"Wyatt."

The voice snapped him back to the present. He turned to see Salem, his ever-reliable agent, striding toward him with a serious expression.

"Boss, we've got a situation," Salem said quietly, his gaze flicking to Isabella before settling back on Wyatt.

"Excuse me," Wyatt said to Isabella, already rising to his feet.

"Oh no, you don't," Caroline's voice rang out, cutting through the low murmur of the hallway. She appeared seemingly out of nowhere, her hands clasped in front of her as she leveled a mock-stern look at Salem.

"Whatever it is, Salem, it can wait," she said, her tone light but commanding. "Wyatt is on a very important mission for me tonight."

Salem's brow lifted slightly, his lips twitching with barely concealed amusement. "Is that right?"

"Absolutely," Caroline said with a bright smile, gesturing toward Isabella. "He's under strict orders to relax and enjoy himself. Isn't that right, Wyatt?"

Wyatt cringed internally, his jaw tightening as Salem gave him a knowing look.

"Of course, ma'am," Wyatt said through gritted teeth, the corners of his mouth pulling into a forced smile.

"Good," Caroline said, clearly pleased. "Now, carry on. And Salem, let the poor man breathe for one night, would you?"

As Caroline disappeared back into the ballroom, Wyatt exchanged a look with Salem, whose grin had widened considerably.

"Good luck, boss," Salem said with a low chuckle before retreating.

Wyatt sighed, sinking back into his seat. Isabella tilted her head, watching him with an amused expression.

"Caroline certainly keeps you on your toes," she said.

Wyatt offered a tight smile, his thoughts already drifting back to the ballroom. He couldn't shake the image of Pixie's tense shoulders, her nervous glance toward the exit. Something was wrong.

And as soon as he could shake off Caroline's matchmaking scheme, he was going to find out what.

Chapter Eighteen

The Valemont Ballroom was suffocating.

Pixie stood near the edge of the glittering crowd, her back pressed against a marble column as she tried to steady her breathing. The grand chandeliers above cast golden light over the polished parquet floors, and the air was thick with the scent of roses, champagne, and perfume — luxury at its most opulent. But none of it felt glamorous to her tonight. It felt claustrophobic. Dangerous.

Her phone buzzed in her clutch again, and she already knew who it was. Ethan Kane.

She hesitated, glancing around the room as she pulled the phone from her bag. The message previewed on the screen.

Santoro's all dolled up. He's definitely heading to something big tonight. Do you want backup? I can be there in thirty.

Her chest tightened, and her thumb hovered over the keyboard. *Do you want backup?* Ethan had asked it like this was any other job, like she was just another client, not someone whose life was dangling on the edge of a blade.

She locked the phone without replying. She couldn't deal with this now.

Instead, she scanned the room again, her gaze landing on the center of the ballroom where Wyatt stood.

Of course, he looked entirely unbothered.

Wyatt was leaning casually against the bar in the dimly lit lounge area, a drink in hand and that damnable smirk on his face. Across from him sat a blonde socialite who couldn't have looked more perfect if she'd been sculpted from porcelain. Her gown shimmered in the low light, her hair was swept into an effortlessly elegant style, and her laugh was light and airy, like she'd never known a single hardship in her life.

Pixie's stomach churned, a sharp bitterness rising in her chest. She clenched her hand around the stem of her champagne flute, trying to ignore the way her heart twisted uncomfortably as Wyatt leaned closer to the woman, saying something that made her laugh again.

It wasn't fair. He looked so at ease, so comfortable flirting and sipping whiskey like this was just another gala, another night on the job. She envied that about him—how he could compartmentalize everything, push the world away when it suited him.

Her gaze flicked away, but it didn't help. Her mind was too full of noise—memories, fears, and the growing certainty that she didn't belong here.

The air suddenly felt too heavy, the room too loud. The chandeliers' glow seemed to press down on her, and she could feel her pulse thrumming in her throat.

I need to get out of here.

Pixie glanced toward the exit, considering her options. Could she fake a headache? Caroline wouldn't question it — she'd probably send Pixie off with a cup of tea and a warm "Take care, dear." Marcy might raise an eyebrow, but she'd cover for her if needed.

But as she thought about slipping away, her phone buzzed again, and her stomach dropped.

You need to be careful, Serafina. I mean it. Santoro doesn't forget faces.

Her chest tightened, and she shoved the phone back into her clutch as panic clawed at her ribs. She forced herself to take a sip of her champagne, the bubbles sharp and biting against her tongue.

Keep it together.

But it was hard to focus, hard to breathe when she felt like the walls were closing in. She tried to tell herself that she was imagining things, that Santoro wouldn't dare come here. But Ethan's words haunted her. *Santoro doesn't forget faces.*

Her gaze was drawn back to Wyatt, unbidden. He was still at the bar, still smiling that crooked smile of his, the blonde leaning closer to him now as she toyed with the stem of her glass.

Pixie swallowed hard, the taste of champagne bitter in her mouth. She hated the pang of jealousy that flared in her chest, hated the way her stomach knotted at the sight of him so at ease with someone else. Someone who, by all accounts, was perfect for him.

She looked down at her dress, suddenly feeling out of place. It wasn't enough. Not tonight. Not when her world felt like it was spinning out of control and Wyatt Steele was halfway to forgetting she even existed.

Maybe that's for the best, she thought bitterly.

The idea of slipping away crept back into her mind. If she could just leave, just find a quiet corner where the ghosts of her past couldn't reach her, maybe she could make it through the night.

But as she took a deep breath, trying to steel herself, her eyes found Wyatt's again. This time, he wasn't looking at the blonde.

He was looking at her.

Her heart stuttered, and for a brief moment, the chaos in her mind quieted. His blue eyes were sharp, focused, and the smirk was gone, replaced by something more serious.

Pixie swallowed hard, her grip tightening on her glass.

Don't come over here, she thought desperately. *Don't ask me what's wrong. Don't make this harder than it already is.*

But deep down, a part of her wished he would.

Pixie wasn't alone for long. Jamie and Marcy, her steadfast partners in the chaos of First Lady operations, appeared at her side like clockwork. They flanked her casually, each holding their own drink, but their watchful eyes caught the tension in her shoulders immediately.

"Okay, spill it," Jamie said, leaning in slightly, his silver-streaked hair catching the warm light of the chandeliers. "You're brooding. And when you brood, you get lines on that perfect forehead of yours, and I'm too tired to remind you about skincare tonight."

Pixie shot him a dry look. "I'm not brooding. I'm observing."

Marcy snorted softly, adjusting the strap of her silver gown. "Observing, huh? That why you've been staring at Wyatt and Blondie over there for the past five minutes like you're planning an assassination?"

Pixie scowled, looking down at her glass as her face flushed. "I wasn't staring."

"Oh, please," Jamie drawled, swirling the whiskey in his glass. "You've been practically burning holes in the back of his head. What's the deal? You mad because Caroline's matchmaking again?"

Marcy grinned mischievously. "Or is it because the match is, let's face it, kind of gorgeous?"

Pixie's lips tightened, and for a moment, she didn't answer. Instead, she glanced up, her gaze inevitably drawn back to Wyatt. Tall, composed, radiating that unshakable tension he always carried like armor. Beside him stood her... Isabella Wentworth.

Pixie had recognized her immediately. Everyone in this world did. Politician's daughter. Art patron. Tabloid darling. She'd once made headlines for throwing a thousand-dollar clutch at a paparazzo outside a gala in Florence, and somehow it only made people like her more.

She looked...*perfect*. All sculpted cheekbones and diamond-drop earrings, her navy gown sliding over her body like it had been poured on. She reached for Wyatt's hand with a smile so polished it belonged on a campaign poster.

Pixie's stomach twisted.

Pixie looked away quickly, the sight making her stomach twist. "Do you think she's beautiful?" she asked, her voice quieter than usual.

Jamie and Marcy exchanged a quick glance, both sensing the vulnerability in her question.

"Well," Jamie began, drawing the word out as he gave Isabella an exaggerated once-over, "if you like that whole glamorous socialite thing, sure. But me? I prefer someone with more edge. She probably cries if her blowout gets wet."

Marcy nodded vigorously. "Exactly. I mean, come on — she's flawless in a way that's almost annoying. No visible pores, no bad angles. It's suspicious."

Pixie raised an eyebrow. "So you're both saying she's perfect."

They both fell silent for a moment before Jamie sighed dramatically. "Fine. Yes. She's stunning. Drop-dead gorgeous, even. Happy?"

Marcy let out a groan of defeat. "And she looks good with him. Like...annoyingly good."

Pixie's chest tightened, and she took a long sip of her champagne to hide the way her jaw clenched. The three of them stood there in shared silence, staring glumly at the impossibly picturesque couple across the room.

"She probably knows how to make perfect soufflés," Jamie muttered darkly, breaking the silence.

"And probably has never once spilled coffee on herself," Marcy added.

Pixie bit the inside of her cheek, a bitter laugh threatening to escape. "She's probably never had a hard day in her life," she murmured, more to herself than them.

Marcy and Jamie glanced at her again, their teasing fading slightly as they saw the tightness in her expression.

"She's probably lovely," Pixie admitted. "She's probably great for him."

"Look," Jamie said softly, setting his glass down on a nearby tray, "so what if she's picture-perfect? You're not exactly invisible, Pixie. Trust me, people notice you."

Marcy nodded in agreement. "Yeah. And you're...you. You're strong, and smart, and people don't forget you. Ever."

Pixie's lips curved into a faint, humorless smile. "Thanks for the pep talk, but I don't think that's going to matter much tonight."

The three of them stood there, watching as Isabella leaned in closer to Wyatt, her laugh ringing out again like a soft chime. The picture of perfection and charm.

"Well," Jamie said finally, taking a long sip of his whiskey. "This is depressing."

Marcy sighed, swirling her champagne. "It really is."

The hour stretched long, and Pixie could feel every second of it. The Valemont Ballroom was starting to show the effects of the night's festivities—champagne glasses abandoned on tables, guests laughing a little too loudly, and the air buzzing with a heady mix of exhaustion and revelry.

Pixie stood near the edge of the room, her fingers clutching the stem of her champagne flute with just a touch too much force. Her sharp gaze flitted to Wyatt once again, as it had far too many times that evening.

He was leaning against the bar, his posture relaxed, his tie loosened slightly. The lines of his usually stern face had softened, and his lips curved into an easy, crooked smile as Isabella spoke to him, her hand brushing his arm in an overly familiar way that made Pixie's stomach churn.

Pixie had spent the last two hours scanning for Santoro...but really just watching Wyatt transform — not into the disciplined head of protective detail she was used to but into a man. A red-blooded, very-much-alive man who, for some reason, seemed utterly magnetic to every woman in the room.

It wasn't just Isabella anymore. A string of women had approached him throughout the evening — women who giggled, leaned in too close, and practically glowed under his attention. But it was Isabella who lingered, laughing at whatever dry joke he'd made, her perfect blonde hair glinting in the soft light.

Pixie clenched her jaw, the champagne glass in her hand. She hated how aware she was of him — the way he stood, the way his hands moved as he spoke, the way his blue eyes crinkled ever so slightly when he smiled.

Why now? she thought bitterly. *Why tonight?*

She turned her back on him, staring out at the room instead. A group of donors danced in the center of the floor, their movements loose and uncoordinated as the jazz band played something lively. She could leave soon. Another twenty minutes, and she could call it a night without raising any eyebrows.

"Ah, there you are."

Pixie turned to see Caroline approaching, her cream gown flowing elegantly around her as she glided across the room. The First Lady's smile was deceptively innocent, but Pixie knew better.

"Enjoying the evening?" Caroline asked, her tone light but her eyes far too perceptive.

Pixie forced a polite smile. "It's been lovely, ma'am. But I was just about to—"

"Nonsense," Caroline interrupted, her eyes twinkling with mischief. "You can't leave before the best part."

Pixie blinked. "The best part?"

Caroline snapped her fingers, and the jazz band seamlessly transitioned into a new melody — something playful, familiar, and impossibly romantic. The energy in the room shifted immediately as couples began moving toward the dance floor, laughter and applause erupting as they paired off.

"It's time for dancing, of course," Caroline said brightly, her gaze flicking to someone over Pixie's shoulder.

Pixie turned just as Wyatt appeared in front of her. She didn't need to look to know it was him — she could feel his presence, the warmth of him, the quiet confidence he exuded without effort.

"Sinclair," Wyatt said, his voice low and even, though there was a glimmer of something in his blue eyes that she couldn't quite name. He extended his hand toward her. "Dance with me."

Pixie stared at him, her brows lifting in disbelief. "Absolutely not."

His smirk deepened, infuriatingly so. "You're going to turn me down in front of the First Lady? Bold move."

Caroline, who had conveniently not moved away, chuckled softly. "Oh, Pixie, don't be such a stick in the mud. A little dancing never hurt anyone."

Pixie shot her a withering look, but Caroline just smiled sweetly and walked off, leaving her alone with Wyatt.

"You should go ask your new girlfriend," Pixie muttered, turning back toward the edge of the room.

Wyatt stepped closer, his outstretched hand still waiting. "I don't want to dance with Isabella. I want to dance with you."

She hated the way her body responded to his nearness. "Why?"

He tilted his head slightly, his smirk softening into something more genuine. "Why not?"

Pixie opened her mouth to argue, but the warmth in his gaze disarmed her. With a resigned sigh, she placed her hand in his.

"Fine," she said tightly, glaring up at him. "But only once."

Wyatt chuckled softly, his fingers curling gently around hers as he led her onto the dance floor.

The music swelled, and Pixie felt her breath hitch as Wyatt's hand settled lightly on her waist. He was warm and solid, his movements easy as he guided her into the rhythm of the song. She forced herself to focus on the steps, but it was impossible to ignore the way his touch lingered, the way his blue eyes locked on hers like they were the only two people in the room.

"You're tense," Wyatt said quietly, leaning just close enough that she could feel the heat of his breath against her temple.

Pixie scowled. "I wonder why."

"Easy, tiger," he murmured, his hand tightening ever so slightly on her waist. "I hate this as much as you do."

Finally, he got a laugh out of her — to which he returned a gorgeous grin of straight white teeth. She never noticed what an incredibly handsome mouth he had before.

Her heart pounded, and she hated how easily he seemed to affect her. But as they moved together, the tension in her shoulders began to ebb, replaced by something softer, something she didn't want to name.

"You're surprisingly good at this," she muttered, glancing up at him.

Wyatt's lips twitched into a faint smile. "Surprisingly?"

Pixie rolled her eyes, but a reluctant smile tugged at the corner of her mouth.

For a brief, fleeting moment, she let herself forget the nerves, the jealousy, and the ghosts that lingered in the shadows of her mind. For a moment, it was just the two of them, moving together in the golden glow of a jazz band.

The dance ended, and Pixie was acutely aware of Wyatt's hand still resting lightly on her waist, his other hand holding hers. The song had slowed to its final notes, the band transitioning seamlessly into another upbeat tune, but Pixie had already decided this was where she needed to end it. She stepped back slightly, attempting to create distance, but Wyatt didn't release her immediately.

"One more," he said, his voice low, a smirk tugging at the corner of his lips.

Pixie shook her head, forcing herself to maintain control. "I think I've humored you enough for one evening, Steele."

"Come on, Sinclair. You were finally starting to relax," he teased, his hand dropping from her waist but his gaze holding hers. "Don't tell me you're running off already."

Before she could respond, her eyes flickered toward the balcony, just beyond the ballroom's grand arched windows. The faint outline of a man caught her attention, his profile sharp under the dim outdoor lighting. Her heart sank. Ethan Kane.

He shouldn't be here.

Pixie swallowed hard, trying to hide her immediate sense of dread. Ethan's presence wasn't casual—it never was. And if he was here, it meant something was wrong. Urgently wrong.

"I'm not running," she said, forcing a calm tone as she glanced back at Wyatt. "I just… I need to check on something."

Wyatt arched a brow, clearly unconvinced. "You have a terrible poker face, Sinclair."

Pixie felt her cheeks flush but managed a small, dismissive smile. "That's not true."

"It absolutely is," Wyatt said, his voice dipping lower as he leaned in slightly. "What's going on?"

"Nothing," she replied quickly, stepping back again and forcing her tone to stay breezy. "Caroline will be looking for you anyway, and you know how she gets if you're not exactly where she wants you."

Wyatt's smirk softened, but his blue eyes stayed sharp, studying her face. She could feel him trying to read her, and she hated how exposed she felt under his gaze.

Before he could press further, the First Lady's voice rang out over the crowd, calling for Wyatt with her usual maternal authority.

"You're lucky," Pixie muttered, gesturing toward Caroline as the First Lady made her way toward them. "Duty calls."

Wyatt glanced at Caroline, then back at Pixie, his expression still skeptical. "This conversation isn't over."

Pixie didn't respond. She used the moment of distraction to step away, her pulse quickening as she weaved through the crowd and toward the balcony. She could feel Wyatt's eyes on her back, but she kept moving, willing herself not to look back.

The air outside was crisp, a sharp contrast to the warmth of the ballroom. The balcony was dimly lit, its ornate wrought-iron railing gleaming under the moonlight. Ethan stood at the far edge, his hands in his coat pockets, his sharp blue eyes scanning the streets below like he was already tracking something.

"Ethan," Pixie said, her voice low as she approached. "What are you doing here?"

He turned, his expression grim. "I told you I'd come if it was serious."

"I didn't reply," she said pointedly, crossing her arms over her chest to shield herself from the chill. "Which should've told you not to show up."

Ethan raised an eyebrow. "I'm not exactly the type to wait for permission, Serafina. You know that."

She winced at the use of her real name, glancing back over her shoulder. The sound of music and laughter from the ballroom spilled into the night, but no one else had followed her out. For now, they were alone.

"What's going on?" she asked, her voice softening slightly.

Ethan exhaled, his breath visible in the cold air. "Santoro."

Her stomach dropped. She didn't need him to say more, but he did anyway.

"He's been asking around," Ethan continued, his tone low but urgent. "I got confirmation earlier tonight—he knows you're in New York. Someone saw you. And I'm almost certain he's trying to figure out where you went."

Pixie's chest tightened, her fingers digging into the fabric of her dress. "He can't... He wouldn't come here. Not to this event."

Ethan tilted his head, his expression both knowing and sympathetic. "If he knows where you are...you and I both know Santoro doesn't play by the rules. If he wants something — or someone — he'll find a way."

Pixie's mind raced, the weight of his words pressing heavily against her chest. She'd been so careful, so meticulous about keeping her past buried. But if Santoro was looking for her, if he knew she was here...

"What do you want me to do?" Ethan asked, his voice cutting through her spiraling thoughts. "You want me to stick around? Handle it if he shows?"

Pixie shook her head, forcing herself to breathe. "No. If he's here, I don't want a scene."

Ethan frowned. "Serafina —"

"I can handle this," she snapped, though her voice wavered slightly. She looked up at him. "Please, Ethan. Just... I don't know what to do."

He hesitated, searching her face before he finally nodded. "You have three options. Confront him. Run from him."

"And the third?"

"Kill him."

Pixie nodded tightly, and the knot in her chest caught fire.

Ethan lingered for a moment longer, his expression unreadable. "You just tell me what you want to do. I can help, or find guys to help."

She chewed her lip, feeling tears spiking her eyes. This was terrible timing. She hadn't worn waterproof mascara.

Ethan turned and disappeared into the shadows of the balcony.

She stood there for a moment, her arms wrapped around herself as the cold air bit at her skin. The sounds of the ballroom felt distant now, like they came from a different world entirely.

One where she didn't belong.

Chapter Nineteen

The door slammed shut behind her with a sharp clang, and Pixie found herself in a dim, cold stairwell that reeked of damp concrete and cleaning supplies. Her heels clattered as she hurried down the metal steps, breath shallow. The borrowed black cloak swamped her, its weight a temporary shield. She hadn't cared whose it was — she just needed to disappear.

The sound of the ballroom — jazz, chatter, laughter — faded as her pulse thundered in her ears, the only noise now the creaking stairs beneath her feet.

This is the right call, she told herself, gripping the railing as she descended. *Get out. Now.*

Her phone buzzed in her clutch. She didn't look. It had already buzzed once when she was with Ethan, and she knew it was Wyatt.

He'd noticed by now. Or maybe he was still caught up in Caroline's matchmaking. Either way, she couldn't deal with him tonight. Not when everything was falling apart.

Finally, she pushed through the fire exit at the bottom of the stairs, stepping into the biting cold of a Manhattan winter night. The street outside the venue was quieter than the front entrance, dimly lit by a flickering streetlamp and flanked by the shadows of the surrounding buildings.

Pixie pulled the cloak tighter around her shoulders and glanced around before heading briskly around the building and to the side entrance of the hotel. Her heels clicked against the pavement, the sound sharp in the stillness of the side street.

The walk felt endless, every noise making her heart race — a car door slamming in the distance, the murmur of voices from a nearby alley, the faint buzz of a neon sign overhead. She couldn't shake the feeling that someone was watching her, that Santoro was lurking just around the corner, waiting for her to let her guard down.

When she finally reached the side entrance, her hands shook as she swiped her key card and slipped inside.

Her room on the ninth floor felt suffocating when she entered, the warmth oppressive against her cold skin. She didn't waste any time, grabbing her suitcase from the closet and throwing it open on the bed.

Her clothes, her toiletries, her few personal items — all of it went into the suitcase in a messy heap. She didn't care about organization. She just needed to leave.

Her phone buzzed again. This time, she couldn't ignore it. Wyatt.

Pixie, what's going on?

She stared at the screen, her breath hitching. For a moment, she hovered over the keyboard, her fingers trembling. She wanted to tell him. Wanted to say something.

But then she remembered Isabella's laugh, the way Wyatt had looked at her earlier in the evening. The way he didn't need the chaos that came with someone like Serafina Romano.

She locked the phone and shoved it into her bag, zipping it shut with a finality that echoed in the room.

Outside, she flagged down a cab, the cold biting at her cheeks as she slid into the backseat. The driver, an older man with a kind face, glanced at her through the rearview mirror.

"Where to?"

"The station," she said, her voice tight.

"Penn?"

"Yes."

The ride was quiet except for the low hum of the cab's heater and the occasional blare of a horn from passing cars. Pixie stared out of the window, her mind racing as the city blurred by in streaks of yellow and white. She could feel her resolve hardening, the plan forming in her mind. She'd take the overnight train south. She'd go back to Florida. She'd fake a family emergency, beg Caroline for forgiveness later.

She had no choice. Staying meant danger—for herself and for the carefully constructed life she'd built.

When the cab pulled up to Penn Station, Pixie handed the driver a few bills and slipped out into the cold. The station loomed before her, its massive glass windows glowing in the night.

Inside, the air was warm but bustling, the low murmur of travelers mixing with the occasional announcement over the loudspeakers. She purchased a ticket for the next southbound train, her fingers shaking slightly as she handed over her card.

As she waited on the platform, her phone buzzed one last time. She glanced at the screen. Wyatt again.

Talk to me. Whatever's happening, you don't have to run.

Her chest tightened painfully, but she shoved the phone into her bag without replying. The message still burned behind her eyes, but she couldn't look at it again. Not now.

The train screeched into the station with a gust of cold wind, brakes hissing like steam escaping a pressure valve. Overhead, a voice crackled through the speaker.

"Departure in two minutes. Please stand clear of the doors."

Pixie stepped on board, her boots clicking against the metal floor as the doors slid shut behind her. The car was mostly empty—just a teenager with headphones at the far end, a man in a suit scrolling his phone, and an older woman muttering quietly to herself near the doors.

She slipped into a window seat, tucking herself against the wall like she could disappear. Her forehead pressed to the cool glass. The platform lights outside cast long, distorted reflections across the steel tracks. Her own reflection wavered in the glass—pale, tired, haunted.

The train's engines hummed to life beneath her, that low mechanical thrum vibrating up through the seat. It felt like it always did—the beginning of escape.

But it didn't move.

There was a pause. A moment of breathless stillness. Then came the hiss of hydraulics — the doors closing. A soft jolt. The lights inside the car flickered once. Twice.

Pixie blinked.

Still no movement.

Then a *sound*.

Not from the train. From outside. From the platform.

Boots.

Running.

Shouting.

She turned just as shapes emerged through the window — figures in dark clothes, masks pulled up, moving fast, too fast.

The man in the suit looked up, confused.

The doors whooshed open again, not by schedule but by force — someone hitting the emergency override, the lock mechanism sparking slightly as it jerked back.

"What the hell?" the teenager yelped, yanking out an earbud.

They didn't speak. They didn't need to.

Three of them rushed inside, moving with precision. One yanked the old woman back by the collar and shoved her out of the way. Another pinned the suited man to his seat with a grunt and the gleam of something metallic flashing in his hand — too dull to be a gun, too cruel to be anything else.

The third came for her.

Pixie bolted upright, heart slamming into her ribs as she fumbled for her bag.

She barely made it to her feet before the figure was on her — gloved hand clamping over her mouth, the other yanking her back into the aisle.

The world spun. Her scream never made it out.

Somewhere, the intercom squawked, "Doors closing. Please stand clear."

Too late.

She was already being dragged off the train.

And the hum of the engine died in her ears.

They dragged her down the far end of the platform, boots echoing against the concrete as the train hissed behind them — doors shut, engine idle, no one daring to intervene. The station was nearly empty, the late hour turning the place into a hollow echo chamber of distant announcements and buzzing fluorescent lights.

Cold air needled her skin, sharper now without the adrenaline to mask it. The platform smelled of rust and old oil, mingled with the faint chemical sting of disinfectant that never quite erased the grime. Somewhere above, a loose wire crackled in the light fixture, casting a sickly flicker across the cracked tile wall.

Then she saw him.

Raffaele Santoro.

He emerged from the shadows like the devil she used to know — still draped in luxury and sin. A long, charcoal-gray coat hung open across his shoulders, the cashmere catching the dim light like a shroud. His dark hair was slicked back in that effortless, arrogant way that made you want to slap him or kiss him or both. Time had only sharpened him. Olive skin like warm bronze, cheekbones like a sculptor's fantasy, and that jaw — set in a lazy smirk that made her stomach turn.

He looked like money and menace.

And she hated that her pulse jumped at the sight of him.

"Serafina," he drawled, like the name was a private joke only he remembered. His voice wrapped around her—low, smooth, unmistakably New York Italian, thick with history and heat. "It is you. I've been wondering when you'd come see me."

Pixie didn't move.

Didn't breathe.

The sound of his voice, that old nickname he always used like a leash—Serafina—slammed into her like a memory she'd locked away in a box and buried six feet under.

But now the box was open.

And Raffaele was standing at the edge of it, smiling like he'd never left.

Pixie's blood ran cold. Her heart pounded against her ribs as she forced herself to keep her expression neutral. "You've got the wrong person," she said, her voice tight. "I don't know who you're talking about."

Raffaele laughed softly, the sound low and mocking. He stepped closer, his polished leather shoes clicking against the platform. "I don't forget faces," he said, his voice dangerously sweet. "And I sure as hell will never forget yours, my love."

"I'm not your love," Pixie snapped, her composure cracking for a moment.

"Not anymore," he admitted with a casual shrug, his smirk deepening. "But you owe me, Serafina. You owe me everything. Your loyalty. Your body. I made you, and you wouldn't have anything without me."

Pixie's hands clenched into fists at her sides, trembling with a mix of fear and rage. "You don't own me," she said.

Raffaele's smile faded, his dark eyes narrowing dangerously. "Oh, but I do. And if you don't come willingly, I'll be forced to take more serious measures to correct this...unfortunate situation."

He reached out, his hand brushing her chin, and she jerked back, her heart hammering in her chest. The two men flanking her tightened their grip, their hands like vises on her arms.

"You're coming with me, Serafina," Raffaele said, his voice like silk wrapped around steel. "You don't have a choice. I have been looking for you for a long time."

Before she could respond, a voice cut through the tense air like a blade.

"Get your hands off her."

Raffaele barely had time to turn before Wyatt appeared, his blue eyes blazing with fury. He moved with the precision of a predator, his fists already flying. The first punch landed squarely on Raffaele's jaw, the impact sending the designer stumbling back with a grunt.

The two men holding Pixie released her to lunge at Wyatt, but he was faster. He spun, his elbow slamming into one man's face before delivering a swift kick to the other's stomach. Both fell to the ground, groaning in pain.

Pixie stumbled back, her breath hitching as Wyatt turned to Raffaele, his jaw clenched, his injured shoulder clearly ignored in the heat of the moment.

"She's under my protection," Wyatt growled, his voice low and deadly. "You touch her again, and I'll make sure you regret it."

Raffaele straightened slowly, wiping a trickle of blood from the corner of his mouth. He chuckled darkly, his smirk returning despite the pain. "Her name is Serafina," he said, his tone mocking. "Do you even know who she really is?"

Wyatt's gaze cut to Pixie for the briefest of moments before locking back onto Raffaele. "I don't care who she is," he said coldly. "She's not yours."

Raffaele's smile widened, and he raised his hands in mock surrender. "I see how it is," he said smoothly. "This is personal. Interesting."

Wyatt didn't take the bait. He stepped forward, his towering frame looming over Raffaele. "Walk away, buddy. Now."

For a moment, the platform was silent, the tension crackling like electricity. Then Raffaele gestured for his men to get up, his smirk never fading.

"This isn't over, Serafina," he said as he backed away. "You'll see."

She stood frozen against the wall, her lungs burning. Raffaele and his men were gone — disappearing into the darkness like smoke — and yet the echo of his voice still curled around her bones.

Wyatt's hand hovered near her arm but he didn't touch her. Not yet. His voice broke through the ringing in her ears.

"Are you hurt?"

She shook her head. Her mouth opened, but nothing came out. Her fingers were still clenched tight — nails digging into her palms like anchors.

"You found me," she whispered, finally. "You came."

Wyatt's jaw flexed. His voice was low, steady. "You think I wouldn't?"

Pixie looked at him, eyes wide, rimmed red. "How?"

He exhaled, scanning her like he was making sure she hadn't shattered completely. "I met your friend. Ethan Kane. He was very concerned. After that..." His mouth twisted. "I asked around. A girl matching your description was seen getting on the 1 train, alone. Wrong platform for the time of night. Wrong kind of alone."

Her breath caught.

"I watched them take you," he said, quietly.

That was the part that undid her. The image of Wyatt—stoic, armored Wyatt—running. For *her*.

"You shouldn't have come," she said, barely audible.

He stepped in close now, close enough for her to feel the heat of him. "Don't say that."

"You don't know what you're in the middle of—"

"I don't care."

"Wyatt—"

"I don't give a damn who he is. Or what he has. You don't walk into a storm like that alone. Not when I can walk into it with you."

Her voice cracked. "You don't understand. It doesn't end with me. He'll come after *you* now."

"Let him," Wyatt said, steel laced through every word. "Let him come. He'll learn fast what it feels like to corner the wrong fucking woman."

That did it.

The last thread of her restraint snapped.

And for the first time in years, she let someone catch her before she fell.

Chapter Twenty

The cold February air bit at Wyatt's skin as he stepped off the curb outside Penn Station. His breath misted in the frigid night, his grip firm on Pixie's bags. Her silence was thick, her eyes darting, tense.

"Salem," Wyatt spoke into his comm, his voice sharp.

The crackle of static, then Salem's drawl. "Lost you there, boss. What's going on?"

"I've got Pixie," Wyatt said, voice low. "She's safe, but something's happened. Stay on First Lady."

A pause. "You good?"

"I'm fine," Wyatt replied, his voice hard. "Just keep things under control. I'll check in when I can."

"Copy that," Salem answered, curiosity laced with concern.

Wyatt tapped his comm off and turned to Pixie. She was shivering slightly, the heavy black cloak she'd borrowed doing little against the icy wind. Without a word, he hailed a cab, his sharp whistle cutting through the hum of the city.

The yellow cab pulled up, its headlights casting a soft glow on the dirty slush piled by the curb. Wyatt opened the door, ushering Pixie in first before sliding in beside her, her bags tucked awkwardly at his feet.

"Where to?" the driver asked, his thick Bronx accent cutting through the tense silence.

Wyatt hesitated, then named a hotel he'd stayed at once during a low-key security job in the city. It wasn't flashy, but it was nice enough and tucked into a quieter corner near the neighborhood Pixie seemed so connected to.

As the cab pulled into traffic, the city came alive around them. Snow flurries drifted down, catching the glow of streetlights and headlights, while the constant hum of engines and honking horns filled the air. Steam rose from manhole covers, and pedestrians in thick coats moved quickly along the sidewalks, their breath visible in the freezing night.

Wyatt glanced out of the window, taking in the towering buildings, the glowing neon signs, the endless movement of a city that never seemed to sleep. It was a stark contrast to the small towns he knew so well, where nights were quiet and the stars were visible in the dark sky.

But as he glanced at Pixie, he realized something—she wasn't out of place here. For all her unease and the fear he'd seen earlier, there was something about her posture now—straight, confident, almost defiant—that told him she belonged here.

"This is you," he said suddenly, his voice breaking the silence.

Pixie looked at him, her brow furrowing. "What?"

"New York," he said, gesturing vaguely. "The noise, the chaos, the cold. You're in your element here."

She didn't respond immediately, her gaze following his. A flicker of something crossed her face — pride, maybe, or nostalgia.

"It's where I'm from," she admitted finally, her voice softer than usual. "Not the fancy parts. In the neighborhoods no one talks about unless there's a headline."

Wyatt studied her, searching her face. There was something different about her here, something raw and unguarded. It was a side of her he hadn't seen before, and it made his chest tighten.

"Is that why you wanted to leave the ball?" he asked, his voice low. "Because of him? Or because of this?"

Pixie's jaw tightened, her gaze flicking back to him. "Both," she said simply, though the weight of her words lingered.

The cab slowed as they reached the quieter streets near the hotel. The buildings here were older, their façades worn but charming in their own way. A mix of mom-and-pop shops, corner delis, and brick apartment buildings lined the snow-dusted streets. The neon glow of a small diner lit up the corner, and a group of teenagers laughed as they huddled near the entrance, their breath visible in the cold.

"This is where I grew up," Pixie said quietly, her eyes on the familiar scene. "Not this exact block, but close enough. It's different now. Cleaner. Safer."

Wyatt watched her, his own questions piling up but staying silent. He could see the tension in her shoulders, the way her hands gripped her borrowed cloak. This place might have been home, but it also seemed to hold ghosts.

The cab pulled up to the hotel, and Wyatt handed the driver a few bills before stepping out. He grabbed her bags and led her inside, the warmth of the lobby a sharp contrast to the bitter cold outside.

It was modest but inviting—plush armchairs in the corner, a small fireplace crackling softly, and a clerk behind the counter who greeted them with a polite nod.

"I'll get us checked in," Wyatt said, his tone leaving no room for argument.

Pixie didn't protest, her arms wrapped tightly around herself as she hovered near the entrance, her gaze distant.

As Wyatt spoke to the clerk, his mind raced. This city wasn't just her element—it was her past. And if he wanted to understand her, to protect her, he'd have to start here. But first, he needed to make sure she was safe.

When he turned back to her, room keys in hand, he saw the faintest flicker of gratitude in her dark eyes. It wasn't much, but it was enough to keep him moving forward.

* * * *

Wyatt set the heavy tumbler of bourbon on the small table beside Pixie with deliberate care, his jaw tight as he straightened and studied her. She hadn't moved much since they'd arrived at the hotel, sitting on the edge of the armchair, her arms wrapped tightly around herself like she was holding her entire world together.

"Something stiff, please," she'd asked. He'd obliged, pouring the bourbon straight, but now he stood there, arms crossed, waiting for her to say something—anything.

She stared at the glass for a moment, then reached for it, her fingers trembling slightly as she brought it to her lips. The liquid glinted amber in the warm light of the room's single lamp. She took a small sip, her throat working, before setting it down with a quiet thud.

"Pixie," he said, his voice low and steady, though he could feel the tension rolling off him in waves. "You've got to tell me what's going on. I can't protect you if I don't know what I'm dealing with."

Her lips pressed into a thin line, and for a long moment, she didn't look at him. The silence in the room stretched, broken only by the faint hum of the heater kicking in.

"Pixie," he said again, more firmly this time.

"It's not my name," she said suddenly.

Wyatt blinked, his frown deepening. "What?"

"My name," she repeated, looking up at him finally. Her eyes shimmered with unshed tears, barely above a whisper. "It's not Pixie Sinclair. It's... Serafina Romano."

Wyatt stared at her, the words sinking in like stones in water. For a moment, he didn't know what to say. "Okay," he said slowly, dragging a chair closer and sitting across from her. "Why does that matter?"

She let out a bitter laugh, wiping at her eyes quickly before any tears could fall. "Because everything about me is a lie, Wyatt. Everything. My name, my life, the person you think I am—it's all fake."

"Start from the beginning," he said quietly, leaning forward, his elbows on his knees. "Tell me what's going on."

Pixie hesitated, her fingers twisting in the hem of the borrowed cloak she still wore. Then, as if a dam broke, the words came tumbling out.

She told him about her childhood in New York, about growing up in a rough Italian-American neighborhood with hardworking parents who never had enough. And then her mom died, followed by her dad. And then she was in foster care. Group homes. Drugs. Gangs. She told him about her first steps into the modeling world, the promise of glamor and escape, and the doors it had opened for her.

And then she told him about Raffaele Santoro.

The words came haltingly at first, her voice trembling as she described how he'd taken an interest in her, how he'd manipulated her trust and used his power to control her. He'd promised her everything she never had. She told Wyatt about the photos, the threats, and the moment she realized she was trapped, with no way to fight back.

"I tried to leave," she said, her voice breaking. "I tried to get out, to tell someone, to do something—but he had everything. Money. Lawyers. Contacts. He told me he'd ruin me if I said a word."

Wyatt's fists clenched on his knees. "And you believed him?"

She laughed bitterly, tears finally spilling down her cheeks. "I didn't have a choice. He had proof—photos, letters. He could destroy me with a phone call. I came from nothing. I believed him."

She went on to describe how she'd fled, cutting ties with everyone she knew, changing her name, and starting over in Palm Beach. How she'd buried Serafina Romano so deeply that even she sometimes forgot who she was.

"But it wasn't enough," she said, her voice a whisper now. "He still found me. He always finds me. And now, he's here, and I don't—"

Her voice cracked, and she buried her face in her hands, her shoulders shaking. "This is it," she said, her words muffled. "This is the end. When he tells people who I am, when those photos come out...it's over. My job, my life, everything I've built — it's gone. And you —" She looked up at him, her tear-streaked face twisting with anguish. "You'll hate me. You'll think I'm disgusting."

Wyatt's heart twisted painfully at the sight of her breaking in front of him. Slowly, deliberately, he reached out and covered her trembling hands with one of his own.

"Stop," he said firmly, his voice low and steady.

She shook her head, her tears falling freely now. "You don't understand, Wyatt. I let him do it. I let him take those photos. I let —"

"Stop," he said again, more forcefully this time. He leaned closer, his grip on her hands tightening. "You didn't let anything happen. He did this to you. You're not to blame for what he is."

Her breath hitched, and she looked away, unable to meet his gaze.

"I don't care who you were," Wyatt continued, his voice softening. "Serafina Romano, Pixie Sinclair — it doesn't matter. What matters is who you are right now. And right now, you're someone who needs my help. So stop trying to push me away and let me do my damn job."

"You don't understand," she whispered.

"Then make me understand," Wyatt said, his voice rough. "But don't think for one second that I'm walking away from you. I'm here, Pixie — Sera — whatever name you want to go by. I'm not going anywhere."

The words broke something in her, and she crumpled forward, her forehead resting against his chest as the sobs overtook her. Wyatt wrapped his arms around her, holding her tightly as she let the pain pour out, his heart aching with every tear she shed.

For the first time, she wasn't hiding. And for the first time, Wyatt wasn't letting go.

"Pixie," she said. "That's who I am now."

* * * *

The bathroom was filled with warm steam, the mirrors fogging up as the shower sprayed water against the tiled walls. Wyatt helped Pixie out of her travel clothes. She wasn't saying much, her movements sluggish and her eyes red from crying.

"Arms up," Wyatt said softly, tugging gently at the hem of her hoodie.

She hesitated for a moment, then obeyed, lifting her arms. He slid the fabric up and over her head, leaving her in a plain tank top that clung to her slim frame. He folded the hoodie and set it on the counter, trying to keep everything calm and methodical, even as his chest tightened at the sight of her vulnerability.

"Shoes," he said next, crouching down to untie her sneakers. His hands moved quickly but carefully, and when he glanced up, he noticed her watching him, her dark eyes glassy.

"Why are you doing this?" she murmured, her voice raw.

Wyatt paused, then met her gaze. "Because you need someone right now," he said simply. "And I'm not going to let you do this alone."

She bit her lip, her hands clenching at her sides as she looked away. He handed her the bourbon to drink while he worked.

He tugged her leggings down gently, trying not to make it feel more intimate than it already was. When she stepped out of them, he straightened and turned toward the shower, adjusting the temperature until it was steamy hot.

He turned back and she was in her tank and panties, downing the rest of the bourbon.

"All of it—off," he said gently, guiding her toward the water. "Let's go."

Pixie hesitated, her arms wrapped tightly around herself. "Okay," she whispered, and let him peel off her shirt, her bra, and her panties. She stood there, fully nude in front of him, tearful and shaking. He held her close, kissing her hair, whispering the things she'd never thought he'd say.

Not Wyatt Steele. Not six months ago.

Wyatt heaved her into the shower first, closing the glass door behind her. She stood for a moment and then peeked back out around the door.

"Are you"—she chewed her lip—"coming in with me?"

Wyatt didn't need to be asked twice. In five seconds, he had stripped out of his pants and jacket, leaving his undershirt and boxers on, and had stepped in behind her.

The water cascaded over them, the sound filling the space between them. Pixie stood under the stream, her eyes closed as the water plastered her hair to her face and ran down her shoulders.

"Close your eyes," Wyatt said softly, reaching for the small bottle of face wash on the built-in shelf.

She obeyed, her lashes fluttering shut as he lathered his hands and began to gently rub the makeup from her face. His fingers were steady but tender, moving across her cheeks, her jaw, her temples.

"I want more bourbon," she whispered, her voice barely audible over the sound of the water.

"I know," Wyatt replied, his voice just as soft. "Have mine."

She opened her eyes then, and the raw vulnerability in them almost undid him as he handed her his drink he had grabbed from the shelf.

He inhaled slowly, steadying his breath, as he watched her suck the glass contents back. He was going to lose his mind watching her doing these things.

"Lean your head back," he said, his voice tightening slightly as he reached for the shampoo. *Focus on the task.*

She turned her back to him, tilting her head into the spray as he worked the shampoo into her hair, his strong hands massaging her scalp. He was careful, slow, his touch firm but soothing.

"Did I tell you how much better it looks like this?" he said. "Natural."

As he rinsed the suds away, she let out a shuddering breath, her body trembling slightly under his hands.

"Come," he murmured, wrapping an arm around her shoulders and pulling her into his chest.

The sobs started again, muffled against his wet shirt as she clung to him. He held her tightly, one hand rubbing slow circles on her back, the other cradling the back of her head.

"I'm so tired, Wyatt," she whispered, her voice breaking. "I'm tired of running. Of hiding. Of pretending."

"I know," he said softly, his lips brushing the crown of her head. "I know, Pixie."

She pulled back slightly, looking up at him with tear-streaked cheeks. "You don't understand. If this gets out—if people know who I really am—everything's over. My job. My life. Us. I mean, sorry, I know there is no 'us' to ruin," she added quickly, her voice defensive.

"Don't do that," he said, his voice low but firm. "Don't push me away just because you're scared."

"I'm not scared," she snapped, though her trembling hands betrayed her.

"Poker face, again. It's trash," he said, brushing away a tear from her cheek with his thumb. "You're terrified. And so am I. But I'm not going anywhere, Pixie. Not now, not ever."

Her breath hitched, her eyes searching his as the tension between them thickened.

"You don't get it," she whispered. "You're loyal, Wyatt. To a fault. But I'm not worth it. I'm not worth you."

"You don't get to decide who or what I find worthy," he said fiercely, his hand sliding down to her shoulder, his lips against her damp skin.

Her resolve cracked then, and she collapsed into his arms again, her sobs shaking them both. Wyatt held her tightly, his own chest aching with the weight of everything she was carrying.

When her sobs finally subsided, he kissed her shoulder softly, his lips lingering against her skin. The steam curled around them, wrapping the small space in a haze as the warm water cascaded down their bodies. Wyatt stood close behind Pixie, his large hands lathered with soap as they moved over her shoulders in slow, firm circles. The tension in her muscles was palpable beneath his fingers, and he focused on easing it away, his touch deliberate and steady.

Pixie tilted her head forward, her wet hair clinging to her neck as her breath hitched slightly.

"I've got you," he murmured. "I promise. No one's going to hurt you again."

"Where was this Wyatt six months ago?" she replied, her voice wavering with the hint of a laugh.

His lips quirked into a faint smile, though she couldn't see it. "Here," he said softly, moving his hands down her arms, his fingers kneading gently. "Waiting for you."

Pixie exhaled shakily, closing her eyes as she let him guide her body. He worked over every knot in her muscles with the same precision he tried to bring to everything he did. He pressed his thumbs into the base of her neck, sliding down her spine, and tried not to react to the soft sigh that escaped her lips.

Wyatt's hands lingered, moving lower across her back, his palms spreading the suds as they traced the curve of her waist. He took his time, his fingers gliding over the damp, soapy surface of her skin, his movements unhurried and deliberate.

The water poured down over her back, warm and relentless, cascading over her skin and masking the sound of Wyatt's sharp intake of breath as Pixie leaned back against him. His cock twitched in response. He had been hard before but now he was a diamond.

Her body fit perfectly against his, her damp hair brushing his chest as the soft scent of her shampoo mixed with the steam curling in the air. His hands, still slick with soap, lingered on her waist, unsure whether to stay or pull her closer.

Her head tilted slightly, her cheek brushing his jaw, and that was all it took. Wyatt's resolve crumbled.

"Pixie," he murmured, his voice rough, raw, her name slipping from his lips like a prayer and a curse all at once.

She turned her head just enough to meet his gaze, her dark eyes wide, questioning. The water clung to her lashes, her lips parted slightly as if she were about to say something—but Wyatt didn't wait. He ripped his wet T-shirt off.

Then he gripped her waist and spun her to meet his face. He dipped his head, his mouth capturing hers in a kiss that was more need than finesse, more hunger than restraint. She tasted warm and sweet, of the faint tang of bourbon still lingering. His lips pressed firmly against hers, coaxing her into responding, into giving him something, anything, that told him this wasn't one-sided.

And then she did.

Her mouth softened beneath his, her lips parting just enough to let him deepen the kiss. He did so without hesitation, his tongue brushing against hers in a way that sent a shiver down his spine.

Wyatt groaned low in his throat, the sound vibrating between them as he shifted to angle the kiss, his hands sliding from her waist up to her back. Her skin was warm and slick under his palms, her body yielding to his as she turned fully toward him, her hands finding purchase on his chest.

She pressed into him, her fingers curling against his wet pecs as the kiss grew deeper, more desperate. Her tongue slid against his, dancing, playing in his rhythm. He could feel the erratic beat of her heart against his chest, her breasts pressed up against him, matching the wild pounding of his own heart.

Her breath hitched when he moved his hands to angle her face, tilting her head to kiss her more thoroughly. He could feel the soft curve of her jaw beneath his calloused palms, the way her breath mingled with his as she gasped softly into his mouth.

She felt like fire in his arms—fierce, consuming. Wyatt didn't want to stop. Couldn't stop. Her taste, her warmth, the way she melted into him—it was everything he hadn't known he needed, and more than he ever thought he could have.

When she finally pulled back, gasping for air, her lips were swollen and glistening, her cheeks flushed. Her eyes met his, wide and searching, her chest rising and falling with each shallow breath. Wyatt rested his forehead against hers, his own breathing ragged as he fought to steady himself.

"You taste…" he began, his voice rough, but the words caught in his throat.

She looked at him, her brows furrowing slightly. "What?" she whispered, her voice barely audible over the shower's steady rhythm.

"Perfect," he finished, his thumb brushing over her cheek, his lips quirking into a faint, self-deprecating smile. "Like I'm already addicted."

Her lips parted slightly, but she didn't reply. Instead, she simply stared at him, her gaze flicking from his eyes to his mouth, as though she was as unsure about what had just happened as he was certain.

And for the first time, Wyatt realized just how far gone he really was.

Chapter Twenty-One

Pixie felt her cheeks flush, though she wasn't sure if it was from the heat of the water or the way his touch was starting to stir something deeper inside her. He kissed her again and again, each time less restrained. The intimacy of it—his hands moving over her as if he wanted to memorize every inch of her—felt like something she shouldn't allow but couldn't bring herself to stop.

He worked his way down again, his hands sliding to her hips, then her thighs, his fingers kneading up gently to her hot slit. The water rinsed away the suds as quickly as he applied them, but he didn't seem to care, his focus entirely on her pleasure. When his hands skimmed up her pussy, his thumbs brushing against her clit, she shivered despite the heat. He was starting to know her spots—too soon for a man she'd barely been intimate with.

Barely.

That was all about to change.

With one hand, he gripped her ass, drawing her up and into him. With the other, he raised her thigh to straddle his hip. He ran his hand up her thigh and back to her clit, finding his way to the place that would drive her over the edge. She leaned on him as he took everything from her—her lips, her pussy, her breath. She moaned as his tongue slid in and out of her mouth, his fingers sliding in and out of her wet pussy.

"Wyatt," she moaned, her voice tinged with something she couldn't quite name.

"Hmm?" he murmured, his hands stilling for a moment.

"This is..." She hesitated, her breath catching as his hands resumed their expert movements. "I'm so close."

He leaned in slightly, and his lips hovered near her ear. "Fall apart for me," he asked, his voice deep and resonant. "I want to see you come."

She swallowed hard, her pulse racing. "God," she prayed, her voice barely above a whisper. "Please, Wyatt." She moaned louder and faster as he increased his pace and determination. Finally, his fingers formed into a come-hither movement, finding the perfect spot inside her, and she nearly fainted.

The warm bourbon, the hot water, the hotter orgasm—and the scorching man standing in front of her. She was going to pass out.

Everything tingled from head to toe. She saw stars.

Pixie closed her eyes, letting herself get lost in his touch, the warmth of the water, the steady presence of him as he caught her. She didn't know what this was or what it meant, but for now, she let herself feel.

He switched off the shower, wrapped her in a towel, and carried her to the bed in one movement—even managing to strip off his wet boxers in the process. The man was damn good.

And when she finally regained her senses, she found herself leaning back into feathery hotel pillows, opening her legs to him, letting the strength of his body anchor her in a way that felt impossibly safe.

The faint golden glow of the city lights softened him above her. He leaned in to kiss her again, finding her tongue with his warm mouth. His rock-hard cock bounced between her thighs, making her mouth water. God, she couldn't wait to feel his full length inside her. She was absolutely aching for him.

And then he flipped her.

Pixie found herself face down on the crisp white duvet, her arms pinned above her head as he sank her into the bed's plush surface. The tension in her body had been building for days, weeks even, and the warmth of his grip on her hips, opening her thighs to him, was both a surprise and an unexpected comfort.

"Bend over," Wyatt growled, his deep voice tinged with irritation — though it wasn't at her.

Pixie smiled against her arm, too relaxed to respond. His hands moved firmly, almost expertly, raising her ass to meet him as he knelt on the bed. He dug into her hips, working in slow, deliberate circles that made her toes curl involuntarily.

His cockhead met her wet opening. Gripping her hips, he slid his length up inside her, inch by inch. She gasped as he filled her, the pressure of feeling so full making her want to lose it all over again.

And then he started fucking her. His thrust was commanding, uncompromising, as though he were conquering her body with sheer will. Each pulse was purposeful, strong, and relentless. When his thumbs traveled down the length of her spine and her ass cheeks, pressing and kneading, her breath hitched and she cried out his name. The bed shook with the force of his movements, and she bit her lip to suppress a scream.

"You like my cock?" he asked, his voice low and gravelly, pausing his hands briefly on her hips.

"Mmhmm," she mumbled into the duvet, her voice muffled but content. "Fuck, babe. Don't stop."

Wyatt huffed a small laugh, though it was more exhale than sound, and he readjusted his position, bringing her ass lower onto him, working with slow, deliberate pressure. Her body shifted slightly with each thrust, the sheer strength of him rocking her against the mattress. It was both grounding and utterly electrifying.

"You're going to be sore tomorrow," he said, his tone almost teasing, but there was an edge of command beneath it. "But you need this."

Pixie cried out, her body melting further into the bed. "I don't think I've ever needed anything more than your glorious cock."

That earned her a reprieve as he chuckled, just a brief slow of pulses before Wyatt resumed his steady work. Each stroke inside her pussy was coursing waves of heat and pleasure through her.

She moaned as he stared groaning dirty things to her—all the things he'd wanted to do to her, all these years.

"Every snide comment of yours, I was this close to bending you over the table and fucking you like the bad bitch you are in front of everyone to see," he growled, and slapped her ass as he penetrated her faster. Rougher. "You'd like that, wouldn't you?" he questioned.

"Yes." She was twisting under his grip as the sensation became so intense.

"You want all the guys to watch me fuck you. Claim you. Make you cream on my cock." He slapped her ass again. Harder.

And as he did it, she started losing it. Her body softened and fell as pleasure exploded in her brain. The only thing holding her up to him was his immovable grip on her hips.

The bed shook more violently underneath them, the rhythm of his thrusts making her acutely aware of just how close he was, of the heat radiating from his body. Pixie let herself sink deeper onto his cock, into the moment, letting go of everything but the feeling of him inside her, all over her.

Pixie felt herself coming to orgasm again. The sensation of his cock pumping inside her and skimming every damn sensitive nerve was officially making her lose her sanity. Her damp skin slid along the sheets as she pushed herself up to his cock, taking the final thrusts, her body alive with the ache of exertion. He grasped her hair and neck, claiming her underneath him. Her heart thundered in her chest, her breaths quick and shallow as she crested the hill. Moaning, she cried out his name again and again. She slowed, turning slightly to glance behind her, watching Wyatt's face grow with intensity as he came to his own edge.

Sweat spread across his broad shoulders and chest, and his dark damp hair hung messily over his forehead. He fucked her harder, rougher, trying to steady his breathing, but his gaze burned with intensity, locking onto hers like she was the only thing keeping him going.

Pixie didn't move. She felt heat radiating off him, the raw energy rolling from his body as he struggled in those final seconds. His chest rose and fell with each labored breath, the sharp lines of his jaw tense, his lips parted slightly. She was struck by the sheer presence of him—wild and untamed, yet grounding her in the chaos of her own thoughts.

He was so damn hot.

"I'm there," he groaned.

"I want to taste it."

"I'm not sure you can handle it."

"Fucking give it to me, babe. Come in my mouth," she said.

In one violent movement, he pulled out, flipped her, and brought her underneath him as he knelt over her.

He pumped his engorged cock and tilted it toward her face. She leaned up, angling her head back and opening her mouth. "Do it."

Wyatt chuckled under his breath, shaking his head slightly before he released his hot cream into her mouth, rich and sweet, filling her senses with the slick texture. It was more than she'd anticipated, the deliciousness almost overwhelming as she clamped her lips shut to keep every drop in.

She swallowed quickly, her laughter bubbling up as she wiped a drip from the corner of her mouth with her finger. "Okay," she admitted. "That was…a lot."

"Told you. I've been holding on for you."

"But it was delicious," she said, grinning as she licked her lips. "And I want more."

Wyatt laughed, the sound deep and warm as he pulled her into his embrace. For the first time in a long time, Pixie felt no tension in her body.

The hotel heater hummed softly in the background, blending with the rhythmic sound of Wyatt's breathing beside her. He held her waist, his touch protective, holding her to him like he was afraid she'd bolt.

Pixie shifted slightly, her cheek brushing against the pillow as she turned her head to look at him. His profile was softened by the shadows, but even in the dim light, she could see the exhaustion etched into his features — the faint lines around his eyes, the tension in his jaw that hadn't quite eased even as sleep beckoned him.

"I always liked you," Wyatt said, his voice low and rough with fatigue. His eyes cracked open, meeting hers in the dark.

"You could have tried being nicer," she whispered back, a faint smile tugging at her lips despite herself.

"I was just defending myself against you, Ms. Sarcasm."

"We all have crutches to protect us."

He huffed softly, his breath warm against her temple as he shifted closer, his muscled leg brushing against hers under the covers.

She grinned and kissed him — long and messy.

"You should get some sleep," she said.

"Hard to sleep with you looking at me like that."

"Like what?" she asked, her voice barely above a whisper.

"Like you're still deciding whether or not I'm real," he replied, his tone light but tinged with something deeper.

Her chest tightened, and she turned her gaze back to the ceiling, the weight of his words settling over her. "I guess I'm just not used to this," she admitted after a moment, her voice hesitant. "Having someone take care of me. Like…really take care of me."

Wyatt's hand, rough and warm, slid up her hip, a reassuring gesture that sent a shiver through her. "You deserve it," he said simply, as if the statement were undeniable.

Pixie let out a quiet laugh, shaking her head. "I'm not so sure about that."

"I am," he countered, his voice steady, even as sleep pulled at its edges.

The silence between them stretched, heavy with the weight of unspoken truths. She wanted to say something, to let him know how much it had meant to her — the way he'd stood by her tonight, the way he'd always seemed to see past her walls, even when she tried to keep him out. But the words felt too fragile, too vulnerable, and so she stayed quiet.

Wyatt broke the silence first. "Pixie, just make me a promise — stay with me. I don't want to wake up and you're gone," he said, his voice quieter now, like the question was more for himself than for her. "No more running."

"Tonight or ever?"

"Ever, for that matter. You have me now."

Pixie turned back to him, her gaze tracing the faint outline of his face. "I don't know if I'd know how," she confessed, her voice barely audible.

He nodded, drawing circles on her side, like he needed the contact to stay grounded. "I get it," he said after a moment. "I've been running too. Just...in a different way."

She frowned slightly, tilting her head to look at him. "From what?"

Wyatt hesitated, his jaw tightening before he let out a slow breath. "From the guy I used to be," he admitted. "I thought I had it all figured out — who I was, what I was good at. And then... Syria...and boom." He let out a humorless laugh, the sound bitter but raw. "Literally."

Pixie's chest tightened at the pain in his voice, and she reached out without thinking, her fingers brushing against his arm. "Wyatt..."

"It's fine," he said, though his voice wavered slightly. "I'm fine. It's just... I don't know. Sometimes it feels like I lost more than just the job. Like I lost...me."

Her heart ached for him, for the vulnerability he was letting her see. She shifted closer, her forehead rested on his shoulder. "You didn't lose you," she whispered. "Not really."

He looked down at her, his blue eyes softening as they met hers. "And how would you know that?"

"Because I see you," she said simply, the words falling from her lips before she could second-guess them. "You're still here, Wyatt. And you're still...good. Even when you don't believe it."

He didn't say anything for a moment, just looked at her like she'd said something he wasn't ready to hear. Then, slowly, he leaned down, pressing a soft, lingering kiss to her forehead.

"Thank you," he murmured against her skin, his voice rough with emotion. "Stay."

Pixie closed her eyes, letting herself sink into the warmth of him, the steady rhythm of his breathing, the quiet strength that seemed to radiate from him even in his most vulnerable moments. For the first time in a long time, she felt safe—not because she was hiding, but because she wasn't alone.

And as sleep finally began to claim her, she realized she didn't want to run anymore. Not from him. Not from this. Not tonight.

Chapter Twenty-Two

Morning light streamed through the hotel curtains as Wyatt stood by the window, sipping black coffee, listening to Pixie singing distantly in the shower. His mind was still grinding over the chaos of the previous night. A knock at the door broke his focus.

He set the mug down and opened the door to find Salem standing there, duffel bag over one shoulder, exasperation in his eyes.

"Morning," Salem said, stepping in without waiting. He scanned the room, noting the unmade bed and the tension hanging in the air. "Figured you'd want your stuff."

Wyatt rubbed the back of his neck. "Thanks."

Salem dropped the bag on the couch, his gaze sharp. "So, you gonna tell me what's going on or should I just guess?"

"She's in serious trouble," Wyatt said, his tone clipped and professional but laced with an edge of frustration. "Her past—you were right. She's been hiding from some guy from New York for years, someone who has the means and the power to damage her, she believes."

Salem's easy demeanor evaporated, his face hardening. "Okay, who is the guy?"

Wyatt nodded. "Raffaele Santoro. He's dangerous — manipulative, well-connected, and vindictive as hell. Last night at the station, he sent his guys after her. If I hadn't been there, god knows what would have happened. He's been hunting her for years, trying to get her under his thumb again. He's not going to stop."

Salem let out a low whistle, his sharp eyes narrowing. "Sounds like the kind of guy who doesn't take no for an answer."

"He doesn't," Wyatt said bluntly. "He thinks he owns her."

"Sex trafficking?"

"Bingo. She was a teenage 'model'. But my guess is she was a gorgeous, unprotected young thing preyed on by lechers."

"Well, fuck." Salem leaned forward, calculating.

"She's terrified of him, but she's more terrified of the fallout if the truth about her past gets out."

Salem's voice dropped to match Wyatt's intensity. "So, what's the play?"

Wyatt straightened, his jaw tight. "We neutralize the threat. Quietly. No scene, no escalation unless he forces our hand. But Santoro needs to understand that she's untouchable now."

Salem frowned, his brow furrowing. "Neutralize how?"

"I have a gun," Wyatt said. "So do you." Wyatt's voice dropped to a near growl. "We make sure he understands there are consequences for coming after her."

Salem studied him for a moment, his expression unreadable. "You're thinking personal, not professional. We took oaths."

"I don't have a choice. I'm doing this."

Salem nodded slowly, his gaze thoughtful. "All right. I'm in. But we have to tread carefully. You know how fast this could blow back, especially with the First Lady in the picture."

"I know," Wyatt said, running a hand through his hair. "But this guy isn't going to stop until someone makes him."

Salem stood, his posture steady and resolute. "Then let's make sure we're those someones."

Before Wyatt could answer, a soft rustle from the bathroom drew both their attention. Salem's brows rose slightly as Pixie appeared, her dark hair still damp from a shower and loosely kissing her shoulders. She wore the hotel's plush white bathrobe, cinched tightly at her waist, and despite her casual demeanor, there was an undeniable confidence in the way she strolled into the room.

She froze for a split second when she noticed Salem, her dark eyes narrowing slightly before softening into something less guarded. Wyatt, already moving to the kitchenette, handed her a fresh cup of coffee without a word, his expression unreadable.

Pixie accepted the cup, her fingers brushing against his briefly. "Hi," she said, her voice husky with sleep as she leaned against the counter and sipped her coffee.

Salem's gaze darted between them, his lips twitching as though he was fighting the urge to comment. "Well, this is new," he said finally, his tone laced with dry humor.

Wyatt shot him a warning look before turning his attention back to Pixie. "How are you feeling?"

"Better," she said simply, her eyes meeting his for a moment before flicking back to Salem.

"I made a promise," she added, her tone firm. "I'm done running. Back to work. Back to reality."

Salem tilted his head, studying her with a mix of curiosity and respect. "Admirable," he said. "But reality isn't exactly safe right now, is it?"

Pixie stiffened slightly, setting her coffee down on the counter. "I'm not going to let him control my life," she said, her voice steady but resolute. "And I'm not going to let you two go off and make it worse by turning this into some...violent mess."

Wyatt crossed his arms, his gaze steady on her. "Pixie—"

"No," she cut him off, her eyes flashing. "I heard what you said, Wyatt. And I'm telling you now—it's not happening. He wants me to be afraid. I'm not giving him the satisfaction. And I'm not sending you guys to prison in the process."

Salem raised an eyebrow, leaning back against the armrest of the couch. "She's got a point," he said, though his tone was cautious. "But ignoring him won't make him go away, either."

Pixie turned to him, her jaw tightening. "Then I will handle it without violence. Without creating a scene."

Wyatt took a step closer, his voice low and firm. "You will not deal with him alone. That's not happening."

Her gaze snapped to his, and for a moment, the tension between them was almost palpable. But then her expression softened, and she let out a quiet sigh. "I know," she said softly. "I know you mean well. But this is my life, Wyatt. My past. I need to handle it my way."

Salem's gaze went back and forth between them.

"You got it, babe," Wyatt said.

Pixie straightened, brushing a strand of hair from her face as she stepped away from the counter. "Good," she said, her voice regaining its sharp edge. "Now, if we're done strategizing, I need to get ready. Caroline's schedule isn't going to manage itself."

Salem watched her as she disappeared back into the bathroom, the door clicking shut behind her. He turned back to Wyatt, his expression a mix of amusement and concern. "You've got your hands full with that one."

Wyatt exhaled, running a hand through his hair. "Don't I know it."

"What's the plan?"

Wyatt clenched his jaw, and turned back to Salem, his voice curt. "She doesn't want me to do this."

"Be realistic. That's not an option."

"So we be discreet. No pistol-whipping...unless absolutely necessary."

Salem nodded, his usual easygoing demeanor replaced with a rare seriousness. "Define necessary."

"He sasses. He gets the barrel."

Salem smirked, but his tone turned serious. "Protecting her like this—it's going to be hard to explain in an inquiry."

"Leave no evidence." Wyatt met his gaze. "She's worth it."

Salem nodded slowly, pushing off the couch. "Fuck yeah. Let's make sure she gets through this in one piece."

"Thanks, man. I always knew you were the 'bury bodies' friend."

"Anytime, brother."

As Salem left, Wyatt leaned against the counter, his eyes drifting to the closed bathroom door. The weight of everything that had transpired settled over him, but amidst the chaos, there was one thing he knew for certain. He wasn't letting her face this alone. Not now. Not ever.

Chapter Twenty-Three

The Metropolitan Museum of Art gleamed in the late afternoon light, its glass façade reflecting the city's pulse. Inside, the space thrived with fashion elites, journalists, and philanthropists, all gathered for the First Lady's sustainable fashion initiative. The air, scented with citrus and cedarwood, hummed with conversation and the click of designer heels on marble floors.

Pixie moved through the crowd, clipboard in hand, her navy dress sharp as her focus. Her hair gleamed under the lights, her poise flawless. No one would guess she'd barely slept, or that last night had been far from typical.

"Headache," she'd told Marcy and Jamie when they'd asked about her sudden exit. The lie had slipped off her tongue, convincing even her. But now, as she stood by a cocktail table, her colleagues' stares felt like a weight she couldn't shake.

"All right," Jamie said, breaking the silence as he swirled his drink. His silver tie glinted under the lights, perfectly complementing his crisp black suit. "We've been patient. Now spill. What happened after you left last night? And don't give me that 'headache' nonsense again."

Pixie sighed, rolling her eyes as she adjusted the strap of her sleek crossbody bag. "Jamie, I told you—"

"Headache," Marcy interjected, her tone laced with disbelief as she pinned Pixie with suspicion. "Pix, you don't just bail on a gala with no explanation. Not with the First Lady in attendance."

Pixie pressed her lips together, her jaw tightening. "It's fine. I'm fine. Nothing happened."

Jamie raised a groomed eyebrow, sipping his champagne. "Nothing happened?" He leaned in, lowering his voice conspiratorially. "Because I heard whispers about you and a certain Secret Service agent disappearing at roughly the same time."

Then a gallery guest breezed past them, champagne in hand, accidentally brushing up against Pixie's behind. She winced—visibly—thanks to the bruises Wyatt had left on her ass.

Marcy's eyes widened, her gasp audible even over the quiet murmur of the crowd. "Wyatt? Oh my God, Pixie, what did you do?"

Pixie's cheeks flushed, the heat spreading quickly as she shook her head. "I didn't do anything," she said, though the memory of Wyatt's hands, his voice, his sheer presence, sent an undeniable shiver through her. "We just—he—"

"Oh my God, you did," Marcy said, her voice an excited whisper as she grabbed Pixie's arm. "You totally did."

Pixie groaned, lowering her clipboard to the table. "Would you two calm down? It's not what you think."

Jamie chuckled, his grin wolfish. "Then why are you blushing like a schoolgirl caught in the act?"

"Because you're both ridiculous," Pixie snapped, but her weak defense only made them lean in closer, their curiosity almost tangible.

"Come on, Pix," Marcy urged, her eyes sparkling. "Just a little detail. Something. Did he kiss you? Or…?"

Pixie hesitated, her defenses cracking under their relentless poking. She glanced around the room, ensuring the First Lady was still engaged in conversation with a designer, before sighing. "Fine," she muttered. "Yes, okay? We… spent the night in a hotel room."

The moment the words left her mouth, both Jamie and Marcy erupted—not loudly, but with enough enthusiasm that Pixie immediately regretted saying anything. Jamie raised his glass in mock toast, while Marcy clapped her hands together, her excitement barely contained.

"Finally!" Marcy whispered. "I mean, come on, Pix. You two have had this…thing for months now."

"There's no thing," Pixie protested, though her flushed cheeks betrayed her.

"Sure there isn't," Jamie said, his tone dry but amused. "Just a night in a hotel room, completely innocent, I'm sure."

Pixie shot him a glare. "It wasn't like that."

Marcy tilted her head, studying her friend. "Then what was it like?" she asked.

Pixie hesitated, the weight of the previous night pressing on her chest. "It was…complicated," she admitted finally, quieter now. "He helped me. Took care of me when I needed it. And…he didn't have to."

Jamie's teasing grin faded slightly, replaced by a look of genuine curiosity. "And how do you feel about that?" he asked, uncharacteristically gentle.

Pixie opened her mouth to respond, but before she could, the First Lady's voice cut through the air, drawing their attention back to the center of the room. Caroline Armstrong stood on a small stage, her elegance commanding the room as she began her address.

Pixie straightened, her walls snapping back into place as she reached for her clipboard. "Time to get back to work," she said briskly, ignoring the knowing looks Jamie and Marcy exchanged.

As she moved toward the stage, the memory of Wyatt's steady hands and the warmth of his voice lingered at the edges of her mind.

The bustling chatter of the museum echoed softly in the distance as the First Lady's speech ended. Pixie and Marcy escaped from the crowd through the quieter side hallway, their heels clicking lightly against the sleek marble floors. Pixie clutched her clipboard tightly to her chest, her mind still half-occupied with the evening's schedule. Everything was running smoothly, but her nerves still simmered just beneath the surface.

Marcy, ever the keen observer, nudged her gently. "You're quiet again. That's never a good sign."

Pixie forced a faint smile. "Just tired."

Marcy gave her a skeptical look but didn't push, instead continuing to chatter about the event logistics. But as they rounded a corner, both women froze in their tracks, their footsteps halting abruptly at the sound of a familiar voice.

Wyatt.

Pixie's pulse quickened as her eyes darted to the small alcove just ahead. Wyatt was standing there with

Isabella — the blonde socialite who'd been glued to his side at the gala. They couldn't see her and Marcy from their angle, and Pixie instinctively grabbed Marcy's arm, pulling her back into the shadow of the hallway wall.

Marcy opened her mouth to whisper something, but Pixie shook her head quickly, her heart pounding too hard to think straight. Wyatt's deep voice was clear, every word cutting through the air like a knife.

"I'm not the marrying type, Isabella," he was saying, his tone calm but firm. "Never have been, never will be."

Pixie's stomach twisted, a dull ache spreading through her chest as she pressed herself closer to the wall. She didn't know why she was listening — why she couldn't make herself walk away — but the weight of his words anchored her in place.

"No commitments," Wyatt continued, his voice steady, like he'd rehearsed this conversation a hundred times. "No kids, no settling down. That's not who I am, and it's not gonna change. So if that's what you're looking for, you're wasting your time."

Pixie's breath hitched, and she felt Marcy stiffen beside her. She didn't dare look at her friend, didn't dare let herself react. The ache in her chest was spreading, sharp and undeniable, but she forced herself to stay still, to stay quiet.

Isabella's laugh broke the tense silence, light and easy. "Oh, Wyatt," she said, her tone dripping with charm. "Who said I was looking for anything serious? You're exactly my type — nothing complicated, nothing messy. Just…fun."

Pixie felt the sting of those words like a slap, her grip tightening on her clipboard until her knuckles turned white.

Isabella's voice turned softer, almost playful. "Call me sometime, okay? I think we'd be good at having fun together."

Wyatt didn't respond immediately, but when he did, his tone was lighter, almost amused. "Not going to happen."

"You say that now. I know how guys like you play."

Pixie felt like the ground beneath her was shifting, unsteady and treacherous. She clenched her jaw, trying to swallow the lump forming in her throat. Marcy's hand touched her arm gently, a silent question in the gesture, but Pixie shook her head, her expression stony.

Finally, Isabella's heels clicked against the floor as she walked away, and Pixie heard Wyatt exhale softly, the sound laced with something she couldn't place. She waited a beat, then another, before turning on her heel and walking back the way they'd come.

Marcy hurried to keep up, her voice a low hiss. "Pixie, what are you —?"

"Drop it," Pixie snapped, her voice cold and brittle as she stormed down the hallway. Her vision blurred slightly, and she blinked rapidly, willing herself to keep it together.

She didn't stop until she was back near the main event space, her breath shaky as she leaned against a column, trying to compose herself. Marcy stopped beside her, her expression unreadable.

"Pix," Marcy said softly, her tone careful. "You okay?"

Pixie let out a sharp breath, her hands trembling as she adjusted her clipboard. "I'm fine," she said tightly, her voice barely above a whisper. "It doesn't matter."

"Girl, not the marrying type? Come on," Marcy said bluntly, her arms crossed. "I saw your face."

Pixie shook her head, her jaw tightening. "It doesn't matter, Marcy," she repeated, her voice firmer now. "He's made it clear who he is. And I'm not going to let it affect me. End of story."

Marcy studied her for a moment, her gaze softening. "He cares about you, you know."

"Maybe," Pixie said quietly, the words cutting deeper than she expected. "But, I'm not here to change anyone."

Marcy didn't respond, and Pixie didn't wait for her to. She straightened, adjusted her posture, and forced herself to step back into the event with her mask firmly in place. Whatever she was feeling — whatever Wyatt's words had done to her — she would bury it. Just like she always did.

Chapter Twenty-Four

Pixie stepped out of the hotel's warmth into the sharp February cold of New York. The city, swallowed by gray clouds, was unnervingly quiet. She pulled her scarf tighter as she made her way toward a neighborhood she hadn't seen in years.

East Harlem hadn't changed much. Cracked sidewalks, weathered brownstones, and the scent of exhaust and roasting chestnuts filled the air. It was a world away from her polished life now, yet the familiar sights pressed on her chest.

She slowed near a small brick building at the block's edge. The old group home was gone, replaced by Marco's Coffee. The grime-covered windows were now sleek, with warm light spilling onto the sidewalk.

With a breath, Pixie pushed the door open. The bell jingled softly. The scent of fresh coffee hit her, rich and inviting, blending with the sound of an old jazz tune. Pastries gleamed under glass domes, and a young barista looked up with a practiced smile.

"Good morning," the barista greeted, her voice bright. "What can I get you?"

Pixie scanned the chalkboard menu above the counter, her fingers tightening around the strap of her bag. "Just a cappuccino," she said, pulling a few bills from her pocket.

As she waited, her eyes roamed the space. The walls were freshly painted, decorated with abstract art and photographs of the neighborhood. But she could still see the bones of the place she'd known — the outline of the old front desk, now replaced by the counter; the corner where she used to sit and read, now a cozy nook with mismatched chairs and a small bookshelf.

When her drink was ready, Pixie thanked the barista and stepped back outside, the warmth of the cup seeping into her gloved hands. She continued her walk, the familiar streets pulling at her memory.

As she rounded another corner, she spotted an older man shoveling snow in front of a modest brick townhouse. His thick coat was dusted with white, and his gloved hands worked methodically as he cleared the stoop. He paused when he noticed her, his weathered face breaking into a wide smile.

"Serafina?" he called, his voice tinged with surprise and warmth.

Pixie froze, her heart skipping a beat at the sound of her given name. She hadn't heard it spoken like that in years, in that familiar cadence, with that unmistakable Italian lilt. Slowly, she stepped closer.

"Mr. Mancini?" she asked, her voice hesitant but hopeful.

"It is you," the man said, leaning on his shovel as he studied her. "Madonna, look at you. All grown up! I didn't believe my eyes at first."

Pixie couldn't help but smile, a genuine one that reached her eyes. "It's been a long time."

"Too long," Mr. Mancini said, shaking his head. "You were just a little thing the last time I saw you. Always running around, getting into trouble with those boys down the block." He chuckled, his breath fogging in the cold. "And now look at you. You look like a movie star."

Pixie laughed, the sound surprising even herself. "I'm just visiting," she said. "I wanted to see the neighborhood again."

"Well, it's not much to look at, but it's home," he said, his voice turning fond. "You don't forget where you come from, no matter where life takes you. I'm glad to see you haven't."

Pixie's throat tightened at his words, and she nodded, her fingers curling tighter around her coffee cup. "It's good to see you," she said. "Really good."

Mr. Mancini waved her closer, pulling a small bag of rock salt from his stoop. "You need anything, you come to me, okay? Still got a lot of friends in the neighborhood. We look out for our own."

Her chest ached at the kindness in his voice, at the familiarity of it. "Thank you," she said, her voice barely above a whisper.

As she walked away, the warmth of their brief conversation lingered, a reminder of a life she'd left behind but never truly forgotten. For a moment, the weight of her past didn't feel quite so heavy.

She reached an intersection and came to a familiar sight. Her church loomed quietly on the corner of East Harlem, its stone façade darkened by time and soot from the endless churn of the city. It stood stoic among the cramped tenements and shuttered bodegas, a relic of something sacred in a place that had seen its share of struggle. The stained-glass windows glinted in the pale winter sunlight, their vibrant colors dulled by grime, but they still managed to cast faint patterns on the snow-dusted sidewalk below.

Pixie paused at the base of the steps, her breath misting in the bitter air as she stared up at the arched wooden doors. They were massive and weathered, their iron handles worn smooth by countless hands. The sight of them tugged at something deep in her chest, an ache she thought she'd long since buried. How many times had she climbed these steps as a child, desperate for answers she never got? For comfort she didn't believe she deserved?

Her fingers tightened on the strap of her bag, the leather cold against her skin. She almost turned back, but then her gaze caught on a small group of homeless men and women huddled near the church's side wall, their thin blankets offering little protection against the biting wind. Their breaths hung in the air like fragile smoke, their faces weary but watchful.

Pixie hesitated, then dug into her coat pocket and pulled out the last few bills she had on her. It wasn't much, but it was something. She folded the bills carefully and stepped toward the group, her boots crunching softly on the salt-scattered pavement. An older man with trembling hands and sunken cheeks looked up as she approached, his bloodshot eyes filled with quiet gratitude.

"God bless you," he murmured as she pressed the money into his hand.

Pixie managed a smile, though her throat tightened as she nodded and turned away. The steps creaked slightly under her weight as she climbed, the sound familiar and unsettling all at once. She pushed open the heavy wooden doors and stepped inside, the warm air and the scent of incense enveloping her immediately.

The church hadn't changed much. The long rows of dark wooden pews gleamed in the dim light, their surfaces worn smooth by years of use. Candles flickered along the walls, their glow soft and inviting. The high vaulted ceiling seemed to stretch forever, its intricate carvings barely visible in the shadows.

Pixie dipped her fingers into the cold holy water near the entrance, crossing herself out of habit more than belief. She chose a pew near the middle, sliding into it quietly and setting her bag down beside her. The weight of the silence pressed down on her, heavy and familiar. She bowed her head, clasping her hands tightly in front of her, and closed her eyes.

The memories came unbidden, sharp and relentless. She'd sat in this very church as a child, her knees tucked against the splintered pews, praying for things she couldn't articulate. For a family that cared. For a place that felt like home. For someone — anyone — to stay.

But no one ever did. People left. Promises broke. Even faith, at some point, had slipped through her fingers like sand.

Now, she was here again, older but no less fractured, with Wyatt's voice echoing in her mind like a wound that refused to close. *I'm not the marrying type. No commitments. No kids. That's not who I am.* His words had cut deep, though she'd pretended they hadn't. He'd made his position clear. She couldn't trust him to stay — not for her, not for anyone.

It would have been nice to know all of that before he made love to her.

Before she lost her heart to him.

The sound of footsteps broke her reverie. She didn't look up at first, assuming it was just another parishioner settling in before the service. But then she felt the shift in the air, a presence familiar and grounding in a way that made her pulse quicken.

She glanced to her right, her breath hitching as she saw Wyatt sliding into the pew beside her.

Good lord. Speak of the devil.

Thankfully, he didn't look at her. His head was bowed, his hands loosely clasped in front of him, as though he'd come here for the same reason she had — to search for something he couldn't name.

Pixie's chest tightened, her emotions a tangle of anger, confusion, and something softer she refused to name. She hadn't seen him since the gala, hadn't answered his messages. And yet here he was, sitting beside her in silence, as if this was the most natural place for him to be.

The priest began the service, his voice steady and calm as he welcomed the congregation. Pixie tried to focus, tried to push Wyatt's presence out of her mind, but it was impossible. The tension between them was electric, his nearness both comforting and maddening.

When the priest began his homily, his words hit too close to home.

"Lent is a time to confront what we've hidden," he said, his voice echoing through the sacred space. "A time to face the truths we're too afraid to admit, to ourselves and to others. It is a time for forgiveness — for others, yes, but also for ourselves."

Pixie swallowed hard, her eyes fixed on the stained-glass window ahead. The vibrant blues and reds of the Virgin Mary seemed to glow in the soft light, a silent witness to her turmoil. She felt Wyatt shift beside her, his posture tense, his breaths slow and measured. She knew he'd heard the priest's words too, felt the weight of them just as much as she did.

When the mass ended, the congregation began to file out, but neither of them moved. The silence stretched between them, heavy and loaded with everything they hadn't said. Pixie stared straight ahead, her hands clasped tightly in her lap, her mind racing.

She wanted to leave, to put as much distance between herself and Wyatt as possible. But a part of her—one she hated, one she'd buried long ago—wanted to stay. Because for the first time in years, she wasn't sitting here alone. And that scared her more than anything.

Chapter Twenty-Five

The church was empty, silent except for the occasional creak of wood as Wyatt shifted in the pew. His gaze was fixed on the altar, but his mind was elsewhere. His hands rested loosely on his thighs, fingers tracing the faint lines in his black jeans. Pixie sat a few feet away, rigid and still, her hands tightly clasped in her lap.

They hadn't spoken since the priest finished. She hadn't even glanced at him. The tension between them felt thick, like a wall pressing against his chest. He exhaled slowly, running a hand through his hair, and finally spoke.

"I know you're upset," he said, voice low but steady.

Pixie didn't move. Her eyes stayed fixed ahead, the candlelight flickering across her face, highlighting the tightness in her jaw, the tremble in her lips.

"Marcy told me," Wyatt added, his tone softening.

Pixie's head snapped toward him, her dark eyes narrowing. "Marcy wouldn't betray me."

"She didn't," Wyatt said quickly, turning to meet her gaze. "Not intentionally. I'm a good interrogator."

"Humble, too."

He shot her a look.

Pixie's shoulders stiffened, and she let out a sharp breath, her voice laced with anger. "So, what? You've come to explain why you said what you said to Isabella? To make me feel better? Because you should just stop now."

Wyatt flinched at her words, guilt twisting in his chest. He looked down at his hands, rubbing his thumb over the faint scar on his palm. "I didn't know you overheard that," he said after a moment. "But yeah, I guess I do owe you an explanation."

Pixie let out a humorless laugh, shaking her head. "An explanation? Wyatt, you made it perfectly clear. No commitments, no marriage, no future. I don't need you to explain that."

"It's not that simple," Wyatt said, his voice rough. He shifted in his seat, leaning forward slightly as he rubbed a hand over his face. "I'm not saying it to hurt you. I'm saying it because…because I can't be that guy. I can't be what you deserve."

Pixie's brows furrowed, her frustration evident. "Why? Because you don't want to? Or because you're too much of a coward to try?"

Her words cut deep, but Wyatt forced himself to hold her gaze. "Because I'm too much like my dad," he said, his voice cracking slightly. "Because I love too hard, and I destroy everything I touch."

Pixie blinked, the anger in her expression faltering for a moment as confusion flickered across her face. "What are you talking about?"

He looked at her then, holding back. His gaze roamed over her as if to memorize her, to lock it away in some unspoken place that didn't—couldn't—exist.

Wyatt exhaled shakily, his hands clenching into fists on his thighs. "My dad… He loved my mom too much. Or maybe it was the booze he loved more. Either way, it got twisted. He'd hit her, over and over, and then cry about how much he loved her. How he'd do better. But he never did. One night, she didn't get up. And he ran. Disappeared. Left me with nothing but the mess he made."

Pixie's breath caught. "Wyatt…"

"I swore I'd never be like him," Wyatt continued, his voice raw. "But I see it in myself, Pix. I get addicted to things. Drugs. Love. Whatever it is, it eats me alive. After Syria, after I got blown up and came home in pieces, I was hooked on painkillers. Couldn't get through the day without them. It took me years to claw my way out of that hole, but the fear never leaves. I know how easily I could fall back into it."

He turned to her. "And now, with you… I feel it, Pix. This…obsession. This need to protect you, to be near you. It's too much. I can't trust myself not to hurt you, not to ruin whatever this is. So yeah, I said that to that chick because it's the truth. I'm not the guy who gets married. I'm the guy who keeps his distance so he doesn't destroy the people he cares about."

"And that means me?"

"Unfortunately."

Wyatt braced the pew in front of him as he watched Pixie. She hadn't said a word since he'd poured his heart out, and the silence between them was both suffocating and electric.

She hunched slightly forward, bowed her head, dark hair shielding her face. Her foot tapped against the stone floor in a nervous rhythm, and her hands were clasped tightly in her lap, as though she was holding herself together by sheer force of will.

He couldn't take his eyes off her. She looked so different from the polished, composed woman he was used to—her casual hoodie slipping off one shoulder, scuffed sneakers peeking out from under her jeans. It was a raw, unguarded version of her that hit him harder than he expected. The set of her jaw, the faint tremble in her lips, the way she kept blinking too fast to hold back tears—every detail pulled at him, igniting something primal and protective in his chest. She was chaos and contradiction, sharp edges and soft vulnerability, and he was drowning in her without even meaning to.

The wait was killing him.

Wyatt leaned back, his heart pounding, the weight of his feelings pressing heavily on him. She was everything he told himself he couldn't have, everything he knew he didn't deserve, but watching her now, he couldn't convince himself to pull away. She was more than he'd let himself admit, and the ache of wanting her—of needing her to be okay—was almost unbearable. As she let out a shaky breath and stilled her tapping foot, he stayed quiet, caught in the gravity of her, unable to do anything but feel.

"You should have told me this before," she said finally, her voice trembling. "Before you slept with me. Before you...made me believe there was something happening between us."

"There is something between us."

"Not in the way I need."

"I didn't mean to hurt you," Wyatt said, his voice barely above a whisper. "I care about you, Pix. More than I've ever cared about anyone. But that's exactly why I can't…"

"Can't what?" she snapped, her anger flaring again. "Can't take a chance? Can't trust yourself to be better than your father? Because from where I'm sitting, you already are."

Wyatt's breath caught at her words, but he didn't respond. He couldn't. The weight of her gaze, her anger, her disappointment—it was too much.

Pixie stood abruptly, her movements sharp as she grabbed her bag. "You know what, Wyatt? Maybe you're right. Maybe you shouldn't get close to anyone. Because if this is how you protect people, I don't want it. I feel like you're breaking up with me before we've even started."

She turned on her heel and walked away, her footsteps echoing in the empty church. Wyatt sat frozen in the pew, his chest tight as he watched her go, her words reverberating in his mind like a drumbeat he couldn't escape.

* * * *

Salem pulled up to the Italian restaurant in Manhattan's Meatpacking District, the sleek black armored SUV idling in the shadows. The neon sign flickered in the cold February night, casting a sickly glow over the snow-covered streets. The air was heavy, still—like the calm before a storm.

Inside, the restaurant pulsed with life, the sound of clinking glass and laughter seeping through the frosted windows, the warm glow of gold reflecting off cocktails, but it did nothing to soften the edge in Wyatt's gaze.

"Time to party," Salem muttered, his voice oozing dry amusement from the driver's seat.

Wyatt didn't take his eyes off the restaurant. "We go in. We get what we need. We leave." His tone was clipped, precise. "Done."

His jaw clenched as he mentally ran through the plan. He adjusted the concealed pistol at his hip under his leather jacket, the weight of it a familiar comfort.

"Let's go," he growled, voice low but sharp as Salem killed the engine and stepped out.

The cold air bit at his skin as he and Salem approached the entrance. The doorman spared them only a glance before his gaze lingered on Salem — a beat too long. A curt nod, and they were in.

The warmth inside hit Wyatt like a slap, the mingling scents of garlic and leather hanging thick in the air, classical music hums blending with the soft murmur of conversation. His eyes cut through the room, immediately locking onto a booth at the back.

"That's him," Wyatt's voice was low, but taut, like the pull of a coiled spring.

Raffaele Santoro sat there, lounging in a tailored suit, his silver hair slicked back with careful precision. Two men flanked him, stone-faced, untouched plates in front of them. Santoro sipped his red wine, watching the room with a bored, calculating smile.

Wyatt and Salem moved through the room like sharks, their presence slicing through the calm, the energy shifting with their every step. By the time they reached the booth, Santoro had already noticed them. His sharp eyes flicked over them, narrowing before a smug, condescending smile curled on his lips.

"Well, well," Santoro said, his voice smooth and tinged with a faint Italian accent. "What do we have here? My friend from last week."

Wyatt didn't sit. He stood at the edge of the table, his gaze locked on Santoro, towering over the booth with a presence that made Santoro's two men stiffen. He didn't glance at them, didn't acknowledge the faint movements of their hands near their jackets.

"You stay away from Serafina," Wyatt said, his voice low but razor sharp. "Or you're dead."

Santoro leaned back, a faint smirk tugging at the corner of his mouth. "Dead? That's quite the statement. You seem to think—"

"I'm not here to think," Wyatt cut him off, his tone a growl. "I'm here to tell you. One more move—one more phone call, one more shadow on her—and I'll make sure everything you've built comes crashing down."

The smirk faded from Santoro's face, his eyes narrowing. "Do you know who you're talking to, *amico*?"

"A fucking goof," Wyatt said, stepping closer, his hands loose at his sides but ready for anything. "A washed-up piece of shit lecher, clinging to old times, hoping no one notices how soft you've gotten. You want to push this? Go ahead. You'll be dealing with me, my gun, and the full weight of some bad fucking dudes on your back."

Santoro's jaw tightened, his fingers curling into a fist on the table. "You have no idea what you're playing with."

"No, you don't," Wyatt snapped, his voice dropping to a menacing whisper. "I'm the guy who ends the game. So this is your one and only warning. Stay. Away. From. Her."

The silence was suffocating, the tension palpable. Santoro's men shifted in their seats, their eyes darting to Salem, who stood casually nearby, his expression unreadable but his posture unmistakably ready.

Santoro stared up at Wyatt for a long moment, the weight of the threat sinking in. Finally, he leaned back, forcing a faint chuckle that didn't reach his eyes.

Wyatt pulled his pistol out and cocked it, his glare boring into the man. "Give me a fucking reason."

Santoro's smirk turned into a scowl.

With that, Wyatt turned on his heel, his shoulders rigid with barely restrained fury as he strode toward the exit. Salem lingered for a beat longer, his gaze sweeping over the table, before following Wyatt out without a word.

The restaurant seemed to exhale as the doors swung shut behind them.

Chapter Twenty-Six

Wyatt stood outside The Birchwood Loft, the sharp winter air biting at his skin. Snowflakes clung to his jacket as he surveyed the scene through the frosted glass. The warm glow of candlelight spilled onto the sidewalk, but it did nothing to ease the tension coiling in his chest.

Inside, Pixie sat across from Caroline at a private table, her posture perfect, her smile polished. She listened intently to a donor, her dark hair falling in soft waves, but Wyatt saw the flicker of tension in her shoulders, the slight tap of her fingers on her wineglass. She was performing—always performing—but he knew better. She was tired. Guarded. And it gutted him that he couldn't be there to protect her.

His gaze lingered on her, the fake smile she wore tugging at his insides. She didn't belong here, surrounded by empty power plays and masked threats. But there she was, navigating it all with grace. He wanted to reach out, to remind her she didn't have to face it alone. But he stayed still, hands clenched in his pockets, the weight of his decision pressing heavily on him.

"Enjoying the show, Steele?"

Wyatt didn't need to turn to recognize Jamie Gray's wry tone. He kept his gaze on the table inside, his jaw tightening. "Just doing my job."

Jamie appeared beside him, bundled against the cold but with his usual sharp edge. Marcy trailed behind, her scarf wrapped tightly around her neck, her expression softer but no less pointed as she glanced between Wyatt and the window.

"Sure," Jamie said, crossing his arms. "Because standing out here in the snow instead of watching the door is definitely in the Secret Service manual."

Marcy sighed, brushing snow from her coat. "Jamie, stop. Wyatt's just—"

"Pining," Jamie finished. "Like a lost puppy. It's almost sweet, if you don't think too hard about it."

Wyatt shot him a look, his voice low and firm. "You don't know what you're talking about."

"Oh, don't I?" Jamie smirked, nodding toward the window. "She's in there, holding it together for Caroline and a bunch of people who don't give a damn about her. Meanwhile, you're out here pretending you're not one breath away from breaking in and pulling her out."

Wyatt's fists tightened in his pockets, but he didn't respond. He couldn't. Because Jamie was right. Every fiber of his being screamed to get Pixie out of there, to take her somewhere safe and far away from the mess she'd been dragged into.

Marcy stepped closer, her voice quieter but no less firm. "Wyatt, you care about her. That's obvious to everyone. But caring isn't enough. She needs stability. She needs someone who can stand by her without making things worse."

Wyatt turned to her then, his blue eyes sharp. "You think I'd make things worse?"

Marcy hesitated, her expression softening. "Not intentionally. But you know as well as I do that Pixie's carrying a lot. If you're not all in, you're going to break her."

The words hit harder than Wyatt wanted to admit. He looked back at Pixie, his heart aching as she laughed at something Caroline said, her mask firmly in place. He thought about everything she'd been through, everything she was still running from. And he thought about himself—the mess he was, the scars he carried, the things he couldn't give her.

But then he thought about the way she'd looked at him in the church, the way her walls had cracked for just a moment, and the way he'd felt holding her in his arms, like she was the only thing that made him feel whole.

"I'm all in," Wyatt said suddenly, his voice steady.

"What's that supposed to mean?"

Wyatt turned to face them fully, his jaw set. "It means I'm done sitting on the sidelines. I'll give her whatever she needs. Stability, safety, a future. If that means marrying her, then so be it."

Marcy blinked, stunned. "Marrying her?"

Wyatt nodded, his voice unwavering. "She deserves someone who's going to stand by her, no matter what. And I'm not letting her run anymore."

Jamie studied him for a long moment before letting out a low whistle. "Well, I'll give you this, Steele. You've got guts."

Wyatt didn't respond. He turned back to the window, his gaze locking on Pixie again. She didn't know it yet, but he was going to fight for her. Even if it meant risking everything.

* * * *

Wyatt navigated the service vehicle through the snowy streets of the Upper East Side, lined with iron streetlamps glowing in the swirling flurries, their light reflecting off the untouched snow. Wyatt barely noticed the beauty of it. His mind was too full of her.

Pixie sat rigid in the passenger seat, her arms crossed tight over her chest, her jaw set in a way that made her look untouchable. But the faint shimmer of light from passing storefronts caught her profile, softening the edges of her defiance. Her lips — painted dark and slightly parted — drew his attention for a beat too long. Her cheekbones, sharp and perfect, glinted under the streetlights. Even in her quiet anger, she was impossibly stunning. And smart — too smart for him, too smart for this.

What the hell are you doing, Steele?

He gripped the wheel tighter, his pulse beating in his ears. The answer should have been simple — he was taking her to tell her how much he wanted her, how much she mattered. But it wasn't that simple. It never was with her. He wanted to protect her, claim her, fix her life — and that was dangerous. He didn't fix things, he ruined them. He wasn't made for this kind of thing, and deep down, he knew it. He was too much like his father, too prone to needing things too badly, too prone to breaking them.

"Where are we going?" Her voice broke the silence, sharp and suspicious.

Wyatt kept his gaze fixed on the road ahead. "You'll see," he said evenly, though his voice felt tighter than usual.

"Wyatt, I'm not in the mood for games," she snapped.

"I'm not playing games," he replied, steady but firm. "Just trust me."

The word trust hung heavy between them, and he caught the way her hands tightened around her crossed arms. She exhaled, the sound of resignation, but didn't push further.

The streets grew quieter as he turned onto a smaller, more secluded lane. Snow clung to the wrought-iron fences and ivy-covered townhouses, untouched and pristine. It was the kind of New York he imagined she'd grown up dreaming of—elegant, timeless, full of promise. But as the SUV rolled to a stop in front of the gates of the Conservatory Garden in Central Park, he knew the promise was a lie. Pixie's world had never been elegant or timeless. She'd fought tooth and nail for every inch she'd climbed, and here he was, about to offer her something she'd never believe in.

Wyatt stepped out into the biting air, his boots crunching against the snow. He walked around to her door, opening it before she could protest. "Come on," he said, holding out a hand.

Pixie glared up at him, suspicion etched into every line of her face. "What are we doing here?"

"Just come with me," he said, his voice softer now, almost raw. "Please."

The faintest flicker of doubt crossed her face before she sighed and slipped her hand into his. Her touch sent a jolt through him, and he hated how much he wanted to keep it there, to pull her closer. She stepped out, her boots landing on the snow-dusted sidewalk, and tugged her coat tighter against the cold. The air was sharp and frigid, her breath visible as she glanced around.

Wyatt led her through the gates, their boots crunching against the fresh snow. The garden stretched out before them, the string lights draped through the bare trees casting a glow that felt almost surreal. The faint scent of evergreen lingered in the air, mixing with the sharpness of frost.

He stopped in the center of the garden, where the path curved around a frozen fountain. The light caught in her dark hair, her lashes dusted with snow, and her skin golden underneath the lights. She wrapped her arms around herself, her breath rising in shallow puffs as she studied him.

"What is this?" she asked, her voice quieter now, but no less suspicious. "Whatever you are doing, please don't."

Wyatt hesitated, his heart thudding in his chest. *What the hell am I doing?* he thought again, but it was too late to back out now. Slowly, he reached into his pocket and pulled out the small box, the velvet edges rough against his fingers.

Her eyes widened, shock flickering across her face before she masked it with a guarded, almost defiant expression.

"Pixie, I have to," he began, rougher than he wanted it to sound. "I'm not good at this. I'm not good at a lot of things. But I know what I feel when I'm around you. And I know I can't keep pretending like this isn't…happening. Marry me."

Her breath hitched, but she didn't say anything.

Wyatt stood rooted in place, the velvet box clutched tightly in his hand as the cold air wrapped around them. The snow was quiet, muffling the rest of the world, but his pulse roared in his ears.

"No."

Her answer hit him harder than he thought possible. That one word gutted him, but it wasn't just the refusal—it was the way she said it. Soft, trembling, like she hated saying it as much as he hated hearing it. Her dark eyes locked with his, shining with unspoken emotion, but her steps backed her further away from him, creating a distance he refused to accept.

"What?"

"I can't, Wyatt," Pixie said again, her voice shaking. She shook her head, her hair falling into her face as she took another step back. "You don't know what you're asking. You said it yourself—you don't want marriage. You don't want that kind of life."

"That was before," he said, cutting her off. "Before I realized what it would mean to lose you."

"That was a few days ago. And now you're willing to try?" Her laugh was soft but laced with bitterness. "I'm supposed to stake my whole future on you deciding you might want this?"

Her words twisted in his chest, raw and cutting. "I'm not asking you to bet on a maybe, Pixie. I'm telling you I'll work every damn day to prove it to you. To be the man you deserve."

Pixie folded her arms, a barrier between them that he desperately wanted to break. "Noble, Wyatt, but I can't afford to be your experiment. I've had too many people promise me things they couldn't deliver."

"Don't lump me in with them," he said, stepping closer, his frustration mounting. "I'm not them. I don't make promises I can't keep."

Her lips pressed together, her chin tilting up in defiance. "You don't even know me. Not really."

"You're wrong," he said, his voice low and taut. "I do know you, Pixie. I know the way you press your lips together when you're about to cry but don't want anyone to see. I know the way you tap your glass when you're nervous, the way you laugh at the wrong moments to cover what you're feeling."

Her breath hitched, her eyes darting away, but he wasn't finished.

"I know you're terrified of letting anyone get close enough to hurt you. And I know you think you're alone in this, but you're not. Not anymore. I'm here, whether you like it or not."

Pixie's jaw tightened, but her voice was trembling when she spoke. "I can't risk this. I can't risk you. And you know why, Wyatt. You know better than anyone how things fall apart."

His frustration boiled over, the intensity of her resistance igniting something primal in him. "Dammit, Pixie, I'm not going to take no for an answer."

Her eyes snapped back to his, fire flashing in them, her breath coming in shallow bursts. She opened her mouth to argue, but Wyatt didn't let her.

He lunged forward, gripping her arms as he pulled her against him. His mouth melted against hers, silencing her words in a kiss that was every bit as desperate as it was consuming.

Her taste overwhelmed him — sweet and electric, a mix of anger and something deeper, something raw. He felt her freeze for a moment, caught off guard, but then her body softened against his, clutching his jacket as though she couldn't push him away even if she wanted to.

The kiss deepened, his lips demanding, his fingers tangling in her hair as the world around them disappeared. She moaned as his tongue found hers, slick and eager. He pulled her hips against him, grinding into her body. His cock pulsed in his pants, desperate for more. He was an animal. Addicted. 'No' was not an option.

And she seemed to feel it, too.

She was kissing him faster, digging her nails into his neck and jaw. The icy air couldn't touch the heat between them, the electricity sparking through his veins as he poured every ounce of his frustration, his longing, his need into her.

When he finally pulled back, both of them were breathless, their lips swollen and cheeks flushed. Her eyes were wide, her lips trembling as though she wanted to say something but couldn't find the words.

"Do you get it now?" Wyatt rasped, his voice thick with emotion. "Do you see how much I want you? How much I need you?"

Pixie's hands slipped from his jacket, her expression a storm of conflict. "I can't..." she whispered, her voice cracking. "I can't do this, Wyatt. I wish I could, but I can't."

Her words hit like a punch to the gut, but he didn't let her go, his hands still framing her face, his thumbs brushing against her damp cheeks.

"Yes, you can," he said softly but fiercely. "You just don't want to believe it yet."

She shook her head, tears slipping free. "I'm sorry," she whispered, her voice breaking.

Before he could respond, she turned and walked away, the snow crunching under her quickened steps. Wyatt stood there, the cold seeping into his skin, watching her disappear into the darkness, knowing he couldn't follow her this time.

Chapter Twenty-Seven

The subway car rumbled along the tracks as Pixie gripped the pole, swaying with the motion. Her mind was elsewhere, still haunted by the feel of Wyatt's kiss, the desperation in his voice as he begged her to understand.

She squeezed her eyes shut. *I can't keep doing this.*

The train screeched to a halt, snapping her back to reality. Pixie stepped onto the platform, boots clacking against the damp tiles. The cold air from Central Park still clung to her coat, the scent of snow and pine lingering, but it couldn't chase away the memory.

She hurried up the stairs, her breath a fog in the chill as she made her way toward Blair House, desperate to leave the night—and Wyatt—behind. Palm Beach called to her, a lifeline to reset, to breathe again.

But as she rounded the corner, a shadow shifted in front of her.

"Sera," Ethan Kane said smoothly, his voice cutting through the quiet like a knife.

She froze, her heart leaping into her throat. "Ethan?"

He stepped closer, his tailored coat immaculate, scanning her face with unnerving precision. "You're hard to keep up with. I've been looking for you."

Pixie took a step back, her instincts flaring. "What do you want?"

Ethan raised his hands, palms out in mock surrender, but his expression was far from innocent. "You. I'm here to help you."

"Help me?" she repeated, her voice sharp. "Pray tell."

Ethan sighed, his tone dropping to something more serious. "Your boyfriend and his buddy paid a little visit to Santoro. They made quite an impression, but you should know—Santoro doesn't scare easily. If anything, they've provoked him."

Pixie's stomach twisted, but she kept her expression neutral. "What do you mean?"

Ethan stepped closer, his voice lowering. "I mean, he's not done with you. He's planning something. Something big. A kidnapping, maybe worse. He's claiming you as his, Serafina. And trust me, when he wants something, he doesn't stop until he gets it."

Her chest tightened, a mix of fear and fury bubbling under her skin. But before she could respond, Ethan leaned in slightly, his hand brushing a loose strand of hair from her face.

"You're beautiful," he said softly, his eyes lingering on hers. "You deserve someone who sees that. Someone who can protect you."

Pixie stiffened, her breath catching for a moment before the words hit her like a slap.

She stepped back, her eyes blazing. "Are you kidding me right now?"

"Sera, I'm just—"

"No," she snapped, her voice rising. "You don't call me 'Sera'."

He froze, watching her intently.

She wasted no time to rip into him. "You're just another man thinking he knows what I need, thinking he has the right to fix my life or control it. I am completely and utterly done with all of you fucking men."

Ethan blinked.

"If Santoro thinks he's going to kidnap me, let him try," Pixie continued, her tone cutting like steel. "I will claw his damn eyes out myself."

Ethan opened his mouth to speak, but no words came out. He took a step back, visibly shrinking under the force of her glare.

"You're right," he muttered finally, his voice smaller now, almost apologetic. "I overstepped."

Pixie's eyes flared with anger, her chest rising and falling with each breath. "Damn right you did. And next time, don't even think about stepping in. If you do, you'll be getting a hell of a lot more than a lecture."

He hesitated, then said, "One more thing—did you want Steele to talk to Santoro?"

"No," she snapped, voice like ice.

"Well, he did. Paid him a visit at his restaurant. Made things worse. Now everyone's talking about it."

Pixie's jaw clenched, fury lighting up her features. "What the hell? I didn't agree to that! What part of no do you men not understand?"

Ethan hesitated for a moment longer before nodding and retreating into the shadows. Pixie watched him go, her pulse hammering in her ears.

She turned on her heel, her pace quickening as she headed back toward Blair House. Her body was still shaking, but for the first time in a long time, it wasn't from fear. It was from power.

No more running. No more depending on anyone else.

She was beyond done.

Fuck everyone.

From now on, Pixie Sinclair would fight her own battles. And she wouldn't lose.

Pixie stepped into her apartment at Blair House, already feeling the tension crackling in the air.

The click of the door behind her seemed louder than usual, almost echoing in the charged silence. And then she saw him.

Wyatt was leaning against the window, his posture rigid, his blue eyes cutting through her like a blade. He didn't move, didn't speak, but the intensity in his stare made her stomach twist. She set her bag down with more force than necessary, hoping to mask the nerves buzzing under her skin.

"What the hell are you doing here?" she demanded.

"Waiting for you," he replied, low, almost cold. He pushed off the wall, taking a slow, deliberate step toward her. "We need to talk."

"No, we don't," Pixie snapped, crossing her arms tightly. "We already talked. I said no, Wyatt. What part of that didn't you get?"

"The part where it made any damn sense!" Wyatt's voice rose, his frustration cracking through his composure. "You didn't even give me a chance —"

"To do what?" she cut him off, her tone biting. "Convince me that proposing out of nowhere was a good idea? That it's some magical solution to whatever the hell this is? That's not love, Wyatt. That's you trying to patch a hole that can't be fixed."

He recoiled slightly, as if her words had slapped him, but he recovered quickly, his expression hardening. "You don't get to tell me what this is or isn't. You don't get to make that call for both of us."

"Oh, really?" she said, her tone dripping with sarcasm. "Because it sure as hell felt like you made the call when you told Isabella you weren't the marrying type. When you told me I was nothing more than an obsession you couldn't shake."

"That's not what I meant, and you damn well know it!" Wyatt snapped, his voice cracking with frustration. "I said that because I'm trying to protect you—"

"From what?" Pixie demanded, stepping forward, fists clenched. "From yourself? Your pathetic excuses? That's all they are, Wyatt. Excuses."

His jaw tensed, his frustration barely contained. "You don't get it," he growled. "You don't know what it's like to carry this weight. To wonder if you'll become the one person you swore you'd never be."

"No," she said, "but I know what it's like to be abandoned. To be left by the people who were supposed to protect me. So don't tell me I don't get it."

"That won't be me," he insisted.

"You promised you'd have my back," she spat. "Yes, I found out. What did you think would happen? You went behind my back and talked to Santoro. You made it worse. Now he's enraged."

Wyatt's mask cracked for a moment, pain flashing across his face, but he quickly hardened. "You think you're so strong? Hiding behind walls, running away from everything? You're just as scared as I am, Pixie."

Her chest tightened, anger burning through her. "You don't get to throw that in my face. Not after everything you've done to push me away."

"I push people away because it's the only way I know how to survive!" Wyatt roared, his voice shaking. "You think I want this? You think I like being this fucked up? I'm trying, Pixie. I'm trying to do the right thing, but every time I get close, you slam the door in my face."

"Because I can't trust you!" she shouted back, her chest heaving. "You don't even trust yourself. How the hell am I supposed to put my life in your hands when you're too busy tearing yourself apart? You need serious help. And it's not me."

Silence fell, thick and suffocating, as the words echoed between them. Wyatt stared at her, his breathing ragged, his eyes glassy with unshed tears.

Then there was a shift. A snap. The air between them crackled with the weight of everything that had just happened — and what it meant.

"You're unbelievable," he muttered, his voice low and full of frustration, his hands dropping from her hips. He turned away, running a hand through his hair, pacing like a caged animal. "You push me to the fucking edge, Pixie, and then what? What happens next? You think we can just go back to normal after this?"

She swallowed hard, her body tingling from his presence, her heart pounding. "I didn't ask for this," she said, her voice trembling. "You're the one who—"

"Don't," he interrupted spinning back to her, his voice sharp, cutting through her words. His eyes snapped back to hers, darker now, full of something she couldn't quite name. Regret? Anger? Desperation?

"Don't pretend you don't know exactly what you are doing."

She opened her mouth to argue, but the words stuck in her throat. Because he was right. She had pushed him. She'd wanted this—wanted him to break, to lose the iron grip he always held over himself. But now, staring at him, seeing the barely restrained fury in his eyes, she realized she hadn't considered what would come next.

"You don't get it, do you?" he said, his voice quieter now, but no less intense. "We can't change what has happened between us."

Her chest tightened, panic rising. "We need to," she said quickly, almost pleading. "We can just...forget it all."

Wyatt's laugh was bitter, humorless. He stepped closer, towering over her again, his presence overwhelming. "Forget it?" he repeated, his tone sharp with disbelief. "You think I can just forget the way you feel, the way you looked at me? The way you fucking moaned my name like you needed me more than your next breath?"

Heat flooded her cheeks, shame and desire warring within her. She turned her head, unable to meet his piercing gaze, but he grabbed her chin, forcing her to look at him.

"No," he said. "You don't get to run from this. You don't get to pretend *we* didn't happen."

Her eyes burned, but she refused to let the tears fall. "What do you want me to say, Wyatt?" she asked. "That I fucked up? That I shouldn't have pushed you? Fine. I'm saying it. But what about you? You think you're innocent in all this?"

His grip on her chin tightened just slightly, his jaw clenching. "I've never claimed to be innocent, Pixie," he said, deadly calm. "But I sure as hell am not throwing you away."

Her chest heaved, her emotions swirling into a storm that mirrored his. "So what now?" she demanded, trembling. "We just tear each other apart until there's nothing left?"

For a moment, silence stretched between them, heavy and suffocating.

"I don't know," he admitted, low, almost broken. "But don't think for a second that I'm letting you walk away from me. Not now. Not ever."

Her heart clenched, the weight of his words settling over her like a physical thing. There was no going back from this—not for either of them. And as much as she wanted to run, to protect herself from the fire that was Wyatt, she couldn't. Because he was right. Whatever this was between them, it wasn't something she could just walk away from.

But it came with consequences. She could feel it in her bones, in the way his eyes burned into hers like a brand. This wasn't just a line they'd crossed—it was a chasm, and they were both falling. Together.

Pixie's throat tightened, her heart aching for him, but her anger wouldn't let her relent. "You have to let me go, Wyatt," she said quietly. "You can't expect me to stay."

His jaw clenched, his fists at his sides. "I am asking you to stay. Not expecting you to."

Her chest constricted, the finality in his words cutting deeper than she expected. "Good," she said, her voice cracking. "Because I won't."

She turned, heading for the door, heavy with the weight of what they'd just destroyed. Wyatt didn't stop her, didn't call after her. He just stood there, his silence deafening. And as the door closed behind her, Pixie felt the sting of tears. This was it. Whatever had existed between them was gone. For good.

Chapter Twenty-Eight

The SUV hummed quietly as it sped down the highway, leaving New York City behind. Snow clung stubbornly to the edges of the road, and the gray sky hung low, as if the city itself was reluctant to let them leave. Wyatt kept his eyes on the road, his grip firm on the steering wheel. The tension in his jaw made his stubble seem sharper, and the air inside the car was thick enough to cut with a knife.

Caroline Armstrong sat in the backseat, elegant as always in her cream coat and perfectly styled hair, but her gaze was harsher than usual, flicking between Wyatt and Salem. Beside him, Salem sat stiff in the passenger seat, hiding behind his sunglasses as the First Lady grilled Wyatt.

"You've been unusually quiet," Caroline said, her tone casual but layered with intent. "Even for you."

"Just driving, ma'am," Wyatt replied, though he didn't meet her eyes in the rearview mirror. "Let's get home safely."

"Hmm," she murmured, a note of amusement. "I'd say you've been doing more brooding than driving."

Salem said. "I'll back her on that one, boss."

Wyatt's hands tightened briefly on the wheel, but his tone stayed even. "Thanks for the feedback."

And then there was an awkward pause.

Caroline finally broke the ice as she leaned forward, her tone light but pointed. "Oh, Wyatt, we see you every day. We both know what's got you in a mood. Or should I say who?"

Salem chuckled low under his breath.

Caroline added, "This is about Pixie, isn't it?"

Wyatt's jaw clenched, but he didn't respond, focusing instead on the stretch of road ahead. His silence only seemed to embolden Caroline.

"She's impressive," Caroline continued, her words thoughtful. "Handling everything with grace despite…certain complications."

Wyatt's knuckles whitened on the wheel. "She's a smart lady."

Salem grinned, leaning back in his seat. "That's one way to put it."

Wyatt shot him a do-not-fuck-with-me glare.

Caroline's laugh was soft but knowing. "I've seen the way you look at her, Wyatt. And the way she has been avoiding looking at you."

Wyatt's mouth twitched, his tone sharpening. "I think I'm good on the matchmaking, ma'am."

Caroline didn't miss a beat. "Well, then you wouldn't want some motherly advice?"

Wyatt pressed his lips together as Salem snorted.

"Yes, I think he does," Salem said.

"I would advise you to do something about it before it's too late."

"Too late for what?" Wyatt snapped before he could stop himself, his frustration bleeding through.

Caroline tilted her head, her gaze sharp. "For her to realize that you're worth the trouble."

The words hit harder than Wyatt expected, and he felt Salem's eyes on him. The silence stretched, broken only by the sound of the engine.

Wyatt didn't respond. His eyes were locked on the private airstrip ahead, the black SUV gliding along the slick tarmac with surgical precision. Floodlights spilled across the empty runway, gleaming off the matte-black fuselage of the waiting jet. Two Secret Service agents stood at the base of the stairs, stone-faced in dark suits, their radios murmuring in low static.

Wyatt kept the motorcade tight as he brought the vehicle to a halt at the designated mark, tires crunching lightly over salted pavement. He cut the engine, the silence in the cabin immediate and cold.

Protocol took over.

He stepped out and moved swiftly to the passenger side, opening the rear door with a crisp nod.

"Ma'am," he said.

Caroline emerged with effortless grace, her coat pulled tight against the wind, her heels clicking softly on the pavement. She didn't look back at the others. Just him.

She paused — barely a second — as the wind tugged at the ends of her silk scarf. "Think about it," she said lightly, but her eyes held that knowing glint. "Didn't you promise me something about happiness once?"

He didn't answer. He couldn't.

The First Lady turned and made her way toward the plane, flanked by agents, her figure quickly swallowed by the glow of the floodlights.

Behind him, Salem climbed out, his boots thudding onto the tarmac. He clapped a hand to Wyatt's shoulder with familiar weight.

"She's not wrong, you know."

Wyatt exhaled through his nose, jaw clenched. "Let's just get back to work before I start regretting not leaving you on the runway."

Salem chuckled, but there was no humor in it.

As they watched the First Lady ascend the stairs, her silhouette framed in the open aircraft door, Wyatt felt something shift in his chest—a pressure he couldn't name, but couldn't shake.

"She doesn't want me," he muttered finally. "She said no."

Salem didn't respond right away. Just nodded, slow and thoughtful, eyes tracking the jet as it roared to life.

But as the plane's door closed with a quiet finality and the cabin lights glowed from within, Caroline's words echoed louder than the engines warming up on the runway.

Didn't you promise me something about happiness?

He had.

But that was before Pixie Sinclair had rewritten every rule in his book.

* * * *

The sliding glass doors of Wyatt's Palm Beach house glimmered in the late afternoon sunlight, framing the rolling waves of the Atlantic in a golden hue. The salty breeze drifted in, mingling with the faint scent of cedar and leather that always seemed to linger in his home. The house itself was minimalistic yet warm—cool gray walls adorned with a few framed black-and-white photos of his military days, sleek furniture softened by throw blankets and the occasional scuff from Nova's paws.

Home.

Wyatt leaned against the kitchen counter, watching as Nova bounded toward him, her nails clicking on the polished wood floor. Dallas had dropped her off an hour earlier after watching her while he was gone. She barked once, her ears perked high, then nudged his hand with her snout.

"Hey, girl," he murmured, his voice softer than it had been in weeks. He crouched, letting her shove her face into his chest, her tail wagging furiously. "You miss me?"

Nova huffed, licking his cheek before retreating to retrieve her favorite chew toy — a battered rubber bone that had survived two deployments and countless games of tug-of-war.

"Yeah, I missed you too," Wyatt said, his lips quirking in a faint smile as he tossed the bone across the room. Nova bolted after it, sliding slightly on the hardwood as she made the catch.

The house felt alive with her there, the silence that had weighed on him the past few days lifting slightly. Still, as he watched her settle into her favorite spot near the sliding doors, the heaviness crept back in. He turned away, heading to the living room where a half-empty glass of bourbon waited on the coffee table.

He didn't sit. He never did when his thoughts were too loud. Instead, he paced, his bare feet soundless on the rug. His gaze flicked to the glass, then to the small box sitting on the table beside it — the ring he hadn't been able to put away since that night in Central Park.

Wyatt ran a hand through his hair, frustration clawing at his chest. *What the hell are you doing, Steele?*

He wasn't the kind of man who could offer someone stability. He'd told himself that for years, and he'd believed it. His past made sure of it—his father's fists, his mother's tears, the unrelenting ache of failure that followed him even after he'd left the battlefield. He'd been taught early on that love didn't build—it broke. And he wasn't about to let that happen to Pixie.

Except he already had.

Her face haunted him—the way her lips trembled when she told him no, the fire in her eyes as she pushed him away. He'd seen fear, anger, and pain in those moments, but there was something else, too. Something softer. Something she was too scared to name.

And he'd walked away.

Wyatt stopped pacing, turning toward the window. The ocean stretched endlessly before him, its waves crashing against the shore in a rhythmic lullaby. It should've been calming, but all he could think about was Pixie. She'd found her way into his mind, into every quiet moment, into the cracks he thought he'd patched up long ago.

He lowered himself onto the couch, his elbows resting on his knees as he stared at the ring box. His fingers itched to open it, to see the simple gold band and the small diamond that had felt so right in the store but now felt like a taunt.

She doesn't need this, he thought bitterly. *She doesn't need me.*

But then he thought about her smile—those rare, unguarded moments when her walls came down, when she laughed without reservation, when she let him see the woman she tried so hard to hide. He thought about her bravery, her stubbornness, the way she walked into every fight with her head high, even when she was scared.

Wyatt exhaled slowly, leaning back against the cushions. He didn't know how to be what she needed, but he knew one thing for sure — he wasn't going to let her face this alone.

Nova padded over, her head tilting as she dropped the rubber bone at his feet. He smiled, running a hand over her fur.

"You think I'm crazy, don't you?" he muttered.

Nova huffed, nudging his knee.

"Yeah," he said, picking up the bone and tossing it again. "You're probably right."

Nova growled playfully at him, her tail wagging her whole body.

He laughed. "All right, you are definitely right. I'm a little fucked up."

But even as the words left his mouth, his resolve hardened. He couldn't promise Pixie perfection. Hell, he couldn't promise her much of anything. But he could promise her this — he wasn't going anywhere.

He would try, dammit, to be what she needed.

And maybe, just maybe, that would be enough.

* * * *

The church basement smelled of coffee and old carpet, the kind of neutral, nondescript place that could have been anywhere in the country. Metal folding chairs were arranged in a loose circle, the overhead lights buzzing. Wyatt adjusted the brim of his ball cap, scanning the room as a few men and women milled around, grabbing coffee or water from the small table at the back.

"Remind me why we're here again?" Salem asked, his voice low and gruff as he stood just behind Wyatt.

Wyatt turned slightly, one brow arching. "Because we're both screwed up, and it's time to do something about it."

Salem snorted, crossing his arms over his broad chest. "I'm not the one dragging you to a damn shrink's circle."

"You're the one I had to bribe with breakfast to get here," Wyatt said, his voice dry but tinged with weariness. "Now shut up and sit down."

Salem muttered something under his breath but dropped into one of the folding chairs, his posture stiff and defensive. Wyatt followed, settling into the chair beside him. His own shoulders felt tight, the weight of his decision pressing down on him.

He hadn't been to a meeting like this in years. Not since the early days of his recovery, when he was still battling the demons of addiction and the aftermath of Syria. Back then, the thought of sitting in a room full of strangers and sharing his pain had felt like torture. Now, it felt like a lifeline.

The door creaked open, and a tall man in his fifties with salt-and-pepper hair stepped into the circle. He wore a worn leather jacket and a calm, steady expression.

"All right, folks," the man said, his voice carrying a quiet authority. "Let's get started. My name's Mark, and if this is your first time here, welcome."

Mark's gaze swept the circle, landing briefly on Wyatt and Salem. Wyatt nodded slightly, his jaw tightening as Mark smiled.

"Tonight, we're talking about the weight we carry," Mark continued, settling into his own chair. "What we bring back from the battlefield, what we carry into our daily lives, and how we let it shape us."

Wyatt glanced at Salem, who was staring at the floor, his jaw set like granite. He could feel his friend's discomfort, but Wyatt wasn't about to let him off the hook.

Mark gestured toward the circle. "Who wants to start?"

For a moment, no one moved. Then Wyatt leaned forward, resting his elbows on his knees. "I will."

Salem's head snapped up, his eyes narrowing. "Oh, for—"

Wyatt ignored him, focusing on Mark. "I'm Wyatt Steele. Former Special Forces. Syria." His voice was steady, but the words felt heavier than he'd expected. "I got hurt. Bad. Got hooked on the pills they gave me to fix it. Took me a long time to figure out how to fight without them. Some days, I still don't know if I'm winning."

Mark nodded, his expression encouraging but not pitying. "What brought you here tonight, Wyatt?"

Wyatt hesitated, his fingers lacing together as he searched for the right words. "Someone I care about. She thinks I'm worth more than I do. And I'm starting to think she might be right. But I've got a lot of shit to work through first."

Mark's gaze softened, and he nodded again. "That's a good reason to start. Sometimes the people we care about are the ones who remind us we're worth saving."

Wyatt glanced at Salem, whose expression was unreadable but not hostile. He could tell Salem was listening, even if he wouldn't admit it.

"I don't want to be the guy who breaks someone else," Wyatt added quietly. "Not her. Not anyone."

The room was silent for a moment before Mark spoke again. "It takes strength to recognize that. And even more to do something about it."

Wyatt leaned back in his chair, exhaling slowly. He didn't feel strong—not yet. But he felt like he was finally moving in the right direction.

When the meeting ended, Salem was the first to stand, grabbing his jacket with a grumble. "You owe me more than breakfast for this."

Wyatt smirked, clapping him on the shoulder. "You're welcome, big guy."

As they walked out into the cold night air, the weight in Wyatt's chest eased slightly. He wasn't fixed. Hell, he wasn't even close. But for the first time in a long time, he felt like he wasn't running in circles.

And if that meant dragging Salem along for the ride? So be it.

Chapter Twenty-Nine

Palm Beach, Florida

Pixie moved quickly through the halls, the cold marble beneath her heels doing nothing to ease the heat crawling up her spine. The Armstrong estate sprawled in the harsh Florida sun, its manicured lawns and palm-lined paths a perfect lie of safety. The salt of the Atlantic clung to the air, carried by the soft ocean breeze. It should've been calming. It wasn't.

The sound of her heels echoed, each step a defiant act against the storm inside her. She clutched her tablet like a shield, her eyes darting to every movement in the estate. The staff bustled, their voices blending into a dull hum. She didn't trust it. Not after what Ethan had said.

Santoro wanted her. To claim her. To own her.

She swallowed hard, her mouth dry despite the oppressive humidity outside. *Not in this lifetime*, she thought, her grip tightening on the tablet. But the shadows felt longer today, the corners darker. Every face seemed unfamiliar at a glance, and she couldn't shake the sensation that eyes lingered on her too long, that someone might be watching.

The morning briefing with Caroline had been a blur. Luncheons, galas, foreign dignitaries—it all felt pointless against the drumbeat of anxiety pounding in her chest. She caught none of the details, her gaze constantly flicking to the door, to the windows, to the staff moving in and out of the room.

"Pixie?"

Caroline's voice snapped her back. Pixie blinked, realizing the First Lady was watching her, concern narrowing her usually warm eyes.

"Are you all right, dear? You seem…somewhere else."

"I'm fine," Pixie lied, her voice sharp and efficient, as always. "Just running through logistics."

Caroline didn't look convinced but let it slide, waving a hand toward the neatly stacked files on her desk. "Good. I trust you to make it seamless."

Pixie nodded and left before Caroline could press further. The door shut behind her, and she exhaled slowly, her pulse thrumming in her ears. The halls stretched endlessly ahead of her, the sunlight streaming through the tall windows doing little to banish the sense of encroaching danger.

And then—she saw him. Standing near the main entrance, his posture all sharp edges and unrelenting focus. Wyatt. The sight of him sent a pang through her, hot and unwelcome. His blue eyes tracked her as she passed, his gaze weighing heavier than the Florida heat pressing in from outside.

Her steps faltered for a split second before she forced herself to keep walking, her chin lifting defiantly. She hated that he could still affect her. Hated that even now, after everything, he looked at her like that. Like she was his problem to fix.

The estate's kitchen was alive with the clatter of pans and the murmur of staff preparing for the luncheon. Pixie leaned against the counter, pretending to scroll through her tablet, her fingers trembling slightly. The sharp scent of citrus filled the air, mingling with the warmth of fresh bread and the faintest tang of coffee. It should have been grounding. Instead, it felt suffocating.

She grabbed a glass of water, the coolness biting against her palms. Her reflection in the window caught her off guard — the tightness around her eyes, the forced set of her jaw. She barely recognized herself.

Get a grip.

When she left the kitchen, she found him again. Wyatt. He was speaking with another agent, his broad shoulders relaxed, though his expression stayed unreadable. He looked up as she passed, their eyes locking for a moment.

His gaze was a question. Hers was a warning.

She escaped to her office, shutting the door behind her with a soft click. The space was quiet, save for the hum of the air conditioning and the distant crash of waves outside. The bookshelves and neatly stacked folders felt oppressive, the order of the room a stark contrast to the chaos swirling inside her.

Her phone buzzed on the desk. She hesitated, dread curling low in her stomach.

How are you? I'm still keeping my eye on things up here.

Pixie's jaw clenched, the knot in her chest tightening. She didn't need Ethan's reminders. She didn't need Wyatt's watchful eyes. And she sure as hell didn't need Santoro's shadow looming over her every move.

Her fingers curled into fists, her nails biting into her palms. She stood and stared at the door, her heart thundering in her chest. *Let him come,* she thought darkly. *Let him try.*

If Santoro thought she would crumble, he was dead wrong.

She paced the room, her movements sharp, her pulse still racing. She didn't want to feel this way — boxed in, controlled, powerless. And yet, wasn't that what had been happening all along? Men like Santoro. Men like Ethan. And even Wyatt, with his protective instincts and his desperate declarations.

They all thought they knew what was best for her.

* * * *

The late morning sun filtered through the towering windows of the Armstrong estate, the golden light bouncing off the polished floors. Pixie sat at her desk in the small office adjacent to the First Lady's wing, her tablet balanced on her knee as she scanned the logistics for the upcoming week. The sound of heels clicking against the marble broke her focus, and she glanced up just as Marcy breezed into the room.

"Pixie!" Marcy sang, her voice light and filled with purpose, her navy sundress swishing as she leaned against the doorframe. "Please tell me you're coming tonight."

Pixie's stomach twisted. She knew exactly what Marcy was referring to. She'd already tried to pretend she hadn't seen the group text buzzing all week with plans for Marcy's birthday celebration.

"I don't know, Marce," Pixie said, trying to keep her tone light as she looked back at her tablet. "It's been a long week."

"Exactly," Marcy countered, crossing her arms and fixing Pixie with a pointed look. "That's why you need to come. You need a night out. A real night out. No schedules, no meetings, no...brooding."

Pixie smirked at that. "I don't brood."

Jamie appeared a moment later, peeking his head in behind Marcy. "Yes, you do," he said with a teasing grin. "And you're not skipping tonight. We've already got a table booked at Maison Soleil. The best oysters in Palm Beach, thank you very much."

"And after that," Marcy added, her eyes gleaming, "we're heading to Opal Room. Dancing, cocktails, the whole nine yards. You need this, Pixie."

Pixie shook her head, anxiety a dead weight in her stomach. Maison Soleil and Opal Room were very much not her scene—trendy, exclusive, filled with people who exuded a kind of effortless confidence she'd never felt comfortable faking. The thought of stepping into that world, with its velvet ropes and sharp laughter, made her palms sweat.

"Guys, I really—" she started, but Marcy cut her off, raising a hand.

"No excuses. None. You've been holed up all week. And don't even think about telling me you're too busy. Caroline has nothing on the schedule tonight, so you're free. Officially."

Pixie sighed, setting the tablet down and pinching the bridge of her nose. "It's not that. I just... I don't know if I'm in the mood."

"Then we'll get you in the mood," Jamie said, his tone breezy but kind. "Pixie, come on. You've been a rock for everyone else. Let us be the fun for you, just for one night. Please?"

Marcy stepped closer, her expression softening. "We miss seeing you like this, Pix. Out of work mode. You deserve to have fun. And you know Jamie and I won't let anything bad happen to you. We've got your back."

Pixie swallowed hard, the knot in her throat hardening. She knew their intentions were pure, but the weight of everything she'd been carrying—Santoro's threats, Ethan's warnings, and the gnawing absence of Wyatt—left her feeling more exposed than ever. She felt like she was walking a tightrope, and one wrong step could send her tumbling.

But she didn't want to say any of that. Marcy and Jamie didn't need to know how fragile she felt, how much she missed having someone—anyone—to lean on. How Wyatt's absence felt like the rug had been pulled out from under her.

Instead, she forced a smile. "All right," she said, her voice quieter than usual. "I'll come."

"Yes!" Marcy clapped her hands, beaming. "You won't regret it."

"Just promise me I don't have to dance," Pixie muttered, earning a laugh from both of them.

"No promises," Jamie said with a wink as he and Marcy left her office, already buzzing with plans for the evening.

"And promise me that there won't be any agents there," Pixie said.

Marcy licked her lips and gave a perky smile. "Of course. It's just us."

Pixie leaned back in her chair, her fingers curling around the edge of the desk. Her heart pounded unevenly, the thought of being out in the open making her stomach churn. For so long, she'd felt shielded in some way—whether by Wyatt's watchful presence or the structure of her job.

But now, for the first time in years, she felt exposed. Alone. And no matter how much she told herself she didn't need him, Wyatt's absence left a hollow ache she couldn't ignore.

Just one night, she thought, steeling herself. *I can survive one night.*

Chapter Thirty

The pulsing bass of the nightclub vibrated through Pixie's chest as she stood near the edge of the crowded dance floor, a champagne flute dangling from her fingers. Neon lights flashed in rhythmic bursts, painting the room in hues of electric blue and magenta. The energy was palpable — laughter, shouted conversations, the scrape of chairs being pushed back, and the unmistakable beat of a DJ spinning tracks that seemed designed to pull everyone to the dance floor.

Pixie felt like she was watching it all through a pane of glass. Marcy twirled in the center of it all, her arms raised as she laughed, her dress shimmering in the shifting light. Jamie, ever the charming wingman, danced beside her, his movements exaggerated and playful as he tried to keep up.

Pixie sipped her champagne, the bubbles sharp against her tongue, but it did little to dull the weight in her chest. The heat of the room pressed against her skin, the faint scent of sweat and expensive cologne mingling with the tang of spilled drinks. The nightclub was alive in a way she couldn't feel — not tonight.

"You look like you could use a dance partner," a voice drawled beside her.

She turned to find a tall, broad-shouldered man leaning against the bar, his tailored suit hinting at money and his grin heavy with confidence. His dark eyes scanned her in a way that felt both familiar and unremarkable — a man used to being noticed, used to getting what he wanted.

"I'm fine," Pixie said politely, offering him a faint smile before turning back toward the dance floor.

But he wasn't deterred. He shifted closer, resting his elbow on the bar as if settling in for the long haul. "Come on, don't tell me you're spending the whole night glued to this spot. You look way too good for that."

Pixie's grip tightened on her glass, her mind racing as she tried to ignore the unease crawling up her spine. He wasn't the first man to approach her tonight. Since dinner, she'd dodged half a dozen conversations that began with compliments and ended with thinly veiled propositions.

Her friends meant well. Marcy and Jamie had insisted on getting her out of her shell, laughing and cheering every time someone approached her. But each interaction only deepened the hollowness in her chest, the stark reminder that the one person she wanted to see — the one person she couldn't seem to stop thinking about — wasn't there.

"Not interested," she said firmly, stepping away from the bar and weaving through the crowd.

The man's voice faded behind her, lost in the thrum of music and laughter. She found herself at the edge of the dance floor, watching as Marcy grabbed Jamie's hands and pulled him into a ridiculous spin. The sight drew a small smile from Pixie, but it was fleeting, quickly replaced by the ache she couldn't shake.

Wyatt wouldn't have let that guy even get close, she thought bitterly. But Wyatt wasn't here. And maybe that was for the best.

Still, his absence gnawed at her. She'd wanted him to leave her alone, hadn't she? Wanted space to breathe, to think, to forget the way his lips felt against hers, the way his voice sounded when he'd begged her to believe in him. But forgetting wasn't as easy as she'd hoped.

"Pixie!" Marcy's voice cut through the haze, and Pixie turned to see her friend stumbling toward her, flushed and laughing. "Come on! You've got to dance at least once tonight!"

"I'm good," Pixie said, shaking her head.

"No, you're not!" Marcy protested, grabbing her hand. "You've been moping all night. Whatever's going on in that pretty little head of yours, you've got to leave it here. Just one dance!"

Pixie let herself be pulled a few steps forward, the energy of the crowd swirling around her like a tide. But even as Marcy spun her around, even as she forced herself to smile, her mind was somewhere else.

The lights, the music, the laughter — it all felt hollow. Every movement felt wrong, like she was trying to fit into a space that no longer belonged to her.

Eventually, she broke away, slipping back to the edge of the room where the shadows felt safer. She leaned against the wall, the cool surface grounding her for a moment. She closed her eyes, letting the music fade into the background, and took a deep breath.

When she opened them again, her gaze fell to the doorway at the far end of the club. For a split second, she thought she saw him — Wyatt. Tall, broad, his blue eyes cutting through the crowd like he could see straight into her.

But it wasn't him. Of course it wasn't.

Pixie swallowed hard, the weight in her chest settling deeper. She'd asked him to let her go, to keep his distance. And he had.

But as she stood there, surrounded by people yet feeling more alone than ever, she couldn't help but wonder if she'd made a mistake.

The bass thudded deep in Pixie's chest as the champagne buzzed through her veins, loosening the tension that had gripped her all evening. She let herself sway to the music, her hips moving in rhythm with the pulsing beat. The flashing lights painted the nightclub in streaks of gold and red, shadows flickering across the sea of bodies around her. Her friends were somewhere nearby — laughing, dancing — but Pixie had slipped into her own head, caught between the music and the faint haze of alcohol.

The floor was packed, the heat of the crowd pressing against her skin, and for the first time in what felt like forever, she let herself move. Her arms lifted, her head tilting back as she lost herself in the beat. A momentary release from everything clawing at her.

And then she felt it.

Strong, warm hands slid around her waist, pulling her back against a solid chest. Her body stiffened, the haze of champagne vanishing as her mind screamed a single thought. *This is it. He's here. I'm being taken.*

Her pulse thundered, fear tightening her throat as she spun around, her heart slamming against her ribs.

But the face she found wasn't a stranger's. It wasn't Santoro.

It was Wyatt.

His blue eyes locked onto hers, darkened by the low light and something deeper, something smoldering. The scent of him hit her next — subtle cologne and the faint burn of alcohol on his breath, mingling with the sweat and heat of the club.

"What are you —" she started, but her voice faltered. "Marcy said you guys weren't coming."

"She lied."

His hands didn't leave her waist, holding her steady as the music swirled around them. The rest of the club seemed to blur, the crowd a distant haze. His gaze pinned her in place, intense and unrelenting.

"I couldn't stay away," he murmured into her ear, his voice rough, almost drowned out by the music.

Her chest tightened, a rush of emotions colliding — anger, confusion, relief. The warmth of his hands seeped through her dress, grounding her even as her mind raced.

"You shouldn't be here," she managed, her voice sharper than she intended.

He smirked, leaning closer. "Neither should you. You should be with me."

The heat of his breath sent a shiver down her spine, her body betraying her even as her mind screamed at her to push him away. But she didn't.

His grip tightened slightly, drawing her closer until their bodies moved in sync with the music. His head dipped, kissing her temple, her cheek, so faint it could have been an accident — but she knew better.

"What are you doing?" she asked, her voice quieter now, her heart pounding against her ribs.

"Whatever you'll let me," he said, his voice low and rough.

The air between them was thick, electric, the thrum of the bass matching the beat of her pulse. His hands moved slowly, one sliding up her back while the other remained at her waist, his fingers splaying possessively against her.

"You've been drinking," she whispered, though it sounded weak even to her own ears.

"Not nearly enough to forget what I want," he replied, his gaze dropping to her lips.

Pixie's breath hitched, her hands pressing against his chest as if to push him away, but they stayed there, caught between resistance and surrender.

She hated him in that moment—hated the way he made her feel, the way her body leaned into his despite everything screaming at her to stop. Hated how desperately she wanted to forget the pain, the fear, and let herself drown in him.

And she hated that he knew it.

"Wyatt..." she began, but the word dissolved into the space between them as his lips hovered just above hers, the heat of him consuming every last coherent thought she had.

"Tell me to stop," he murmured, his voice edged with something raw, almost pleading.

But she couldn't. She didn't want to.

The music swelled, the lights dimming around them, and for that moment, there was no one else. Just them. Just the unrelenting pull of something she didn't want to name, something she didn't know how to fight.

Wyatt held her hand, pulling her into the dark. He walked her down a hall and pushed open a shadowed door with one hand, his other firmly gripping Pixie's wrist as he led her inside. The air was cooler, quieter, almost intimate in its isolation.

It was a private champagne room, dimly lit, a golden haze of muted light casting long shadows across the sleek, minimalist furniture. The hum of the nightclub's bass was muffled here, a distant pulse that felt more like a heartbeat beneath their feet.

Pixie barely had time to protest before the door clicked shut behind them. Her breath caught as Wyatt turned, his towering frame silhouetted against the soft glow of the city lights filtering through the balcony doors. His blue eyes burned with something raw, something that made her pulse quicken and her knees weaken.

"Abducting me?" she said, pulling her wrist free, though her voice lacked conviction.

Wyatt didn't answer. Instead, he stepped closer, his presence consuming the space between them. His hand found her waist, pulling her toward him as his lips crashed into hers. The kiss was fast, fierce, and unrelenting, all the restraint he'd shown in the past burned away in an instant.

He pulled them both down on the plush couch, holding her in his lap. He ran his hands up and down her thighs, inching her skirt up higher each pass.

Pixie gasped against his mouth, her hands instinctively pressing against his chest before fisting in his shirt. The heat of him was overwhelming, the taste of bourbon and salt on his lips intoxicating. He kissed her like a man starved, his other hand tangling in her hair, tilting her head back to deepen the connection.

"God, I missed you," he murmured against her lips, his voice rough, almost desperate. "You have no idea."

Pixie's heart raced, her body betraying her as it melted into his. She wanted to push him away, to yell at him for his audacity, but her mind blurred under the sheer intensity of him—his warmth, his strength, the unyielding way he held her like he never wanted to let go.

"Wyatt," she breathed, her voice trembling, half a warning, half a plea.

His lips moved to her jaw, trailing a path of fire to the sensitive spot below her ear. "Don't say no," he whispered, his voice raw. "Not this time."

Her hands slid up to his shoulders, gripping tightly as she tried to ground herself. The balcony doors were ajar, letting in a cool breeze that kissed her flushed skin, but it did nothing to quell the heat between them.

"You don't get to do this," she said, her voice cracking even as her body leaned into his touch. "You don't get to disappear and then—"

"I didn't disappear," Wyatt cut her off, pulling back just enough to look her in the eyes. His gaze was intense, unwavering, his thumb brushing against her cheek. "You left me. But I never stopped wanting you."

The words hit her like a blow, her chest tightening as she tried to look away, but he wouldn't let her. His fingers tilted her chin, forcing her to meet his gaze.

"I've been losing my damn mind without you, Pixie," he admitted, his voice softer now but no less raw. "I can't stop thinking about you. And I'm done pretending I can."

Pixie swallowed hard, her lips parting to speak, but no words came. She hated how much she wanted to believe him, hated how his touch made her feel like the world wasn't so broken, like she wasn't so broken.

"I don't know if I can do this."

"You don't have to know," Wyatt said, his forehead resting against hers. "You just have to let me try."

His lips found hers again, slower this time but no less consuming. It wasn't a question, but a promise — a vow wrapped in heat and desperation, in the unspoken truths they both refused to name. For a moment, just a moment, Pixie let herself believe him. Let herself fall.

As if sensing this, Wyatt pushed her down onto the couch.

Pixie lay back, arms loosely by her side, watching his next steps. He lowered himself to his knees, pushing up her skirt and pulling down her panties. He angled her pussy to his face, smirking, his body relaxed in a way that only infuriated her more.

Wyatt leaned in, both hands under her ass, and slowly, he raised her to his mouth, his tongue darting out to lick a bead of juice that had gathered in her hot slit. His movements were unhurried, deliberate — taunting.

Her nails dug into the couch as she fought to keep her composure. "Are you seriously doing this right now?" she moaned.

Wyatt's eyes flicked to hers, amusement sparking in the stormy depths. He didn't answer right away, taking another slow, deliberate lick along the curve of her pussy as he started to pulse his fingers into her. A drop of her liquid slid down his fingers, and he caught it with his tongue, his gaze locked on hers the entire time.

"What's the problem?" he drawled, his voice infuriatingly calm. "We're alone."

Her cheeks flushed hot, anger mixing with something far more dangerous. "You're doing this on purpose," she accused, her words biting. "To punish me."

"Doing what?" he asked innocently before resuming his work. He massaged her clit with his thumb, then sucked the liquid off with a smirk that made her want to throw something at him.

Her frustration bubbled over. "You're such an ass!" she exploded. "You know exactly what you're doing."

He chuckled, the sound low and teasing, as he leaned toward her, bracing his hands on either side of her. "And what exactly am I doing, Pixie?" he asked, his tone laced with mockery. "Enlighten me." While he waited for an answer, he dove in again, faster and stronger, licking and pulsing her pussy with one goal in mind.

She moaned in pleasure, trying to twist underneath him. But he wouldn't let her. Her fists clenched at her sides, her entire body taut with anger. "You're trying to punish me for leaving you," she bit out. "And guess what? It's working."

He tilted his head, angling to lick her clit better, his smirk widening. "Good to know," he said, his voice dropping an octave. "Because if I'm under your skin, it means you're thinking about me. And that's exactly where I want to be."

Her breath caught, her pulse racing as his words sank in. But she wasn't about to let him win. "You're so full of yourself," she snapped, though her voice wavered under the intensity of his gaze.

"And you're so easy to rile up," he said. "It's almost too much fun."

He was sending her crashing over the edge. She cried out his name again and again, moaning harder as he pumped his fingers into her sweetest spot. He had driven her to orgasm—and she was melting in his hands.

Her chest heaved, her anger mixing with the undeniable pull he had on her. "I don't want you," she spat, her voice trembling with the lie. "Please stop."

He pulled back. His smirk softened, his eyes darkening as he leaned down, his mouth just a breath away from her clit. "Then why are you shaking?" he murmured, his voice low and dangerous.

She froze, her entire body betraying her as the truth of his words settled over her. She hated him for it — for knowing her, for seeing right through her walls, for wielding his control over her with such maddening precision.

But most of all, she hated how much she didn't want him to stop.

Chapter Thirty-One

Wyatt pulled back quickly, pulling down her skirt as the door to the room creaked open behind them.

"Whoa, sorry — didn't realize someone was in here," a man's voice interrupted, his tone half-apologetic, half-curious.

Pixie froze, her heart hammering in her chest, but Wyatt reacted in an instant. He spun, his broad shoulders blocking her from view as he slammed the door shut with enough force to rattle the frame.

"Room's taken," Wyatt growled, his voice low and menacing. The footsteps outside hesitated for a moment before retreating, the muffled music from the club swallowing them up.

Pixie blinked, her breath shallow, as she looked at Wyatt. He turned back to her, his jaw clenched, his blue eyes alight with something dangerous. "That's it," he said, his tone decisive. "You're coming with me."

"What?" Pixie managed, but before she could protest further, Wyatt's strong hands gripped her waist, lifting her as if she weighed nothing.

"Wyatt—put me down!" she said, her hands pushing against his chest, but he was already marching.

He didn't answer, his movements quick and deliberate. They exited through a side door, slipping into the cool night air. The streets buzzed with activity — cars honking, distant laughter, the faint hum of the ocean in the distance. Wyatt flagged down a cab with one hand, still holding her close with the other.

The yellow cab screeched to a halt, and Wyatt opened the door, practically depositing her inside before sliding in after her. "Palm Beach," he barked to the driver, giving the address of his oceanfront house.

Pixie glared at him, her chest heaving. "Have you lost your mind?"

"Probably," he muttered, his gaze fixed ahead. "But I'm done waiting for you to run again. I've had enough of you looking over your shoulder and pretending you don't need help."

She opened her mouth to argue, but the look on his face silenced her. His jaw was set, his eyes stormy and determined, and the weight of his words hung heavy in the air between them.

The cab sped through the quiet streets, the city lights casting fleeting shadows inside the car. Pixie stared out of the window, her arms crossed tightly over her chest, her mind racing. She hated how safe she felt next to him, hated that even now, with her world spinning out of control, Wyatt still managed to make her feel grounded.

The ride to Palm Beach felt both endless and fleeting, and when the cab pulled up in front of Wyatt's house, Pixie's heart sank further. The modern structure loomed against the backdrop of the dark Atlantic, its sleek lines illuminated by soft, exterior lighting.

Wyatt paid the driver and stepped out, pulling Pixie with him before she could protest. She barely had time to register the cool sea breeze on her skin before the front door opened, and Nova bolted out to greet them, her tail wagging furiously.

"Nova," Wyatt said, his voice softening for the first time all night. The German Shepherd barked happily, circling them before nuzzling Wyatt's side. He crouched briefly, ruffling her fur before standing again and guiding Pixie inside.

The warmth of the house enveloped her immediately, the faint scent of cedarwood and salt mingling in the air. Pixie stood stiffly in the entryway, her arms still crossed as Nova sniffed her curiously.

"This is insane," she said, her voice tight. "You can't just abduct me like this."

Wyatt turned to face her, his blue eyes unyielding. "Why not?"

Her chest tightened at his words, the fight draining out of her as she looked at him. His hair was disheveled, his shirt wrinkled, and there was an intensity in his eyes that both terrified and comforted her.

Nova nudged her leg, her warm brown eyes full of curiosity and affection. Pixie exhaled slowly, her fingers brushing against the dog's fur as she knelt to pet her. "This is insane," she repeated, though her voice was quieter now.

"Yeah," Wyatt admitted, his lips curving into a faint smirk. "But it's the kind of insane I can handle."

Wyatt didn't give her time to think — hell, he barely gave her time to breathe. Wyatt's strong hands gripped her waist and spun her around. Her back hit the edge of the kitchen counter with a jarring thud, and he was on her, crowding her space, towering over her with an intensity that stole her breath. His smirk was gone, replaced by a look so fierce and commanding it sent a shiver racing down her spine.

One second she was glaring up at him, her heart pounding with fury, and the next his mouth was on hers, desperate and searching. His tongue twisted inside her mouth, tasting and claiming. He ran his hands up and down her chest, tummy, ass, and thighs with a ferocity that made her gasp.

"You've been asking for this," he growled, his voice low, rough, and dangerous as he kissed her. His eyes burned into hers, dark and wild, like a predator staring down its prey. "Pushing me, taunting me, running that sharp little mouth of yours. Well, sweetheart, now you're gonna see what happens when you push too far."

Her chest heaved as she received his lips on hers, her body trembling under the intensity of his presence. "You think I'm scared of you?" she spat, though her voice betrayed her, trembling with something far more dangerous than fear.

He pressed harder against her, making his arousal crystal clear, his breath hot against her lips. "No," he said, his voice a low rasp. "You're not scared. You're fucking desperate for me, and you hate it. That's why you keep fighting me. You want to see how far I'll go."

Her heart thundered in her chest, her hands gripping the edge of the counter as if it was the only thing keeping her grounded. "You're so full of yourself," she snapped, though her voice lacked conviction, her pulse racing under his scrutiny.

His lips curled into a feral grin, his hands tightening on her hips. "And you're so full of shit," he said, his voice sharp and biting. "You can lie to yourself all you want, Pixie, but your body doesn't lie. I can feel the way you react to me. You like this."

Before she could deny it, he grabbed her wrist, spinning her around so quickly her head spun. He hauled her up and marched her to his bedroom. He pressed her chest-first against his bedroom wall, his hands pinning hers flat against the surface. His body crowded hers from behind, his heat overwhelming, suffocating in the best way.

"Wyatt!" she snapped, twisting under his grip, but it only made him press against her harder, his cock throbbing at her ass. His strength was unrelenting, and the sheer force of it sent a thrill racing through her.

"Stop fighting me," he growled, his voice rough in her ear. "We both know you don't want me to stop." He ran his hands across her arms and to her neck, holding her in place like he commanded every inch of her body. And then he ripped off her shirt.

Her breath hitched, her body betraying her as her pulse thundered in her ears. "You're fucked up," she bit out, though her voice was weaker now, trembling under the weight of his presence.

"And you're driving me fucking crazy," he said, his teeth grazing the shell of her ear before he pulled back just enough to speak.

His hands slid down her, rough and deliberate, leaving a trail of fire in their wake. He settled on the waist of her skirt and pulled it down. He gripped her waist again, spinning her against him with a force that made her gasp. "You're mine, Pixie," he growled, his voice fierce and unyielding. "And I'm done letting you pretend otherwise."

Then he kissed her again. Powerfully. Like he was never going to let her go.

Her body arched instinctively into his touch, her mind screaming at her to push him away, but she couldn't. Because he was right. She didn't want him to stop—she didn't want to win.

So, she took everything he wanted to do to her. His tongue danced in and out of her mouth, kissing, biting, and licking down her throat.

"Say it"—he tore off his own shirt—"admit it. Admit you want this."

There he stood before her, half naked. Almost as nude as her. She clenched her teeth, refusing to give in, but the way he stared at her, the raw power in his touch, left her trembling. "Go to hell," she bit out, though her voice was shaking now, her body betraying her resolve.

His laugh was low and dark, full of challenge. "Already there, sweetheart," he said, his voice dripping with ferocity. "And you're coming with me."

Before she could respond, he threw her down on his bed, finding the edge of her panties and tearing them down her thighs, slamming her back against the mattress as his lips crashed down on hers. The kiss was furious, consuming, a battle that left her gasping for air. His teeth nipped at her lower lip, his tongue sweeping inside, demanding everything she had to give.

Her hands flew to his shoulders, not to push him away but to hold on, to anchor herself against the storm he was unleashing. His grip on her was possessive, almost bruising, and the sheer intensity of him made her body hum with need.

"You're mine," he growled against her lips, his voice a harsh rasp that sent a thrill racing through her. "And I don't care how much you fight it. You're not walking away from this."

Her chest heaved, her breath coming in shallow gasps as she stared up at him, her anger and desire blending into something she couldn't control. "You're impossible," she whispered, her voice trembling.

"And you're fucking mine," he said, his lips curling into a wicked smirk. "Get used to it."

"Fuck you." She moaned as he found her hot opening with his fingers, already aching from when he licked her open at the bar.

He wasn't going to give up. His cock pulsed between her thighs, rock hard and ready.

"You think I'm playing with you?" he growled, his voice rough as his hands slid to her hips, gripping them with bruising force. "Think you can run your mouth and walk away without consequences?"

Her breath hitched, her pulse pounding in her ears as she stared up at him, her lips parting to respond. But nothing came out. She couldn't think, couldn't breathe, not with the heat of his body pressing against hers, pinning her in place.

"I didn't—" she started, but he cut her off with a low, dangerous laugh. "Please, just fuck me."

And so he did.

He thrust his cock up her pussy in one fluid motion. Her body hummed under his touch, her skin alive with every rough movement of his hands. She cried out his name at first but as he quickened the pace she found herself screaming. He leaned in close, his lips hovering just above hers, his voice dropping to a dark, taunting rasp. "What's the matter, Pixie? No smart-ass comeback now?"

Her eyes narrowed, defiance sparking to life despite the heat pooling low in her belly. "You're so full of yourself," she bit out, though her voice trembled under the weight of his intensity. "And I hate you for it."

He pulled her thigh up, holding her leg in the air as he penetrated her more deeply, faster. She watched his muscled frame, glistening with sweat, as he pumped relentlessly into her. She licked her lips, head tilting back, losing her mind. His sense of humor returned, dark and dangerous. "Oh, sweetheart," he murmured, his hands sliding to her thighs, spreading them just enough to step between them. "You don't hate me. That's the problem."

Before she could respond, he pulled out, grabbed her by the waist and spun her again, this time pressing her chest-first against the mattress. His hands gripped her wrists, pinning them behind her as his body crowded her from behind. She gasped, her heart racing at the roughness of his movements as he entered her from behind, the edge of orgasm coursing through her.

"Wyatt!" she cried, but it wasn't snark in her voice — it was something else entirely. Something desperate. Something she didn't want to admit.

"Say my name," he growled, his lips brushing against her ear, his voice a dark promise. "Say it again."

"Wyatt."

Her breath came in short, shallow gasps as his hands moved, gripping her hips and thumping her ass against him. His strength, his dominance, sent a thrill racing through her that she couldn't deny, no matter how much her mind screamed at her to fight it.

"You like this," he muttered, his voice low and rough. "Don't fucking lie to me, Pixie. I can feel it."

"Babe, I'm coming," she moaned, though her voice was weaker now, trembling with the force of what he was doing to her. "Slow down."

He let out a dark chuckle, his fingers digging into her hips just enough to make her gasp. "Not a chance," he said, his voice dripping with dark amusement. "Not until you admit it. Admit you love the way I handle you. The way I make you feel."

She clenched her teeth, her pride warring with the undeniable pull of him. "You're an asshole," she bit out, though her body betrayed her, leaning into his touch.

"And you're a goddamn menace," he said, as his cock thickened even more inside her. "But you're my menace. And I'm not letting you go."

She could barely take it anymore, coming hard on his cock as he pumped into her. Her heart thundered, her body trembling as his words sank in. He wasn't just tossing her around—he was claiming her, consuming her in a way that left no room for doubt. And as much as she hated to admit it, she didn't just like it—she craved it.

Her breath hitched as his hands slid up her sides, his touch rough and unapologetic. "Say it," he growled, his voice low and commanding. "Tell me you want this. Tell me you want me."

She swallowed hard, her pride screaming at her to fight, to push back, but the heat in his voice, the intensity in his touch, left her undone. "I want you," she whispered.

His grip tightened. "Damn right you do," he murmured, his voice thick with satisfaction. "And feel how much I want you too—" And with those final words, he let out a low groan that turned into a growl. He stopped pumping, gasping for air, releasing his seed inside her.

Breathless, he collapsed onto the bed, pulling her into him and kissing every inch of her shoulders and hair—holding her like he'd never, ever let her go.

The room was dark, illuminated only by the soft glow of moonlight streaming through the cracks in the curtains. The sound of the ocean outside was a steady rhythm, like a heartbeat, soothing and constant. Pixie lay curled against Wyatt, her head resting on his chest, the slow rise and fall of his breathing lulling her into a state of hazy calm. His arm was wrapped protectively around her, heavy and warm, anchoring her to him.

Pixie lay still in the crook of his arm, eyes open, staring past the ceiling.

The sound of the ocean drifted through the open window—soft, pulsing, indifferent. Moonlight spilled in across the rumpled sheets, painting them silver-blue, ghostlike.

Wyatt's fingers moved lazily across her back. Possessive. Gentle. Unrelenting.

She could still feel him inside her, phantom-like— the echo of his body claiming hers, the way he'd growled her name like it belonged to him.

And gods help her, she'd *let* him.

Worse—she'd *wanted* it.

A deep shiver ran through her, but not from the cold. From something older. Wound-tight. *Instinct.*

Her body had responded to him without hesitation. That was the problem. Her mind — the part that had clawed its way out of every trap, every lie, every man who thought he could own her — was slower to follow.

Wyatt was nothing like Raffaele. She knew that. He didn't lie. Didn't manipulate.

But he *controlled.*

Every inch of a room, every situation, every moment he stepped into — Wyatt Steele took command like it was breathing.

And now here he was. Wrapped around her like armor. Or chains. She wasn't sure which yet.

She shifted slightly, just enough to breathe without his chest rising under her cheek. He didn't stir. His grip tightened reflexively.

Her heart kicked in her chest.

No one owns me anymore.

The thought struck like lightning — hot, defiant, ugly in the quiet of this perfect scene. She should've felt safe. Cherished. But what she felt was *cornered*. Not by him. Not really.

By herself.

By the way she'd folded under the weight of his want. The way she'd said *yes* and meant it — and still felt like she was slipping back into something she'd sworn she'd never be again.

It wasn't fair to blame him.

But it was there.

Gnawing at the edge of her bliss.

Wyatt shifted in his sleep, exhaling deeply, his fingers smoothing up her spine in a sleepy, instinctive gesture that felt too much like ownership.

* * * *

The pale blue light of dawn spilled across the sheets, the kind of light that made everything feel too honest. The room smelled like bourbon, sweat, and something rawer—sex, yes, but also confession. Unasked-for closeness.

Pixie was already awake.

Wyatt stirred behind her, one heavy arm still draped over her waist, his chest warm against her spine. She didn't move. She just stared at the window, jaw tight, every part of her humming with a sharp, restless energy she couldn't shake.

"Pix," Wyatt murmured, voice rough from sleep and drink, "you awake?"

Her fingers stilled, and she tilted her head to look up at him. His blue eyes were fixed on the ceiling, his jaw tight, as though he were holding back something he didn't want to say. She waited, her heart beginning to ache with the weight of whatever he was carrying.

"I push people away," he began, his voice strained. "Not because I don't care, but because... I'm scared."

Her chest tightened as she listened, her fingers slipping down to entwine with his. "Scared of what?" she asked softly.

He exhaled, his eyes closing for a moment as if summoning the courage to continue. "That if I let anyone in—if I let you in—you'll see how broken I really am. And you'll leave."

His words hung heavy in the air, and for a moment, Pixie couldn't breathe. The raw vulnerability in his voice cut through her, and she gripped his hand tighter.

"Wyatt..."

"I don't want to be like him," he said, his voice cracking. "My father. He'd let people in, just enough to screw them over. Just enough to hurt them. And when things got hard, he bailed. I swore I'd never be like him, but…there are days I wonder if it's already in me. If I'm just one mistake away from becoming him."

Pixie sat up slightly, her hand cupping his cheek, forcing him to meet her gaze. His eyes were glassy, his expression guarded but crumbling.

"You're not your father," she said firmly, her voice trembling with conviction. "You're not even close to him, Wyatt. You're a good man. You care about people — you care too much, and that's why you're so afraid. But that fear doesn't define you. It doesn't own you."

He shook his head, his lips pressing into a thin line. "You don't know how many times I've screwed up. How many people I've let down."

"I'm not trying to fix you," she continued, her voice softening. "You don't need fixing. I just want to be here. To stand beside you, whatever that looks like. You don't have to carry this alone."

His jaw tightened, and for a moment, she thought he might argue. But then his hand came up to cover hers, his fingers trembling slightly as he held her palm against his cheek.

"You don't know how much that scares me," he admitted, his voice barely audible. "Letting you see me like this."

"And yet here we are," she whispered, leaning down to press a soft kiss to his forehead. "You let me in, Wyatt. That says more about who you are than anything else."

His arms tightened around her, pulling her back down against him as he buried his face in her hair. She felt the faint tremor in his body, the silent struggle as he fought to keep himself together.

Pixie stared at the ceiling. "You know what scares me?" she said, her voice flat. "That I let you in without even realizing it. And I'm waking up now wondering if I just handed over pieces of myself without reading the fine print."

He sat up slightly, the sheet falling away from his chest. "I'm not trying to control you—"

"But you do," she cut in. "You *do*, Wyatt. You command every room. You decide who gets in, who stays out, when to move, how far. Even with me."

His jaw tightened, but he didn't interrupt.

They sat in silence for a beat, the early light washing over their naked skin like some cruel, divine interrogation lamp.

"I'm not him," Wyatt said, his voice low. Tired. "I know that."

"I know that too," she said. "But I also know I've spent years crawling out from under men who needed to be in control. Who convinced me that surrender was safety."

Her voice wavered for the first time. She hated that it did.

"I don't want to be owned," she whispered. "Not even by someone good."

"We agree then. I don't deserve you," he muttered, his breath warm against her skin.

"Maybe. Maybe not." Pixie closed her eyes, her heart breaking for him and all the pain he carried. "All I know is you deserve more than you let yourself believe."

The words hung heavy, breathless between them.

He looked like he wanted to speak, to argue—but didn't.

She turned away, curling onto her side.

The silence returned, thicker than before.

But underneath it all, love still pulsed. Not clean. Not simple. But there.

Like a wound that hadn't yet decided whether it would scar — or rupture.

Chapter Thirty-Two

Pixie lay there for another moment, tangled in the sheets, her body warm but her thoughts already running. Sleep hadn't stuck—just dozed around the edges of her, too fragile to settle. Wyatt was beside her, still as stone, except... he wasn't asleep. She could tell.

The tension in him had returned. That locked-in stillness that only men like him had—soldiers, fighters, protectors too tired to fight but too wired to rest.

She rolled onto her back, letting the silence stretch.

"We should get up," Wyatt said finally, voice gravel-thick, not a whisper—just...low. Resigned.

She didn't answer. Just sat up, dragging the sheet with her. The air in the room was cold. Not just temperature—something else. She could feel it in the space between them.

Wyatt sat up too, rubbing a hand down his face. His hair was rumpled, his mouth a thin line. He didn't look at her. He stood and pulled on his boxers, his back turned as he grabbed a shirt off the chair. She watched him, jaw tight.

"You couldn't stay in bed another hour?" she asked, her voice cool.

"I can't lie next to you pretending nothing's cracked open," he said, finally glancing at her. "I don't have the talent for that."

Pixie laughed, sharp and joyless. "Good. Because I'm not pretending either."

His eyes flicked to hers—steady, blue, unblinking. "Didn't think you were."

She stood and reached for her clothes without shame, tugging on her underwear, his old T-shirt, her fingers moving quickly, efficiently. The silence buzzed.

"What now?" she asked, not softly.

Wyatt hesitated. Then he crossed the room, opened a drawer, pulled out a fresh pair of socks like they weren't standing in the wreckage of something they'd set fire to a few hours ago.

"I make coffee. You pretend you don't want to bolt," he said, too tired to coat it in sugar. "Then we see what's left."

She paused, one hand on her hip. "Wow. Romantic."

"You want me to lie?"

"No," she said. "I want you to stop trying to manage me."

That stopped him. His head turned slowly, eyes narrowed.

"I'm not managing you, Pix."

"Aren't you?" she shot back. "You show up at the bar, you pull me out of that train station like some white knight, you decide when I sleep, when I talk, when I break." Her voice cracked, bitter and hot. "I didn't ask for a bodyguard. I asked for a goddamn moment to *breathe*."

Wyatt said nothing. Just stared at her with a tension she couldn't read—anger, hurt, or maybe just restraint.

She shook her head and walked out.

The kitchen was still cool, the smell of yesterday's coffee long gone. She opened the fridge and grabbed water, twisting off the cap with too much force.

Nova padded in, tail wagging, sensing the shift in the room. Pixie let her out with a muttered, "Go on," watching the dog vanish into the yard.

The house was quiet.

When she turned, Wyatt had followed her in. He leaned against the doorframe, shirt half-buttoned, eyes darker than before.

He didn't speak. Just watched her, like he wasn't sure which version of her he'd find now.

Pixie set the bottle down and crossed to the table.

That's when she saw it—a notebook half-tucked under some printed handouts. Her fingers hovered, then pulled it free.

The handwriting caught her off guard.

Not the clean, blocky scrawl she expected. It was…careful. Almost cursive. Like he'd taught himself how to write properly a long time ago and never unlearned it.

She scanned the first line, heart pinching.

Admitting the problem doesn't make me weak.

She read more. Notes about guilt. About change. About holding himself accountable.

Pixie looked up at him. "You don't talk like this," she said quietly, lifting the notebook.

Wyatt stepped forward. "No."

"But you write it."

He shrugged. "It's easier when no one's watching."

Her chest tightened.

"I'm not trying to fix you," she said.

"I didn't ask you to," he replied.

She set the notebook down gently, her hands still on the cover. Her voice was lower now. "But I *am* trying to survive you."

That made him flinch.

Pixie walked past him, back toward the door, and paused.

"I'll stay for coffee," she said over her shoulder. "But after that, we talk. For real. No more shields. No more control."

Wyatt nodded once. "Deal."

They stood there, both exhausted, both bracing for what came next.

The kind of morning that didn't forgive anything — but demanded everything.

An hour later, the coffee had long since gone cold, untouched in her hands.

She sat cross-legged on Wyatt's couch, wrapped in one of his worn sweatshirts, the sleeves pushed halfway up her forearms. Her hair was still damp from the shower, her thighs bare against the cool leather, but she didn't move. Couldn't.

Wyatt sat across from her, elbows on his knees, watching her like she was going to bolt if he blinked.

He wasn't wrong.

"Pixie, I know I've been a mess," he said, his voice low and steady. "Hell, I *am* a mess. But I'm trying."

She stared at him for a long beat, her fingers wrapped tight around the ceramic mug like it might anchor her. "I've heard that before."

"I know." No defensiveness. Just quiet acknowledgment. "But this isn't a grand gesture. It's not a line. I'm not trying to trap you into some fairytale ending."

"Good," she said flatly. "Because I don't do fairytales."

He nodded, jaw tightening. "I don't want to push you. I just need you to know where I stand."

Her eyes flicked to his face — God, that *face* — all stubble and war-hardened lines and a mouth that looked too damn soft for someone so relentlessly capable of violence.

She hated how beautiful he was.

Because it made it harder to remember the red flags. The control. The way he moved like he *already knew* what was best for her. The way he didn't ask — he just acted. Protected. Possessed.

And yet here she was.

On his couch.

In his sweatshirt.

With his scent still on her skin.

"I won't lose you," he said, something raw slipping beneath the words. "But I'm not going to force you into anything. Don't decide now. Don't decide at all. Just know — I'm here. Whenever you're ready."

Her fingers twitched around the mug. "That's a lot to put on someone, Wyatt."

"It's not pressure," he said. "It's choice."

She stared at him. This man who had seen her at her lowest. Who'd held her through the worst kind of shaking, who knew the weight of her secrets and still *looked at her like this*. Like she was worth staying for.

It pissed her off.

And it pulled at something soft and stupid and deeply buried inside her.

Without thinking, she set the mug down and crossed the distance between them in two quiet steps. He looked up just in time for her to grab the collar of his T-shirt and kiss him.

It was soft. Then it wasn't.

Her lips dragged against his like she was trying to figure him out through taste and friction alone. And he let her. He let her take whatever she needed. His hands stayed at his sides until she pressed harder, until her fingers slid under the hem of his shirt and her body folded into his like she couldn't help it.

Then he moved.

His hands found her hips. Her waist. Her spine. Grounding her and undoing her all at once.

She pulled back, just an inch. Her breath was ragged.

"This is so fucking stupid," she whispered.

He touched her cheek, thumb brushing along the hinge of her jaw. "Then don't do it."

"Don't tempt me," she shot back, but there was no fire in it. Only heat. Only ache.

Wyatt smiled, small and rueful. "You're impossible."

"So are you," she murmured, and kissed him again—slow this time, aching.

When they broke apart, she rested her forehead against his. His breathing was just as wrecked as hers.

"I have something for you," he said.

She pulled back slightly, wariness flickering through her eyes. "Is this the part where you hand me a pair of handcuffs?"

He reached for the table beside the couch, opened a drawer, and pulled out a small silver key.

He held it out between two fingers, offering it like it was something sacred.

Pixie didn't move.

"What is that?"

"It's the key to this place," he said. "No conditions. No questions. You don't owe me anything. But if you ever want to come back—if you ever need to—you can."

Pixie stared at the key like it might burn her.

Her mouth parted. But no words came.

The key sat in his palm, gleaming in the early morning light. Small. Unthreatening. But heavy with something she wasn't ready to name.

She took it.

Because she was *already falling*.

Because she didn't know how to stop.

And because a tiny, traitorous part of her—the same one that used to dream in quiet, impossible moments—*wanted* to believe it could mean something else. Something safe. Something hers.

Her fingers closed around it slowly, and she didn't look at him when she whispered, "You're getting to me."

Wyatt didn't move. Didn't smile.

But his voice was rough when he said, "I know."

And the worst part?

So did she.

Chapter Thirty-Three

The late afternoon sun dipped low over the sprawling gardens of the Palm Beach Historical Society, casting warm, golden hues over the crowd gathered for the annual Preservation Gala. Pixie stood just behind the First Lady, the rhythmic murmur of conversation and clinking glasses creating a backdrop of polite sophistication. She scanned the crowd methodically, every detail registering in her mind — the placement of the security team, the high-profile guests in attendance, the way the president casually conversed with donors under the shade of the pavilion.

But despite the serene façade of the event, Pixie couldn't shake the tight knot of unease building in her chest.

Her phone buzzed in her clutch. She hesitated, stealing a quick glance around to ensure she wasn't being watched too closely before fishing it out. The name on the screen sent a chill down her spine. Ethan Kane.

Her stomach flipped as she opened the message.

Santoro hasn't been seen in New York for days. No private appearances, no public sightings. Be careful.

Pixie's breath hitched, her pulse pounding in her ears. She typed back quickly.

Do you know where he went?

The response was almost instant.

Not yet. He's either laying low or planning something. Either way, keep your guard up. He's not the type to let things go.

She locked her phone, tucking it back into her clutch with trembling fingers. The air suddenly felt too heavy, too close. The laughter of the nearby guests grated on her nerves, and she caught herself glancing toward the First Lady, hyper-aware of her responsibility to remain composed. But inside, her mind raced with possibilities.

Where was Santoro? Why had he gone silent? Was he here, in Palm Beach? The thought chilled her to the bone.

A hand touched her elbow lightly, pulling her out of her spiraling thoughts. She turned to find Marcy, dressed impeccably as always, her bright smile betraying none of the tension Pixie felt. "You good?" Marcy asked, her voice pitched low enough that no one else could hear.

Pixie forced a nod. "Fine," she lied. "Just making sure everything is in place."

Marcy gave her a knowing look but didn't press. Instead, she gestured toward the First Lady, who was now mingling with a prominent environmental philanthropist. "Mrs. Armstrong's got this under control. You could probably relax for a second."

Pixie's eyes darted back to the crowd, her unease spiking. "I'll relax when the night is over," she muttered, her tone sharper than intended.

Marcy's expression softened, and she leaned closer. "Whatever's got you so on edge, I hope you know you're not alone in this."

Pixie swallowed hard, unable to muster a response. She didn't feel like she wasn't alone. If anything, she felt more isolated than ever. Ethan's warning hung heavy in her mind, a shadow she couldn't shake. And then there was Wyatt—his absence, his silence. She hadn't heard from him in days, since she slept over, and she couldn't decide if his distance was becoming a blessing or another source of torment.

The First Lady turned toward her, signaling with a subtle glance that it was time to move to the next cluster of guests. Pixie straightened, smoothing the fabric of her dress, her mask of composure sliding firmly into place. She fell into step behind Caroline, the picture of professional poise.

But inside, her thoughts were a whirlwind. Something was coming—she could feel it. Santoro's silence wasn't a retreat. It was a warning.

As they moved through the crowd, Pixie couldn't stop her eyes from flicking to the edges of the event, scanning for anything out of place, any sign that the storm was about to break.

The air was humid, thick with the salty breeze blowing in from the Atlantic. Wyatt stood at the edge of the event, his sharp eyes scanning the bustling crowd beneath the marquee lights of the Palm Beach Historical Society. He could hear the faint hum of conversation, the occasional burst of laughter, but his focus was elsewhere.

Something wasn't right. He could feel it.

Wyatt shifted his weight, his hand brushing the concealed pistol at his side as he scanned the perimeter. The Secret Service detail was in full force, stationed at key points around the property, but none of them seemed to notice the subtle crackle in the air that set Wyatt's nerves on edge.

Then, a black SUV pulled up just outside the gates, its tinted windows gleaming under the streetlights. Wyatt narrowed his eyes, his gut tightening. It wasn't just the vehicle — those were a dime a dozen in this part of town — it was the way it idled, the way the driver made no move to exit, the way two more identical SUVs rolled in right behind it.

It screamed trouble.

Wyatt murmured into his comms, his voice low and calm despite the adrenaline surging through his veins. "Salem, status check on the north perimeter."

Salem's voice crackled back. "All clear on my end. You see something?"

Wyatt didn't answer immediately. He watched as a man stepped out of the first SUV, his build stocky, his suit tailored just enough to suggest money, but the bulk beneath his jacket hinted at something else entirely. Another man followed, then another, their movements deliberate, their gazes sharp as they surveyed the crowd.

"Mafioso," Wyatt muttered under his breath. His grip tightened on the comm. "Keep eyes sharp. We've got guests who weren't on the list."

"Copy that," Salem replied, his tone serious.

Wyatt's pulse pounded in his ears as he moved toward the gate, his steps quick and purposeful. The men didn't flinch when they saw him approaching, their gazes cool and calculating. Wyatt didn't like it. He didn't like it one damn bit.

"What's your business here?" he demanded, his voice flat and hard, carrying just enough authority to force a response.

The stocky one smiled, his expression one of casual disinterest. "Just here to enjoy the gala," he said, his accent Italian, his tone mocking.

Wyatt's jaw tightened. "Don't lie to me. Who sent you?"

The man didn't answer, his smile widening ever so slightly, as if amused by Wyatt's tension. Behind him, one of the others opened the back door of the SUV slightly, as if readying for someone to step out. Wyatt's blood ran cold, the edges of his vision sharpening as his instincts screamed at him.

Santoro.

He was here. He had to be.

Wyatt moved without thinking, his hand slamming against the open door to stop it from opening further. "Stay in the car," he barked, his voice a growl. "This isn't the time or the place."

The man didn't flinch, his smile fading into something darker, colder. "You're playing a dangerous game, Agent Steele."

Wyatt leaned closer, his grip tightening on the edge of the door. "You want to see dangerous? Try me."

He yanked the door open fully, his heart pounding as he scanned the interior. Empty. His gaze said to the first man, then to the other SUVs. The second vehicle's passenger side door opened slightly, just enough to make Wyatt's stomach twist.

Breaking protocol entirely, Wyatt darted to the second car, yanking the door open before the occupants could react. Empty again.

"Where is he?" Wyatt growled, his voice low but deadly.

The stocky man behind him chuckled, the sound grating on Wyatt's already frayed nerves. "I don't know what you're talking about."

Wyatt turned, cutting through the man's façade. "I don't care who you're working for or what your plan is. You so much as breathe wrong in this direction, and I will bury you under a mountain of federal charges so fast you won't even see it coming."

The man didn't respond, but the faint flicker in his eyes gave Wyatt everything he needed to know. Santoro wasn't here—not yet. But this was a message. A reminder. A threat.

Wyatt stepped back, his gaze scanning the SUVs one last time, his chest heaving. He keyed his comm, his tone clipped. "Salem, tighten the perimeter. Double-check all points of entry. I want no surprises."

"Copy," Salem replied, his voice steady, though Wyatt could hear the tension underneath.

Wyatt turned his back on the SUVs, his fists clenched at his sides. He had to get back to Pixie.

The air inside the Palm Beach Historical Society was alive with murmurs and music. Wyatt didn't register any of it. His boots pounded against the marble floors, his breath short, his heart racing. He was a bullet tearing through the halls, blind to everything but one thought— *Find Pixie.*

Guests froze as he thundered past. Some gasped. Others pressed themselves against the walls, whispering in alarm. Wyatt didn't care. Couldn't care. The unease in his gut had turned into a roar, drowning out everything else.

"Wyatt!" Salem's voice cracked over the comms, tense and urgent. "What the hell are you doing? You're making a scene!"

"Where is she?" Wyatt barked, his tone sharp enough to cut.

"East wing. Still with the First Lady," Salem replied, a hint of panic in his voice. "But you—"

Wyatt ripped out the earpiece. He didn't have time for caution. Those SUVs outside. The men with their cold eyes and quiet smiles. Santoro's men. He knew it. Felt it deep in his bones. This wasn't just a warning. They were here.

And Pixie was in danger.

The ballroom came into view, golden light spilling into the hallway like fire. He skidded around the corner, his gaze snapping to the stage. The First Lady was speaking, her voice calm and commanding. Wyatt barely glanced at her. His eyes locked on Pixie, standing just off to the side. Her tablet was clutched in her hands, her expression focused as she worked with Marcy.

Relief slammed into him like a freight train, but it didn't last. Her phone buzzed in her hand. Once. Then again. Her brow furrowed as she silenced it, her lips pressed tight. He couldn't tell who was calling her but Wyatt's pulse surged. He couldn't deny his instincts. The way she was reacting. Something wasn't right.

Wyatt closed the distance between them in seconds, his presence like a storm bearing down. Pixie turned as he reached her, her confusion flashing into concern when she saw the wild look in his eyes. He immediately guided her away from the crowd, down a hallway where no one could see them.

"What are you doing—" she said.

"Santoro," he said between heavy breaths.

"He's here?"

"I don't know. Maybe." Wyatt tried to explain his instincts but ended up spinning them in circles.

Wyatt watched as Pixie's face turned pale, her breathing shallow and erratic. Her hand trembled around her phone, her lips moving but no sound coming out. The crowd around them blurred into nothing—all he could see was her panic.

"Pixie," he said, his voice low but firm.

She didn't respond. Her gaze darted around the room, unfocused, her chest rising and falling too fast. She pressed a hand to her stomach, like she was trying to anchor herself, but it wasn't working.

"Pixie, look at me," Wyatt said again, stepping closer, his hand hovering near her arm. He wanted to grab her, to shake her out of it, but something stopped him. She didn't need fixing. She needed space.

"I—I can't," she whispered, her voice trembling. "I—I don't know—" Tears fell from her eyes.

"You're safe," he said softly, keeping his voice steady. "Right here. Right now. You're safe."

Her eyes flicked to his, wide and glassy. She shook her head, her panic bubbling to the surface. "It's never over."

"I know," Wyatt said, his chest tight. "But you're not alone in this. You've got me."

Her knees wavered, and he reached out instinctively, but he didn't pull her close. He just braced her, steadying her with a hand on her arm, giving her the choice to lean in or not. "Just breathe," he murmured. "One breath at a time."

Her lips trembled, but she followed his lead, her breaths slowly evening out as her focus zeroed in on his face. "I can't," she said, small but raw. "I can't."

"You can," Wyatt said. "I got you."

"You don't get it. You don't—"

"Then tell me," he interrupted, his tone sharpening with frustration.

Pixie's breath hitched, and for a moment, she just stared at him, her vulnerability laid bare. "Because everyone leaves," she said finally, her voice cracking. She chewed her lip as her chest heaved.

The words hit him like a punch to the gut. He stepped closer, his voice steady but filled with an edge of desperation. "Fuck that. Not me. I'm not going anywhere."

She looked at him, her dark eyes swimming with doubt and something deeper. She just watched, steadying her breathing.

His jaw tightened, the frustration and pain warring within him. But he forced himself to breathe, to hold steady for her. "I stay," he said firmly. "I stay when it's hard. I stay when you're too much. I stay because you're worth it. All of it."

Her lips parted, her tears finally spilling over as she searched his face for something—anything—to prove he was telling the truth. "Can I believe that?" she whispered.

"Doesn't matter. Just let me prove it," he said, his hand finally settling on her cheek, his touch gentle but

A Patriot's Promise

resolute. "One day at a time. One breath at a time. Just let me prove how much I love you."

She turned up to him.

And then he whispered in her ear, "Because I do. I love you."

For a long moment, she didn't move, didn't speak. The weight of their emotions hung heavy between them, but something shifted in her gaze—something small, but undeniable. She didn't have to say it. He saw it in the way her shoulders eased, the way her breathing calmed. She was letting him in, inch by inch.

And Wyatt sure as fucking hell was never, ever going to let her down.

The noise of the crowd faded into static, like her ears had been dunked underwater. Everything moved in slow motion—blurry faces, flurries of movement—and through it all, her phone buzzed like a ticking bomb in her fist.

Pixie couldn't breathe.

Not fully.

Wyatt's arms circled her, solid, heat and pressure at her back. She should've felt safe in it—God knew part of her did—but another part...the part that remembered being trapped in luxury penthouses and velvet cages...*flinched*.

"Pixie." His voice cut clean through the fog.

Firm. Commanding.

She turned as he gently took her by the shoulders and looked her dead in the eye.

"Breathe." The word landed like a weight. "With me. In. Out."

She obeyed—not because he demanded it, but because she *chose* to. And that difference mattered more than she could articulate.

Her lungs trembled. She inhaled slowly, like breaking the surface after drowning.

The pressure in her chest began to crack, just slightly, as her gaze locked on his.

And that's when she saw it—*he* was different.

This wasn't the Wyatt who had stripped her bare and made her come undone beneath him with that terrifying, exquisite control. This wasn't the man who always took the lead without question.

This man…was *waiting*.

"What do you need?" he asked. Not a demand. Not a command.

A *choice*.

The tears welled before she could stop them.

"You're different," she breathed. "You're not—"

"Because of you," he said simply.

It shattered something brittle in her. Something she'd been white-knuckling for years.

She nodded, voice raw. "We fight. Together."

Wyatt stepped in, arms wrapping around her—not like a wall, but like a net. "Together."

Her phone buzzed again in her hand.

Pixie looked down. Her stomach flipped.

Ethan Kane.

Wyatt's body tensed behind her.

"Why the hell is he here?" he growled, already on alert.

She hesitated. Her thumb hovered.

Wyatt didn't demand. Didn't rip it from her hand.

He just said quietly, "Take it."

She did.

"What?" Her voice was ice. No emotion. Just steel.

Ethan's voice was crisp. Clipped. No bullshit.

"Santoro is dead."

Everything stopped.

Pixie couldn't move. Couldn't think. The words didn't compute.

"What?" she whispered.

"Executed. Penthouse. This morning. Clean. Professional. It's done."

Her knees buckled.

Wyatt caught her before she could fall, both arms locking around her, holding her upright like scaffolding.

"Pix," he said urgently, voice low against her temple. "What is it?"

She choked it out. "Santoro. He's dead."

Wyatt froze. Just for a breath. Then, without hesitation, he cradled her face in his hands and kissed her.

It wasn't dominance. It wasn't control.

It was relief. It was raw. It was a *thank you* and a *you're safe now* and an *I'm here*.

And she kissed him back—full, slow, grounding herself in the press of his mouth, the way his hand trembled slightly where it cupped her jaw.

When they broke apart, she stared at him, dazed.

"I should be relieved," she said hoarsely. "I should be dancing in the street."

"But you're not."

She shook her head. "He's gone. But the shit he did to me? The version of me he created? That's still in here. Still clawing to the surface."

Wyatt didn't flinch. Didn't try to erase it.

He just held her.

"Then we keep clawing back."

Silence.

Then—

"I need to ask you something," she said, staring at the sidewalk, voice low. "Back at the hotel… that night. In the shower. In bed. You were…"

"Too much."

She nodded.

"And you still said yes," he added gently.

"I did," she said. "But I need to know… if that's who you are. All the time."

He didn't answer right away. His thumb brushed her cheek.

"No," he said. "That's who I *was*. Before I knew how much you needed to breathe."

She looked up at him. The storm in her chest began to ease.

"I don't want to be overpowered, Wyatt," she said quietly. "Not even in bed. Especially not there. That place has to be mine too."

He leaned in close. "Then you tell me when to touch. When to stop. When to *give it up to you* instead."

Her breath hitched.

And, goddammit, she *wanted* him again.

Even now.

Because this man—this *version* of him—was her weak spot.

Wyatt reached into his jacket pocket. Held out something small.

A key.

"Yours if you want it," he said. "No expectations. No surveillance. Just… a door that's open."

Pixie stared at the key in his palm.

It was nothing. It was everything.

It meant safety. Or danger. Or both.

She took it anyway.

Because she was already in love with him. Even if she still wasn't sure she could *trust* him with all of her.

But maybe love came first. And the rest — *

That was the fight.

And they'd fight it together.

The hallway still echoed with the sound of Ethan's voice — *Santoro is dead* — even though the call had long ended. The tremor in Pixie's hand had settled to a dull throb, her fingers now laced tightly with Wyatt's. Not clenched. Not clenched at all.

She wasn't falling this time.

She was *walking*.

Wyatt squeezed her hand, his thumb brushing over her knuckles as they moved down the corridor in step. Back toward the buzz of the gala. Toward glass chandeliers and champagne flutes and curated laughter.

The double doors of the Palm Beach Historical Society opened again — and this time, they didn't slip in unnoticed.

Warm light spilled through the grand ballroom, golden and honey-soft, catching in the sequins of floor-length gowns and the gleam of polished tuxedo lapels. A jazz quartet played low and lilting in the far corner. Silver trays floated past on the arms of servers in white gloves. Everything was perfectly rehearsed.

Until they entered.

Heads turned.

Slowly at first.

Then all at once.

Pixie's pulse kicked up, but Wyatt's hand in hers anchored her. He didn't let go.

Not this time.

He led her with quiet certainty into the heart of the crowd, where the center of gravity shifted. Guests murmured, some trying not to stare, others openly gawking. She caught glimpses — familiar faces, a senator's wife blinking like she couldn't believe her eyes, a gossip columnist lifting her phone halfway before thinking better of it.

Pixie kept her chin high.

Her heels struck the marble floor with purpose.

Wyatt wore his usual look of detached steel, but she could see the pride simmering under his skin.

He was standing next to her. *With* her.

And he was done pretending he wasn't.

The music slowed as the First Lady herself glided toward them through the parting crowd, her signature diamond pin winking beneath the golden chandelier.

Caroline stopped a few paces away, her eyes flicking from their joined hands to Pixie's face.

The room held its breath.

And then —

"I always knew it," Caroline said, her voice rich and smooth. "You two burn too bright to hide."

A hush broke like glass across the room.

Pixie opened her mouth to speak, but Caroline stepped forward and clasped both of Pixie's hands in hers.

"I'm so glad it's *you*," she said softly, with something like fierce affection behind her eyes. "And I'm even more glad you're choosing to be seen."

Wyatt didn't speak. He just inclined his head, respectful. But his thumb brushed Pixie's hand again, barely there, a signal only she felt.

Caroline turned to the crowd with a practiced smile. "Ladies and gentlemen, I believe the Preservation Gala just got a bit more historic."

Laughter bloomed around them—polite, surprised, electric.

Caroline leaned in and whispered, just for Pixie, "You make him better. Don't let him forget it."

Pixie swallowed hard, eyes stinging.

She nodded.

As Caroline drifted away to work the room, Wyatt turned to her. "You okay?"

Pixie exhaled, tension bleeding from her shoulders. "I think I just came out as your girlfriend to the First Lady of the United States."

"She *called* you my girlfriend?" Wyatt asked, one brow raised.

Pixie smirked. "No. But the sparkle in her eye said it."

Wyatt's mouth curved. "I'll take it."

They stood together, wrapped in golden light and a thousand watching eyes. But none of that mattered.

Not now.

Not when she finally knew what it felt like to stand in public and still belong to herself.

She leaned into him, her voice low. "I still don't know where this ends."

He leaned down, brushing his lips just against her temple. "Good," he said. "Because I don't want it to."

And under that vaulted ceiling, surrounded by marble and murmurs and a dozen unanswered questions—

Pixie let herself smile.
For real this time.

Chapter Thirty-Four

The Palm Beach Presidential Residence was a fortress draped in luxury — colonnades, security checkpoints, manicured grounds, and a perimeter monitored by a silent choreography of agents in suits with coiled earpieces.

Wyatt stood inside the eastern foyer, dressed in his black-on-black detail uniform, earpiece clipped, arms crossed as he scanned the updated security grid glowing across the mounted tablet near the window.

Wyatt hadn't slept much in the past few days. Not since the hallway. Not since Pixie.

He rubbed a thumb over the tension building between his brows and was about to step into the west corridor when the gate intercom buzzed.

"Unscheduled arrival. No plates in system."

Wyatt froze.

His gaze lifted to the feed — and he straightened instantly.

A car. Sleek. Deep black. No logos. No diplomatic flags. The kind of vehicle that didn't belong to anyone...unless you knew better.

It slid to a stop at the base of the stairs like it had every right to be there.

A moment later, the rear door opened.

A familiar man stepped out.

Tailored charcoal coat. Navy slacks. Crisp white shirt, collar open. His movements were fluid, precise. His face—clean-shaven, angular, cool—betrayed nothing. His eyes, though...

Piercing. Calculating.

He took one long look around the courtyard.

And then walked straight inside.

Wyatt stepped forward as the man entered the marble-floored hallway, the air cooling between them like something unseen had just slipped in behind him.

"Steele," he said, smooth. Polished, but low. Quiet authority.

Wyatt blinked once. "Kane."

The man didn't look like a PI. He looked like a weapon. And sure as hell Wyatt immediately hated that Pixie ever associated with him.

Kane stepped closer, glancing briefly at the paintings on the wall, at the subtle surveillance points in the ceiling.

"Three days. Dead." Kane nodded. "Penthouse. Precise work. No witnesses. Cops can't trace back to anyone."

Silence stretched between them.

Kane's hands remained in his pockets, casual, but his body read like a man used to anticipating violence.

"Does she know?" Kane said finally.

Wyatt's jaw flexed.

"Only that he's dead," Wyatt responded. "Bury the rest."

Kane's eyes flicked over him, like he was measuring something. Then, he nodded. "Good. That was the deal."

A longer pause this time.

The kind filled with things they wouldn't say aloud.

Wyatt glanced toward the hallway that led to the south wing.

To *her*.

"You did what you had to," Kane said.

Wyatt looked at him then. Really looked. "I did what she couldn't."

Something unreadable flickered in Kane's expression. Approval, maybe. Regret. Or something colder.

"You love her," he said — not a question, just a truth laid bare.

Wyatt didn't answer.

Kane stepped back, pulling something from the inside of his coat. A slim flash drive. He held it out between two fingers.

"I had to pull favors for this. You'll want to destroy it."

Wyatt took it without a word.

"Anything on it that connects back to me?" he asked, voice low.

"No," Kane said.

Another beat.

And then Kane smiled again. Not warm. Not unkind.

But final.

"I've got other business now," he said. "You won't see me again."

Wyatt studied him, the flash drive still pinched between his fingers.

"And her?"

Kane's gaze flicked away — just for a second. "She was worth saving," he said simply. "You better not fuck it up."

Then he turned, walking back toward the front entrance with the same effortless grace he'd arrived with. A shadow slipping back into the cracks of the world.

The black car pulled away seconds later, disappearing down the drive, gone before Wyatt could even track which direction.

And just like that — Ethan Kane was gone.

Wyatt looked down at the flash drive in his hand.

He didn't need to plug it in.

He already knew what it contained.

And he already knew what needed to be burned.

Wyatt moved along the southern perimeter wall, the crisp rhythm of his boots falling into time with Salem's beside him. They both wore suits and earpieces, identically dressed, blending into the curated calm of the president's private estate like ghosts with clearance levels.

Above them, palm trees swayed in the late afternoon wind, casting long shadows across the manicured lawn. They were due to swap out surveillance rotations, but for now, it was just the two of them — walking, scanning, listening.

And thinking.

Salem adjusted the strap on his shoulder and cut a sideways glance toward the circular driveway.

"That guy," he said, nodding casually toward the black car now pulling out through the gate. "Slick coat, untagged sedan. Quiet. Who was he?"

Wyatt's jaw tightened.

Salem kept walking, unfazed. "Was that the PI? The one from New York? The guy who helped track Pixie?"

Wyatt didn't answer right away.

He just kept walking.

The name echoed through him like a slow-burning fuse. *Ethan Kane.*

Yeah. That was him.

The man who left no digital footprint. No return address. No past.

Just one clean line from *Pixie*…to *Wyatt*…to *what had to be done.*

Wyatt finally exhaled, gaze sweeping across the rose hedges and marble lions flanking the back patio.

"Yeah," he said quietly. "That was him."

Salem hummed low. "Didn't think he was real. I mean, I knew you had eyes everywhere, but *that* guy? He looked like he could dismantle a foreign government and still be home in time for steak and Jim Beam."

Wyatt huffed a faint laugh, more breath than humor.

Salem didn't push. But he didn't stop, either.

"You ever gonna tell me what went down with Santoro?"

Wyatt slowed, fingers curling at his sides. "No."

"Copy that," Salem said simply.

They walked a few more paces in silence before Wyatt stopped entirely, staring out at the edge of the garden where the wrought iron fence met the sea cliffs.

He felt it then.

The sharp, perfect moment where the world snapped into focus—and he finally saw what he'd become.

When Pixie disappeared off that train platform, something inside him cracked wide open.

Not because he failed.

But because it *wasn't his decision*. He hadn't seen it coming. Hadn't planned for it. Hadn't *controlled it*.

And for a man like Wyatt Steele, control was god.

The same way it had been for his father.

He remembered the way his mother used to flinch when she heard the garage door open. The sound of whiskey being poured like it meant war. The chill of silence at the dinner table. His father's voice—always calm, always cold, always the final word.

Wyatt had sworn he'd never be like him.

And then Pixie looked him dead in the eye and told him *I don't need a protector — I need to breathe.*

And he'd realized he *already* was.

Control disguised as devotion.

Obsession dressed up like loyalty.

He would've burned the world to keep her safe. And maybe… maybe he had.

Ethan Kane was proof of that.

The man didn't operate in moral absolutes. He delivered outcomes. And Wyatt had let him.

Never said it aloud. Never wrote it down.

But they both knew the language of implication.

Pixie would never know. She couldn't. Because he had done something she would never forgive.

And he'd done it anyway.

Not to protect her.

To *possess* the one thing he'd never been able to keep safe before—love.

She broke him the moment she walked into that gala in a black dress and didn't flinch under pressure.

She broke him when she bled and didn't call it weakness.

She broke him when she looked him in the eye and said *You don't get to decide who I am.*

Now he was a man without armor. Just skin. Just scars. Just her.

Salem adjusted his earpiece. "Hey. You good?"

Wyatt nodded slowly. "Yeah," he said. "Yeah, I'm good."

But something in him was still shaking.

And maybe that was the point.

Because the control was gone.

But *she* wasn't.

And maybe that was enough.

* * * *

The scent of peonies and polished marble clung to the air, the final notes of another long day settling into the quiet hush of evening. Pixie closed the ornate double doors to the First Lady's private study with a gentle *click*, the soft rustle of her silk blouse brushing against her ribs. Her clipboard hung at her side, her heels clicking with measured grace as she made her way down the corridor, hair still perfectly knotted, expression still neutral.

But inside?

Inside, her stomach was doing cartwheels.

The gala had been three days ago. Three *very* public, *very dramatic* days ago—where Wyatt had kissed her in full view of the crème de la crème of Palm Beach society. Where the First Lady had raised one elegant eyebrow...and *approved.*

Pixie had barely had time to breathe since.

"Pix!" came the delighted shriek from somewhere to her left.

Pixie winced. No hiding now.

Here they come.

Jamie rounded the corner first in a whirlwind of coral linen and lip gloss, practically vibrating with joy. Marcy followed behind, her arms already extended for a hug like this was a red-carpet reunion and not a Tuesday.

"Oh my *god*," Jamie said, grabbing her by the shoulders and shaking her gently. "You *did it.* You *really* did it."

"Did what?" Pixie asked dryly, raising a brow. "Successfully managed event logistics for the Florida Land Preservation Society?"

"*No,*" Marcy deadpanned. "You bagged the sexy, grumpy Secret Service demigod. In public. With *tongue.*"

Jamie gasped. "There was tongue?"

"Jamie," Pixie groaned, "can you *not* say tongue in a government building?"

They both dissolved into laughter, collapsing on either side of her like the chaos fairies they were. Jamie linked arms with her, Marcy grabbed the clipboard and promptly started fanning herself with it.

"So," Marcy said, lips quirking. "Are you moving in together yet or just christening every surface of the Palm Beach estate after hours?"

"Jesus Christ," Pixie muttered, but she was smiling now — reluctant, embarrassed, glowing.

Jamie leaned in. "Tell me *everything*. What does he look like naked? Wait — no, don't tell me. *Tell me later*. In detail. Over tequila."

Pixie rolled her eyes but her cheeks flushed warm. "You two are impossible."

"And you," Marcy said, jabbing a finger at her, "are *in love*. Like, actual, inconvenient, soul-altering love."

Pixie's smile faltered.

Her throat tightened. Just for a beat.

Jamie noticed instantly. "Hey," he said more softly. "Too much?"

Pixie hesitated, staring out of the hallway window, watching the Florida sky turn that deep apricot-blue before dusk. "I don't know what to call it," she murmured, voice low. "I just know... I don't want to lose him. Even when he drives me completely insane."

Marcy grinned. "Welcome to real love, babe."

Jamie squeezed her hand. "You can do hard things. We've seen you. He's lucky to have you."

Pixie blinked rapidly, brushing a strand of hair behind her ear. "I'm still figuring it out. The whole... trusting someone enough to stay."

Marcy bumped her shoulder. "He stayed, Pix."

Pixie nodded slowly. "Yeah," she whispered. "He did."

From down the corridor, one of the First Lady's aides called her name. She turned slightly, catching her reflection in the gilded mirror — lipstick faded, eyes still bright, heart still hammering like it didn't know whether to fight or fall.

"Go be a badass," Jamie whispered. "We'll text later."

"Group chat's already titled *Pixie & the President's Bodyman: A Love Story*," Marcy added.

Pixie groaned. "I'm deleting both of you from my will."

But as she turned to leave, the warmth of their affection wrapped around her like armor. Maybe this was what it meant to be held — not just by him, but by people who knew her, who *saw* her, who stayed.

And maybe, just maybe...

She was starting to believe she was worth staying for.

An hour later, the sun was slipping low behind the estate's sculpted palms, gilding the gardens and white stone corridors in molten gold. Palm fronds whispered above like they were passing judgment. The scent of orange blossoms hung thick in the air, sharp and sweet, refusing to be ignored — like memory. Like him.

Pixie moved through the marble hallway, her steps soft on the carpet runner. The post-gala hush had fallen over the residence — staff bustling quietly, laughter fading behind closed doors, secrets passed along silver trays and polite nods. Her blouse clung to her back with the heat of the day. Her heart was no calmer than it had been that morning.

She'd thought she'd feel lighter once the truth was out. But the weight hadn't lifted. It had shifted. It lived in her ribs now — in the space where old fear met something terrifyingly new.

Because falling for Wyatt Steele hadn't come easy.

It had meant forgiving him for that night at the train station, when control had snapped into command. It had meant unlearning every sharp rule she'd built for herself — *never need him too much, never lose yourself in the way he looks at you, never believe a man when he says he's changed.*

But Wyatt *had* changed. Not overnight. Not cleanly. Not without setbacks. He still clenched his jaw when she challenged him. Still reached for control when the silence between them grew too loud.

But he was trying.

And she had compromised—God, *how* she'd compromised.

She'd stopped keeping a bag packed.

She'd stopped treating every moment as a possible goodbye.

She'd let herself be kissed in public. Held. *Claimed.*

And not because she belonged to him.

But because, somehow, impossibly, he had earned his way into her life.

Even now, it stunned her.

She rounded the marble corner—and there he was.

Wyatt Steele.

At the center of a cluster of agents, arms folded, his voice low and commanding as he spoke with two regional leads and a visiting DHS attaché. He wore his duty like a second skin—tall, still, a pillar of control. He'd pulled his tie loose, the top two buttons of his shirt undone just enough to make her stomach tighten.

But then—he turned.

And his whole face changed.

His mouth curved. His sharp blue eyes softened. And before the agents could finish their briefing, he cut through them like a blade, walking straight toward her.

"Wyatt—" she started, brows lifting.

He didn't hesitate. He reached for her hand, pulled her in like she belonged there, and pressed his mouth to hers in a firm, unapologetic kiss. Warm. Real. *Public.*

Eyebrows raised. Someone cleared their throat behind them. A cough. A shift.

Pixie's cheeks flamed. "Wyatt," she said as he finally pulled back. "You're going to start a rumor mill that'll never end."

He just smirked, the edge of his smile smug as hell. "Don't care. I have you now."

And then he laced their fingers together, turned toward the arched glass doors, and led her straight into the garden like they hadn't just thrown gasoline on every protocol handbook in the building.

Outside, the estate glowed.

Low hanging lights twinkled in the olive trees. Marble paths wound between rose trellises and limestone benches. It was like stepping into a painting—old money charm draped in Southern heat.

"Wyatt," she said again, tugging at his hand as they walked. "We're still on duty."

He glanced at her sideways. "Then fire me."

Her laugh escaped before she could stop it. "You're the most stubborn bastard I've ever met."

He stopped walking. Turned. And with the golden light painting his skin and the sea air tousling his hair, he looked like a man pulled from a dream she didn't trust—but couldn't stop returning to.

"What's this about?" she asked, voice low, pulse loud in her throat.

He stepped toward her, hands in his pockets, gaze drinking her in like she was something he wasn't sure he deserved to look at for too long.

"I've been thinking about what you said," he murmured, each word precise. "About letting go of the past. About choosing to move forward."

Her throat tightened. Her hand slipped from his as she stepped closer.

"Wyatt..."

"I found him," he said.

The words hung there, suspended in jasmine and sun.

"My father," he clarified, voice steadier now. "I went to see him the day after you slept over at my place."

Pixie stilled.

"You did?"

"I didn't know how to tell you." He nodded. "It wasn't what I thought it would be. He's...not the man I remember. Older. Bitter. Small."

He didn't let her respond. He took her coffee from her hand — when had she picked it up again? — and set it on the low stone wall beside them. Then he stepped in, gripped her hips gently, and pulled her flush against him.

Not possessive. *Present.*

"But I didn't go for him. I went for me. And for you."

"For me?" she breathed.

His hands were warm through her dress. His voice was low and reverent.

"You told me to stop running. To face it — even if it hurt." His thumb brushed her jaw, tilting her face to his. "You were right. And if I can survive that...then I can survive this. *Us.*"

She felt herself tremble beneath his touch. Not from fear. From recognition.

"You drive me insane," he whispered, dropping his forehead to hers. "You strip me down and rebuild me all in the same breath. I've fought every kind of battle, Pixie, and none of them ever made me feel like *this.*"

Her chest ached.

"Wyatt..."

"Don't," he murmured, his thumb brushing her lips. "Don't say you don't feel it."

302

She didn't.

She couldn't.

Because she *did* — so much it scared her breathless.

"I'm not easy," she choked out. "I'll break you."

He laughed softly, but his eyes were dead serious. "Sweetheart...you *already* did. When you walked into my life, I cracked wide open."

She swore under her breath and kissed him before she could talk herself out of it.

His lips were soft and sure. The kiss tasted like citrus and sunlight, and she gripped his shirt like it might be the only thing keeping her anchored. His hands cupped her face, steady and reverent. No control. No demands.

Just *choice*.

When they broke apart, breathless, trembling, he leaned in and whispered against her cheek, "You're mine. Not because I claimed you. Because you *own* me."

She let out a shuddering breath, eyes glassy, body vibrating with everything she hadn't let herself believe.

And then he stepped back.

Her skin went cold where his heat had been. Her lips were still tingling from the last kiss, swollen and parted as she watched him reach into his jacket pocket.

Her heart *stopped*.

No velvet box. No dramatic speech. Just *him*, lowering himself slowly, reverently, onto one knee — right there on the cool stone path, beneath the orange trees, where anyone from the President's security team could walk by.

But in that moment, there was no one else.

Just him. Just her. Just this.

Wyatt looked up at her, all that brute confidence stripped bare, nothing but heat and hope in his eyes.

"I'm not perfect," he said, voice raw as gravel, gaze locked to hers. "You know that better than anyone. I lose control. I push too hard. I love you too much." He exhaled hard. "But I'm not asking you to be easy, or soft, or anything you're not. I'm asking you to *stay*. To choose me the way I've already chosen you."

The world slowed. Tilted. Vanished.

Pixie's knees hit the stone before she even realized she was moving.

"Yes," she gasped, voice thick, eyes swimming. "Yes. Wyatt, *fuck,* yes."

He let out a laugh—half-wild, half-sob—and slid the ring onto her shaking finger, his hands rough and gentle all at once. The band was cool against her skin, but his palms were fire. His mouth was on hers a second later, all heat and hunger, no hesitation.

She moaned into the kiss as his arms locked around her, dragging her against him, their bodies a mess of tangled limbs and unspoken need. The stone beneath her knees was hard, but she didn't care. Not when his lips were parting hers, not when his tongue was sliding into her mouth with slow, claiming pressure.

She kissed him like she'd never kissed anyone in her life. Like she was starving and he was the only thing that would fill her.

Her hands fisted in his collar, pulling him down with her, crushing their bodies together until there was no space left between them—just heat and sweat and breath. His hand slid beneath her blouse, over the bare skin of her back, and she arched into it, needing more.

God, she wanted him.

Right there, in the garden, with the sun dying behind the trees and the scent of oranges pressing in around them like a spell. She wanted him to ruin her lipstick and hike up her skirt and remind her, with every inch of his body, why she'd said yes.

But more than that — she wanted the *after*.

The slow mornings. The whispered fights. The second chances.

Wyatt kissed her again — deep, desperate, a little reckless — and when he finally pulled back, his forehead dropped to hers, his breath ragged.

"I don't care who's watching," he murmured. "I'm yours. Always."

Pixie was trembling, lips kiss-bruised, thighs aching from kneeling. But for the first time in her life, she didn't feel like she had to run. Or pretend. Or guard every inch of her heart like a war zone.

She just felt...*home*.

"Then take me home," she whispered against his lips, her voice thick with heat and promise. "Because I'm saying yes to all of it. Even the parts that scare me."

Wyatt smiled — slow, wicked, reverent.

And then he stood, pulling her up with him, wrapping her in his arms like a man who didn't plan to let go again.

As twilight bled into night, and the Secret Service whispered into their radios from the hedges, Pixie kissed the man who'd once tried to save her —

And now simply *loved* her.

On duty. In public.

And was finally, *completely* hers.

Sign up for our newsletter and find out about all our romance book releases, eBook sales and promotions, sneak peeks and FREE romance books!

Want to see more from this author? Here's a taster for you to enjoy!

Unbreakable Heroes: Under Control
Zoe Normandie

Excerpt

"Moose, hold up. I haven't cleared the area," Delta called out to the man jumping out of the passenger side of the armored black SUV.

Former Navy SEAL and decorated war hero Carrick Byrne tilted his head back, giving Delta the usual 'don't even start' expression.

"Relax, big rig. This is just a little 'find and retrieve' contract," Carrick said in a skeptical voice tinted with the slightest Irish accent as he leaned back into the idling SUV. "I don't think we need to worry about one little girl."

Delta narrowed his brown eyes, and a lock of his slicked-back dark-blond fell onto his unimpressed face. "She's been on the run for years. Don't underestimate her."

Carrick looked around with obvious sarcasm at the fact that they were literally about to walk through a park on their way to finish the job. Glancing back, Carrick raised his eyebrow to his friend, recognizing the face of someone who wanted to punch him.

"Come on. How much trouble could one chick cause?"

"Your client seems to think she can cause a lot of trouble," Delta reminded him. "And our intelligence suggests the same. She's slippery, Carrick—and I don't think your client is very forgiving."

"Don't overdramatize this," Carrick warned. "This is a nothing contract."

The two strong, opinionated men exchanged looks before Delta backed off, seemingly knowing that at the end of the day, Carrick was the CEO of Sea-to-Sky Security.

"Have it your way," Delta said, leaning back. "You're the boss."

Moving away from the SUV, Carrick slung his old black hockey skates over his shoulder, heading toward the rink. He flipped up the collar of his black work coat, even further concealing his identity. He had a target to follow. Years of urban reconnaissance and black ops had given him more than enough tactical training to handle the job.

Popping a black baseball hat on and smoothing back his black hair that was peppered with gray, the dark Irish-American moved stealthily.

Delta took off behind him with gusto, but Carrick didn't care. He just needed to get the job done and over with, then move on to the next one. It should be in and out—quick and easy. Those were the types of cases Carrick needed to build his client base and his reputation as the premiere private security firm in LA.

And, damn it, he was going to do the best job he could—because after losing everything that mattered to him, this new business venture was all he had left.

Carrick focused on the scene before him. The crowd had thinned. It was growing quiet. As he came up to the skating rink, a young couple passed him on the other side of the pathway leading out of the park. They seemed happy — in love. His only instinct was to scowl, and he pulled down the brim of his hat farther as he stooped to put on his skates.

The target was on the ice. It was time to get *closer*.

Then retrieve.

Out on the rink, it was nearing closing time, and everyone was clearing out. He was the only one heading in. *Good.* He needed the space. It was much easier to keep eyes on the target.

At least, that was what he told himself. He wouldn't admit it, but at that moment — Valentine's Day night — he wanted nothing else than to have a reason to be alone — alone and away from everything to do with his life, away from the memories. *Is this my second Valentine's Day alone?* He shuddered, pushing the thought aside. That wasn't something he was prepared to feel.

He didn't have to. The girl was in sight.

Hockey skates on, Carrick moved hard down the bumpy outdoor ice — as hard as the restrictive leather strap of his shoulder holster would allow. Wearing a pistol was like wearing boxers. He did it every day, no matter what. It had come to feel like a second skin.

Keeping his eyes on the ice, not on her, his blood pumped to his engorged muscles and a sated grin crossed his lips. There were very few things in life that served to alleviate his stress — hockey being one. The other was a similar cardio-exhausting exercise that elevated his endorphins, pumped his blood and left him satisfied and spent.

Pushing forward, he observed her — the lone woman skating in the opposite direction, once again nearing his position. Her long brown hair had escaped her pink toque, and her warm breath visibly illustrated her panting chest, even from afar. Carrick had to admit that her form was more than pleasing to look at. Athletic and swift—he didn't doubt she could give him a run for his money in a race, but he kept his gaze down. He made sure to give her enough space so that he wouldn't scare her away.

Danica Petrova.

As she was skating past him, he stole one glance of her face, locking eyes. He *had* to see her face in person. All he'd seen was a picture.

He wasn't disappointed.

Her red cheeks flashed at him and her eyes sparkled. *So youthful and full of life.* What he'd seen in a blink of an eye held the promise of an eternity of pleasure as he took in her beautiful face.

But then, in an instant, just as her body floated by him, her skate hit a groove in the ice, an unmistakable sound—and common. Turning immediately, he thrust forward and reached out, catching the young woman as she fell. He quickly heaved her back onto her skates, rescuing her from a hard fall. As he held her, she fluttered her dark lashes at him, enchanting and stunning him.

"You okay?" he asked, looking her over, hoping she hadn't been hurt.

"I'm okay." A sweet, feminine voice escaped her full lips.

Holding her close, he realized that her eyes hadn't been sparkling. They were wet.

Has she been crying?

"I just caught an edge," she explained, like she'd been caught doing something wrong. "Thank you."

As she made to push away from his arms, he realized that he had been still holding her all this time. *I never let her go.*

She frowned as she probably realized the same thing. He released his grip on her thick sweater, letting her float back a foot into her own space. Silence filled the rink. Their gazes did not break, and she continued to blink at him, likely assessing him, given the look in her eyes.

There was something distrustful about the way she was evaluating him. Her body language screamed that she was scared and threatened that she was about to run. Before thinking, he threw out his hand, just knowing she was just about to pop smoke and disappear — and knowing he couldn't allow that. His client had warned him that she was a runner — and that she could slip out of any situation.

His client had also warned him of the importance of not letting her go.

"Carrick," he introduced himself, keeping her there.

She took his hand, though hers remained limp, and she retracted it right way. Clearly, she didn't know what to make of him — but her manners shone through.

"Dani."

Cute. She seemed very sweet, and not at all like the client had described. That was the first thing that brought on his suspicion that something might be wrong and not as he'd been led to believe.

"Nice to meet you," he replied with a little more meaning than he'd expected.

She responded slow and shy, her voice cracking, "I really do appreciate you saving me from the fall."

"Forget it." He shrugged as instinct urged him to back off a little.

But the caveman inside him couldn't take his eyes off her. Lithe and pert, she almost glowed under the soft lights. There was something different about this target. She continued averting her gaze, looking down at the hard ice and shaking her pretty heart-shaped face.

Something was brewing in his mind that he was unwilling to accept, and his strategy shifted. This was not how he'd planned the operation to go, but he had to adjust on the fly — right?

Carrick checked his watch and turned in the direction she was going. "Heading this way? Last five minutes."

He motioned, nearly regretting it as he did. Really, he knew better. They didn't have time for leisurely skating.

"I was." Her words poured out nervously, responding to his invitation. "But…"

"You aren't anymore?"

"I mean, I am." She toyed with her gray sweater buttons as she looked away, seemingly just as conflicted as him. She was a smart little coyote, and he wondered if she was ready to bolt.

She is definitely *ready to bolt.*

"Well, let's go then." He took the lead, pushing off the ice and gliding away from her.

If there was one thing Carrick was good at, it was controlling a situation. After a pause, there was the distinct sound of skates on the ice behind him, and she caught up to glide alongside him. He'd been sure she would follow — had just known it.

A sense of intrigue tugged at his senses as a cold burst of wind blew her long brunette locks across her shoulder.

So he decided to lay it on thick.

"Looks like you've got tough luck tonight," he said.

"It certainly wouldn't have been the worst thing to happen to me on Valentine's Day." The rebellious words seemed to slip from her mouth, and she glanced up with an embarrassed expression.

"That sounds like a good story," he replied.

Her wide gaze betrayed discomfort. The effect? He was able to observe her eye color more closely. They were a lighter brown, but mixed. *With green? Like camouflage.* He'd never seen a color like that before.

He continued looking around. "We must be two sad cases — out here alone on Valentine's night."

She brought her gloved hands together, rubbing them and offering him a shy smile. "Or, we must both just love skating."

He couldn't help but smirk, his chest flexing, *Guilty. I'm a hockey guy.*

What the hell am I doing? He wiped the smile off his face, feeling like an idiot. However, it seemed her guard was lowering — and in return her shy tiny smile grew a bit.

"I can't believe you...*caught me.*"

"Come on. I couldn't let you take a nosedive." He shrugged, pumping harder down the ice.

She kept up, showcasing just how good she was on blades.

She cocked her head and offered the slightest grin, tepid and testing. "You have quick reflexes."

He shrugged again. "Yeah, when I need to."

Built from years of Special Forces tactical training.

She shook her head again in apparent disbelief, then looked away. It was almost like she didn't believe someone *would* save her.

The bumpy ice on the rink was overdue for maintenance, which tended to be the case at the end of the skating day. There weren't many rinks in California — and fewer outdoor ones. Her skate caught an edge again, which she was too distracted to see. As she yelped and almost fell, he lunged instinctively, grabbing her against his body one more time.

"Christ." He exhaled.

Holding her in his arms again, he gazed down on her young, golden face. She bit her lip as she glanced up at him. He was aware of his great height and wide frame, which could be intimidating for some, especially when he was on skates.

"Want to keep going?" he asked, offering his arm.

"Or should we head off?"

Danica grinned up to him, making him wait far too long before she answered, her glittery, innocent gaze flickering left and right. Never before had he wanted someone to take his arm so badly. As much as he hated to admit it, he had her exactly where he wanted her. He was forcing her to make a choice. It was going to play into the job nicely.

"One more round." She grinned her little smile, but her cooperation was tentative at best.

She slipped her hand in the crook of his elbow, only to then avert her gaze from his. The flush in her cheeks grew, and he guessed it was more than just the cool night wind coming in off the Pacific Ocean.

Comfortable silence found them briefly as they pushed along the ice by side. She never let go of his arm, and for the first time, it felt like they were skating *together*. Something stirred inside him that hadn't been there before.

"How long have you been skating?" he asked, propelling the conversation forward.

"Oh, for as long as I can remember," Danica began, revealing more and more. "I grew up on skates and dreamed of becoming a figure skater."

Again, the admission was followed by caution that flashed across her eyes. She didn't want to share much, but she *was*. She recoiled slightly, as if realizing her mistake, and tried to create space between them until he decided he wouldn't let her. He didn't want her to withdraw.

Changing the tempo, he pushed her out a little from him, allowing her hand to slide down his forearm and slip to his just as he twirled her around on the ice. It was so smooth, so natural—like they'd been skating together for years. He didn't miss the wide smile that crossed her lips.

"It never hurts to dream," Carrick said as he pulled her back into him, running his gaze over her form for the hundredth time, his curiosity at maximum. *What does Danica want? What does she do?* Questions sprang to the front of his mind. *Why did my client lie to me?*

"I have no shortage of dreams." Her sweet smile betrayed a longing, and it was clear she noticed the way he was looking at her.

"What do you do for work?" He pressed on as he ushered them farther down the ice.

"I'm a nurse."

"At the hospital?" His gaze caught the city worker beginning the process of closing the rink.

"No, at a family clinic," she replied.

"What else?" he probed. "Tell me more."

She let out a low laugh, as if in disbelief he would even say that. "I think it's time to go."

Then she let her hand slip out of his arm, gliding one perfect white skate in front of the other on her way to leave the rink. As he followed, he couldn't keep his eyes off her, watching her closely as she moved. It was like he'd never met a woman before, never seen one. If he were a wiser man, he'd notice that his chest didn't feel as tight as usual for the first time in too long.

If he were a wiser man, he'd notice that he'd grown very distracted.

"What about you?" She cut into his thoughts as she held on to the wall of the rink, stepping one foot through the gate. "Are you…?"

If it weren't for the sound of a man shouting as he sprinted toward them, Carrick would have caught what she said after that. The shouting was unmistakable, and for a second he felt like he could kill Delta for the interruption.

Danica snapped her eyes open like a doe caught in the headlights, clearly frightened by the six-foot-five man running up to the gate. Delta grabbed onto the side of the rink with his meaty SEAL-build as he spoke to Carrick in low tones.

"Moose, there's a situation. We have to go."

About the Author

A little snapshot on who is Zoe Normandie…

After ten years working with the police and attending a military university, I weave stories filled with danger, heart, and the grit of those who serve. An army brat, I grew up on military bases across the country, giving me front-row seat to the world of duty and sacrifice. With a veteran husband, my passion for writing military-themed romance, suspense, and mystery is rooted in real-world experience, supporting him through every mission.

Zoe loves to hear from readers. You can find her contact information, website details and author profile page at https://www.firstforromance.com

ENTWINED PUBLISHING

www.ingramcontent.com/pod-product-compliance

Lightning Source LLC
Chambersburg PA
CBHW032206030726

47494CB000020B/637